An Engaged Grand Tour

VICTORIAN GRAND TOUR SERIES
BOOK TWO

LISA H. CATMULL

SALTAIR PRESS

To Susanne and Half Zantop,
my own chaperones in Mainz,
teachers who held me to the highest standard,
demanded excellence from me,
and shared their love of scholarship.

ACKNOWLEDGMENTS

Thanks to my husband for listening to every chapter and laughing at my mistakes. Thanks to Minecraft and Stardew Valley for entertaining my adorable, intense, worldbuilding children.

Thanks to my extended family members, who talk about movies, analyze stories, and discuss creativity and storytelling with me.

Thank you to Lorie Humpherys, Judy Olsen, Marianne Siegmund, and Sara Hacken, whose line and copy edits teach me the finer points of grammar and sentence construction. Thanks for reading the version with the commas in the wrong places.

Speaking of commas, thanks to my developmental editor, Michele Paige Holmes, for guiding me through the writing process and reading the rough drafts, and Heather B. Moore of Precision Editing.

Thanks to Allison Lane, Nancy Mayer, Karen Pierotti, and Mindy Burbidge Strunk for help with titles, peerage, and precedence.

A shout out for Mackenzie Kincaid's book, *The Writer's Guide to Horses*. I used it. Super awesome and helpful.

CHARACTER LIST

Miss Lucy Maldon
Mr. Arthur Maldon
**Mrs. Ellen Palmer, Lucy's widowed aunt

Miss Rachel Wickford
**Mrs. Edith Wickford, her mother

Miss Alice Loughton
Colonel Curtis Loughton (Alice's brother)
Mrs. Glenn, Alice's chaperone

Mr. Frederick Kempton

Lady Julia Chelmsford, the dowager viscountess
Lord Walter Chelmsford, Viscount of Chelmsford
Mr. Peter Chelmsford, second son of Lady Chelmsford
**Mr. Arthur Chelmsford, third son of Lady Chelmsford
***Mr. Benjamin Chelmsford, fourth son of Lady
   Chelmsford*

Lady Eleanor Shelford
Lord Shelford, Percy Hauxton

Herr Theodor Fliedner, the director of the Institute
*Florence Nightingale

Mrs. Smith, a widow
Mr. Ford

Miss Cecelia Duxford
Mr. Albert Duxford

*Mrs. Elizabeth Barrett Browning
*Mr. Robert Browning

Mr. James Oxley, a lawyer

Stout, a butler at Eleanor's apartments in Florence
**Coombs, the head groom at Lucy's stables
**George, a stable boy at Lucy's stables

The Duke of Woodford, Guy Claybury

*Historical figure
**mentioned in the book, but not an active character

CHAPTER 1

Mid-August, 1856

Lucy Maldon intended to hunt down her missing fiancé, and if attending nursing school in Germany was the only way to do it, she would.

She tried to tamp down the rising excitement. *Finally here!* After months of waiting, after the humiliation of Walter leaving for a Grand Tour without her, she was in Mainz at the Deaconess Institute. Lucy gazed at the dome of the city's lofty cathedral through the drab windows on the chipped plaster walls.

The bare classroom was the least likely place to feel exhilarated, especially when she had not seen Walter since May, but she wanted to run in circles around the stark lecture hall. Traces of sunlight fought their way into the dim hall. The rough wooden floor matched the condition of the worn chairs and simple desks. The stifling heat made her wonder why so many layers of clothing were necessary. At least she wore a cotton muslin dress today.

Lucy played with her fountain pen and tapped her foot, trying to maintain a calm demeanor.

Papa liked all the newest inventions, like innovations in mining or new drilling procedures, but had branched out and invested in the fountain pen company when it first started twenty-nine years ago, before she'd been born. It was one of his many instincts that had paid off in dividends over the years. Using one of Poenaru's pens felt comforting, like having family nearby.

But she quickly tired of spinning the pen between her fingers and couldn't help squirming a little to get a view of the other students. The stark white plaster on the walls and thin curtains around the windows gave her little else to study.

It was such a contrast to her own home. Aunt Ellen ran the household for her papa, and Papa spared no expense. Aunt Ellen furnished every room lavishly and redecorated often. There was not a spot without a clock, a fern, a Grecian bust, a gilded frame, an urn, or a lamp. It was rather stifling in its own way, and Lucy couldn't wait to be on her own in Europe with her traveling companions.

Lucy sat sandwiched between her dearest friend, Rachel Wickford, and another Englishwoman, Miss Alice Loughton. Her older brother, Colonel Loughton and his friend, Mr. Kempton, occupied the seats behind them, ready to translate the lecture. The colonel was nearly ten years older than his eighteen-year-old sister. The perfect age to marry, or so he seemed to think.

Everyone around Lucy chattered in German. She couldn't make out a word of their conversations. She shifted a little to the left, closer to Rachel. Now the colonel would be certain to translate for both Lucy and Rachel. Ever since they'd volunteered to attend the Institute, the colonel had been most attentive toward Rachel.

Lucy appreciated the chance to look for Walter. She ought to help the colonel's cause any way she could. After all, without Colonel Loughton and Mr. Kempton's invitation, she would still be at home in England. The colonel and Mr. Kempton intended to help Miss Nightingale establish a new training program in London, so they were taking close notes on the education at the school "The Lady With the Lamp" had attended herself.

Lucy felt a little guilty. She might not complete the course. She hoped she would not still be in Mainz six months from now, but at least Rachel would. Lucy's only concern was to find her fiancé and marry as soon as possible.

Rachel's hands were folded primly in her lap, her posture stiff and starched as a nurse's cap, but her eyes gleamed with excitement. "Have you attended any medical lectures before?" she asked.

Next to her, Miss Loughton answered. "Curtis drags me everywhere he goes, so, yes, I have attended several lectures." Her eyes held none of Rachel's enthusiasm.

"Really? And have you also met Miss Nightingale?" Rachel asked.

Miss Loughton nodded. "Yes, she made a favorable impression on my brother and Mr. Kempton. They are quite devoted to her cause."

Rachel leaned across Lucy. "Will you tell me more about her? What is your impression of her?"

Miss Loughton scooted her chair closer to talk to Rachel. Lucy felt trapped between the two women and quickly lost interest in the conversation. She had no idea whether she would finish the six-month course or even stay more than a few days. The nursing school was a means to an end: Walter. Surely, now that she'd arrived, she would find him any day.

They'd had only two days to unpack their trunks and settle into their rented rooms before classes started.

She glanced around the room. Eighteen other women filled the wooden chairs, ready to learn nursing at the Mainz Deaconess Training Institute. Even though she wasn't a Lutheran or planning to take vows, she could still learn to care for others, for a few days at least, if it took that long.

A man entered the room. White-haired but kindly, the pastor Theodor Fliedner reminded Lucy of her father. He shuffled to the lectern and began speaking German so rapidly she couldn't catch a single word.

Some of her excitement waned. She felt a rising panic instead.

She would never last a single day if everyone spoke like this, even with the colonel and Mr. Kempton to help.

Colonel Loughton, sitting behind her and Rachel, whispered to them. "He's welcoming all of you. This is an important charge. The sick and the needy are everywhere among us. Especially poor women."

Lucy had a hard time listening to Colonel Loughton translate while also watching the pastor. Mr. Kempton whispered the lecture in English to Miss Loughton. She could hear the pastor speaking, the scratch of chalk on the enormous blackboard that covered the front wall, the colonel speaking in low tones, and Mr. Kempton's indistinct voice. All at the same time. The overlapping sounds made her head ache.

"Our... joy is to find them. He and the other instructors will teach you the skills to care for them," the colonel said. "This is a little awkward, trying to find the right words."

Lucy exchanged a glance with Rachel. Rachel's face glowed with anticipation. She had wanted to study medicine her whole life. Lucy wanted to put her head in her hands and groan. She couldn't understand a word of this German, even though she'd tried to learn a little before she left England.

But she promised herself she would do anything to find Walter. If it meant getting a headache every day until she could quit this school, then she would do it.

Lucy squinted at the diagram Pastor Fliedner had unrolled. She leaned closer to Rachel, so she would only hear one set of translations. She was going to need every bit of patience she possessed to see this through.

۞

"How was the first day of classes?" Eleanor asked. "They should call us into dinner soon. Tell me everything."

Lucy tried to listen to Rachel speak in measured tones as she related the subjects of each lecture. Colonel Loughton leaned casually against the fireplace mantle and watched. Miss Loughton waited quietly on a sofa with her hands in her lap, while Mr. Kempton and Lord Shelford occupied a different corner of the drawing room.

She just wanted to go to bed with a cold compress and some lavender water. Soon. How long was that? Five minutes or twenty? Why couldn't people speak more precisely?

And who took care of nurses? Now that she attended the school, would this mean she could never become sick or weary herself? If she was going to minister to the ill and the fatigued, would she always have to be in perfect health?

"And you, Lucy?" Eleanor asked. "What did you think?"

She hadn't been listening. She tried to pay attention to the conversation around her.

"The quality here is excellent," Miss Loughton was saying. "Some of the finest lectures I've heard. If Curtis is going to force me to take classes, these really are superb."

"Alice," Colonel Loughton began, "you know we need at least one English-speaking nurse to train with us."

Lucy hated conflict or tension of any kind. She quickly tried to stop the argument between Miss Loughton and her brother.

"I am enjoying classes," Lucy lied. "The colonel does a fine job of helping us understand German."

Colonel Loughton nodded. "*Herr* Fliedner speaks quickly and with a strong accent. It's hard to catch everything, but we're getting enough."

"The diagrams help," Rachel said. "The body is the same in any language."

Lucy hadn't understood any of the diagrams either. This undertaking was too large, and she didn't have the passion Rachel did to put in the hours and effort to understand the material. Why had she thought this was a good idea? Leaving her quiet, comfortable home to chase Walter across Europe?

She knew why. Because she was emotionally depleted. Because Walter had delayed their wedding for six months. Then eleven months. She had nothing left to lose, and at least Papa had plenty of financial resources.

She nodded and kept up a polite conversation during dinner, but her thoughts kept returning to Walter. His last letter came from Mainz. He must be close. Maybe on the same street. But if he wanted to stay hidden from her, how could she find him?

Finally, the impossibly long dinner ended, and the Loughtons left with Mr. Kempton.

"Lucy, a moment," Eleanor said. "Will you stay and chat before you and Rachel retire?"

What a relief. She needed to unburden herself. Lucy settled on a plush sofa in the drawing room. "Gladly. I need some time with my friends."

Lord Shelford leaned over and kissed Eleanor on the cheek. "Then I shall find some business to attend to."

Lucy tried to push away the yearning she felt every time Eleanor's husband showed his affection. She wanted Walter to care for her like that, but he never had. Not even before he ran away.

Eleanor reached out a hand toward her husband. "Oh, don't, Percy. Stay and gossip."

"Yes, do," Rachel said. "You're one of us, now."

"But you can kiss me goodbye as often as you wish," Eleanor said.

Newlyweds. Although it hurt Lucy when she saw the tenderness between the couple, it also gave her hope. She was determined to have an affectionate and loving marriage, not merely a cold business relationship between two mutually disinterested parties.

Turning to Lucy, Eleanor asked, "Do we need a round of True Confessions? How did your day really go?" She peered intently at her. "Tell me the truth, now that the Loughtons have gone."

Lucy laughed. "You know me too well. True Confession. I hated it. I'm sorry, Rachel. I don't understand a thing."

Rachel's smile was barely perceptible, modest and contained, just like Rachel. "I loved the lectures. True Confession. I've never been happier in my life."

"That's not a Confession," Eleanor said. "Now, if you tell us how much you enjoyed having Colonel Loughton translate for you, that would be a good start."

Rachel wove her fingers together. "Nonsense. He was planning to translate for his sister, until we decided to attend the Institute."

Rachel's impassive face gave nothing away, but the tight fist in her lap told Lucy enough. She leaned over and prodded Rachel. "That doesn't mean you aren't enjoying it."

Rachel shook her head a little too emphatically.

"He is handsome," Lucy said. "I'm already engaged, so I can say that. And you seem to be making a dear friend of his sister."

Rachel also had that little twitch when she lied. The side of her mouth barely moved, and Lucy watched Rachel fighting to control it. Rachel pursed her lips and didn't respond. Coming from her, that was a strong reaction.

Eleanor clapped her hands. "Well, if you're not going to confess, then we'll just have to wait. But I'm already married, so I can agree that he's handsome."

Lord Shelford glowered at his wife.

She pulled him down on the sofa beside her. "But obviously, I chose Percy over him. Colonel Loughton must have a hidden defect somewhere. Hideous toenails."

Lord Shelford chuckled and tucked Eleanor into his side.

Lucy felt that now-familiar pang of loneliness and longing. Even before Walter had left for the Continent, he had never once treated her with the same fondness as Lord Shelford showed Eleanor.

"I want a Confession from you, Lord Shelford," Lucy said. "I need to find Walter. Tell me that you know something."

"I get to play?" Lord Shelford asked.

They all nodded.

"How do I do this?" He glanced around at the three waiting faces.

Eleanor put a hand on his cheek. "You simply say these words:

'True Confession.' And then you tell us something wonderful that we don't already know. Preferably something scandalous."

Lord Shelford tapped his forehead and smiled. "Aah, I have it. True Confession. I have indeed corresponded with a Mr. Duxford, an old friend from Vienna. He still works for the Foreign Office and lives in Mainz himself."

"Does he?" Eleanor asked. "Oh, we must find him and visit Cecelia. Miss Duxford."

"He says that the Chelmsfords came by to ask for help with the local currency. They are likely to still be in the area, judging by the amount they exchanged, although he hasn't met them personally."

Lucy couldn't believe he had delayed the news for even one minute. One hour. How long had he known? Probably since this afternoon. Lucy appreciated his discretion in waiting until the Loughtons and Mr. Kempton left, but she didn't care who knew her concerns. She just wanted answers. "Oh, my! Where precisely? Yours is the best Confession of all, Lord Shelford."

He puffed out his chest ridiculously far. "Thank you. Connections. The Foreign Office likes to help its visitors abroad."

"In other words, you got lucky," Eleanor said.

Lord Shelford gaped. "I don't believe in luck. It was hard work."

"You wrote a letter."

"And opened it when I received a response," he said. "I nearly sliced my finger open on the paper." He held up his hand and Eleanor squinted at it unsympathetically.

Lucy rose from the sofa, some of the morning's excitement returning. "I'll leave you two to argue," she said. "I feel so much better, knowing that Walter is here. I haven't seen him since May. Three months." He'd left for Europe only a month or so after signing their marriage contract and had never come back, despite repeated promises to return. Now his letters suggested a return for next Easter, almost a full year after he left.

Eleanor's eyes were full of understanding and compassion. "You'll find him any day now."

Rachel joined her by the drawing room door. "We'll check the plaza by the cathedral and the marketplace this weekend."

"Enjoy your classes, Rachel," Eleanor said, "and the translations."

Rachel's lips twitched to one side as they left Eleanor's apartments. Lucy couldn't tell whether she was repressing a smile or trying not to respond.

Rachel led the way to their own rented rooms, one floor below. She paused on the landing. "It's strange to think of Walter and Peter here in Germany," she said. "I'm used to seeing them at dinner parties and out riding in the neighborhood. Peter always looks so good on a horse."

Lucy followed Rachel into their entryway. "Everything's so much more romantic here, just being in Europe. I haven't told Eleanor, but I'll tell you. Another True Confession. I don't only want to find Walter so he can fulfill his marriage contract. I want to make him fall in love with me."

CHAPTER 2

Peter Chelmsford paused in the door to the Mainz cathedral. "We're not Catholic," he said to his brother. "Isn't it wrong to go into their churches during a worship service?"

"We're visiting," Walter said. "No one's going to ask about your religion. Just sit down and watch."

Walter pushed his way past Peter and found a bench at the back of the cathedral. Peter joined him and studied the structure. It was a magnificent building, brilliant with its red sandstone walls. Nothing like their grey stone church at home, the small church that Walter intended for him.

Columns towered above them, leading to a vaulted ceiling. Murals adorned the upper portion of each wall. Friezes in memory of past bishops projected from each pillar near the base. Colored light streamed through the stained-glass windows, casting a web of kaleidoscopic shadows onto the floor.

A vicar. Walter expected him to take orders. As Peter examined the statues of archbishops in the central nave, he squinted to examine the deterioration of the stone. How long had ago had the carvings been made? What type of corrosion had begun on the surface? He laughed to himself. He'd much rather attend the chemistry lectures in London than spend his weekends writing sermons. Walter always prevailed, though. He was Lord Chelmsford now and Peter's oldest brother.

A small choir started singing in the chancel at the front of the cathedral. The unearthly tones drifted back in the perfect acoustics of the building. Peter squinted. The singers were short and squat. Elderly. Grey-haired. Humble people, in everyday work clothes. Just practicing.

At least they hadn't interrupted Mass. It was only a choir rehearsal. But how did those ordinary-looking people create those celestial sounds?

One voice rose above the others. Clear, high, pure. It resonated throughout the cathedral, filling the transept and every side chapel.

"Do you hear that?" Walter rose from the bench. "It is the voice of an angel."

Before Peter knew what was happening, Walter had walked the length of the nave and up to the chancel. He stood, transfixed, watching the singers.

Peter joined him, watching his brother. It was never a good sign when Walter got that mesmerized look on his face.

Peter shifted restlessly on the hard stone floor. Walter ignored him, as usual.

"I've seen enough of the building," Peter whispered.

"Sssh," Walter said. "I see her. The one in front. The tiny one."

He looked. A short blond woman sang with the choir. Unlike the others, she was young. Pretty. And clearly expecting a child. Her voice pierced through the others with its clear, high tune.

She noticed Peter and Walter and stopped singing. She gathered her things, whispered something to an elderly woman, and rushed out of the cathedral.

Walter approached the elderly woman.

Peter wanted to groan. "Don't interrupt their rehearsal," he said quietly.

"Translate for me," Walter replied. "Ask her who the young woman is."

Always imperious. Never asking, always telling him what to do. Walter had always been the oldest and the heir, so his orders were as binding as Father's. Father always made that clear. If Walter said something, his word was law. He was Lord Chelmsford now, just as self-assured as Father had been, and just as quick to withdraw Peter's quarterly allowance if he complained or failed to comply.

"Excuse me," Peter said in German. "I apologize for the intrusion. Who is the woman who just left?"

"Who are you?" the woman replied.

"I am Mr. Chelmsford," Peter said, "and this is my older brother, Lord Chelmsford, from England."

The woman nodded. "Naturally. She is British, too." She motioned to Peter to sit down on a bench. "I am *Frau* Berger."

Walter followed them as the *Frau* began to explain in rapid German.

"She says that the woman is Mrs. Smith. A widow. Very sad story. Very good singer. But she is a psychic and God sends her messages through her dead husband." Peter tried to translate without laughing. It was too ridiculous.

"Really?" Walter asked, his voice full of interest.

Peter knew that tone. The one his father had used during trips to London when his mother remained home. The one reserved for widows and women in loveless marriages. The one that meant the chase had begun.

"*Wirklich*," *Frau* Berger replied in German.

Walter stared at the doorway where Mrs. Smith had left. "Ask her more."

Peter's frustration mounted, but he hid it. He asked the old woman and translated for Walter. "*Frau* Berger says that Mrs. Smith is a medium. She holds séances."

Walter said, "*Wirklich*?" and the *Frau* nodded vigorously.

"For money," Peter added. Of course. She put on a spectacle and earned her living through fraud.

"How much?" Walter demanded.

"*Wie viel*?" Peter asked. Walter never spent a farthing more than he had to. Perhaps this would dissuade him.

Frau Berger shook her head and wagged her finger. "*Nein!*"

Walter raised his eyebrows. "Why not?"

But the look failed to intimidate or impress the woman.

"Evidently her dead husband does not send messages to men. Only to women," Peter said. "She's quite emphatic." He felt relief. Hopefully, Walter would consider this a momentary distraction, and they could leave.

"Get her address anyway." Walter smiled at the *Frau*. "I've always wanted to attend a séance. This might be my chance."

They rode back toward their rented cottage on the outskirts of Mainz. The Rhine river wound through the city and along the outskirts of a forest. Sunlight flecked the tree branches, casting dappled shadows over their path.

Peter worried about the effect the woman's charm had on Walter. He needed to get Walter away from the lure of Spiritualism and ground him in reality.

But he had to tread lightly with his brother. He'd had his funds restricted too many times to risk a direct confrontation.

"How much longer do you intend to stay here?" Peter asked. "Where are we heading next?"

Walter shrugged. "Maybe Vienna or Hungary before Italy for the winter. I don't know."

Peter tried not to let his irritation show. This was supposed to be *his* Grand Tour. He had just graduated from Cambridge, but his brother made the decisions.

And he'd felt a little conflicted about going on this Grand Tour in the first place. Someone should be home with Mother, who still grieved her neglectful husband's passing. Walter *should* be getting married, not hiding in Europe. Yes, Peter wanted a Grand Tour, but every day they were gone was another day that Mother mourned alone while his younger brothers were at school, and another day that Walter left Lucy in the lurch.

Another one of Walter's messes for Peter to clean up. Peter always carried the burden while his brother did whatever he wanted without regard for anyone else's feelings. The sooner they could leave Mainz and finish this trip, the better.

"There's a technical institute in Vienna I'd like to visit," Peter said. "We could leave Mainz and head there now."

Walter stared ahead, not even bothering to look at him. "No. I'm going to get my séance."

Peter also knew that tone. The one his father had used before he died. The one that Walter used now. No discussion. No argument.

They rode in near silence as the horses' hooves crunched the gravel underfoot. Walter would remain in Mainz for as long as it took him to chase another ridiculous fascination. Unfortunately, Walter never could resist magic tricks or anything illogical. Perhaps Mrs. Smith would turn them down, and they could move on.

But he had a feeling that his brother would not relent so easily.

CHAPTER 3

The group meandered through the crowded marketplace. The cobblestone square was filled with wooden carts covered with brightly colored cloths. Merchants called out from individual stalls to advertise their goods: grapes, melons, plums, tomatoes, marinated olives in a range of colors and flavors, brilliant flowers in every hue, fragrant herbs, and freshly laid eggs. Live chickens squawked in cages. Dried garlic hung from wooden pegs, and there was even fresh cheese. White, soft, a kind Lucy had never seen before. Mozzarella, they called it.

Buildings ringed the marketplace, six stories tall. The façades were colorful: pink, cream, green, and blue, with decorations. The tops looked like stairs with the cut-out rectangles that led to the roof. Gleaming windows and overflowing flowerboxes covered the buildings. Small tables and wooden chairs lined the sidewalks around the marketplace.

Lucy loved the crowds and people. She could hear the chatter of conversation, even if she didn't understand any of it. They stopped at several stalls, sampling the fruit and foreign foods.

She felt giddy. The bright colors. The people. The energy in the air. Today was the day. She knew it.

Miss Loughton and Rachel walked behind her with Mr. Kempton and Colonel Loughton. Lord Shelford had Eleanor on his arm. Lucy was alone. But not for long.

Her eyes kept scanning the crowds. He was here. Somewhere close. Walter. The man her father had picked for her to marry. She tugged at her dress and readjusted her bonnet. She'd worn a white dress to stand out in the crowd. None of her dark-colored traveling dresses today.

Lord Shelford bought a huge bunch of sunflowers for Eleanor. His arms were overflowing with packages to take back to their rented rooms. Nuts, fruits, sweets. So many foods were in season and ripe right now. The grapes especially.

Lucy wondered what fruits Walter liked. What fruits did any of her friends like? There would be plenty of time to get to know her husband-to-be, a lifetime to do so, as soon as they found him.

They made their way back to the cathedral at the entrance to the marketplace. A small choir of elderly singers was exiting. Lord Shelford held the door open for them. Lucy waited distractedly for them to leave, checking the faces of each person in the crowd as they passed.

Finally, she could delay no longer. She followed the others into the cathedral, enjoying the coolness of the building's interior.

The group formed a knot at the back of the building and craned their necks to take in the splendor and size of the church. The others wandered off, and Lucy slipped onto a bench at the back.

Maybe this would be a good place to pray. As the others wandered off, Lucy sent a prayer to heaven. *Please, help me. I want to be part of a family again.*

And she couldn't have a family without a husband. She began reworking her strategies. What hadn't she tried yet? Where could she look next?

After a few minutes, the others returned.

Eleanor joined Lucy. "Haven't you seen anything? Have you been here the entire time?"

Lucy nodded.

Eleanor waved to Lord Shelford and the others, who left the cathedral. "How are you?"

Lucy realized it was late afternoon, and they hadn't found Walter, despite an entire day spent searching every face in the crowd. There must have been hundreds of people in the crowded marketplace, and yet, what good were her efforts?

"How will I ever find him?" she whispered. Even so, her small voice seemed to echo in the enormous building. No response. Just emptiness.

Eleanor put a hand on Lucy's arm. "Come, dear heart. It is the first day you looked."

"It's all wrong," Lucy said quietly. "Why am I doing this?"

"Because you could not do anything else," Eleanor said. "Sitting at home, waiting, has never been your way. You're like an egg simmering in hot water. That would never be you. Did I tell you that I learned how to boil water?"

Lucy laughed.

Eleanor drew her up from the bench. "I admire your determination. I always have. You're a human steam engine."

They made their way toward the exit. Eleanor held open the enormous bronze door. "Once you've made up your mind, no one and nothing stands in your way."

"But I've always envied you," Lucy said. "You're so quiet and reserved. You don't get yourself into trouble with reckless behavior."

"This is why we're perfect friends," Eleanor said as they crossed the threshold and rejoined the others in the plaza. The bright sun stung their eyes. "You nudge me out of my comfortable drawing room."

Lucy blinked in the bright light. "And you rein me in when I go too far afield." She threaded her arm through Eleanor's. "I've really done it this time. Why ever did you agree to let me come to Europe with you?"

"Because you convinced your papa, because you knew Rachel could not afford to come without you, and because I love you, dearest. We're going to have a spectacular trip, Walter or not. You may as well see Germany instead of moping at home."

⋙⋘

Lucy determined she would try again the next day, since there were no classes, but Rachel didn't want to go anywhere. Miss Loughton had come over to visit again. Lucy felt a pang of jealousy. Rachel had always been her closest friend, but now Rachel and Miss Loughton talked to each other all the time.

Lucy had nothing new to discuss, yet she wanted to talk about Walter. Analyze every possibility. There were currently seven theories at least and seventeen possible locations. She could tell that Rachel was tired of hearing her worries and her "what ifs." Still, it was hard to think about anything else.

"We've got to study," Rachel said. "You should, too."

Lucy set down her tea cup. "I can't concentrate on anything."

"Perhaps Mrs. Glenn could accompany you," Miss Loughton said. "She gets as bored as I do with Curtis's medical lectures, but she's able to escape them."

Her chaperone and companion, almost as old as Lucy's father, leaned in conspiratorially. "It's true. I evade them like the plague. I should be happy to take a walk."

Lucy closed the medical textbook on the table beside her. "Thank you. But where should I start looking? I tried to think like Walter."

Rachel snorted.

"Exactly," Lucy said. "I realized he's not the type to look at flowers in a marketplace."

"What would he do?" Miss Loughton asked. "You must know him well."

Lucy drummed her fingers along the edge of a sofa. "Not really. I know Peter better. He's closer to our age, so we spent more time with him. What would Walter do?"

"Go to the most prestigious places."

"But he's been here three weeks at least," Lucy said. "He must have already seen them."

"Perhaps the museums?" Rachel suggested. "The most important ones first."

"That's where Peter would go, but not Walter."

Rachel nodded. "If you find Peter, you find Walter."

❧

Lucy crossed another site off her list. She had methodically searched Mainz with Miss Loughton's chaperone for three hours. To her credit, Mrs. Glenn truly did love to walk, but Lucy was beginning to panic. Why had she thought she could find one man in all of Europe? As if she had merely misplaced him and a simple search would be sufficient?

"What haven't I considered?" Lucy asked.

"Oh, dear," Mrs. Glenn said. "We've seen most of everything. I'll tell you where I go while Miss Loughton is in class with you."

"Please." Lucy slipped the list and guidebook into her reticule. Eleanor had faith in her. And, she reminded herself, if they didn't find Walter, at least she was living in Europe and enjoying a Grand Tour. A short one, but still, it was better than listening to Aunt Ellen feel sorry for her.

They walked toward a bright pink building that jutted from one corner of the street. Circular scrollwork adorned the fluted columns on the façade. Intricate carvings decorated the space below the windows.

Lucy stared. "That must've cost a lot."

"It belonged to the Archbishop of Mainz, the Prince Elector of the Holy Roman Empire," Mrs. Glenn said.

"Sounds important enough to me." Lucy hesitated. "Can we take our time? Instead of rushing? I quite like the look of this one." She might as well enjoy her day and take Eleanor's advice. Mainz was a magnificent, historical city, full of wonders to explore.

Mrs. Glenn looked pleased. "Of course. This is one of my favorites."

Lucy followed her into the museum.

Mrs. Glenn indicated the rooms ahead of them. "They have exhibits from the prehistoric ages, the Romans, and the Middle Ages. Where shall we begin? The prehistoric hoard?"

"Yes, let's see the coins," Lucy said. "They sound promising."

But she couldn't read anything. The explanations were in German. Mrs. Glenn left her, and Lucy stared at the corroded metal disks, thinking about the passage of time. About objects and people and emotions long buried and forgotten.

Although she and Papa had buried Mama ten years ago, they'd never forgotten her. Papa had buried his grief in piles of paperwork, but he refused to allow Lucy the same luxury. While he often left for London, she stayed home, alone with Aunt Ellen, with nothing to do. No distractions from the pain and loneliness.

No matter how many times she asked or tried to get involved, Papa steadfastly refused to allow her any part in his business empire. She listened to the explanation of his dealings and eagerly asked questions about the details of transactions. Papa liked to talk as much as she did.

But he insisted that she learn to embroider. And pour tea.

Instead, she spent as much time riding horses as she could. At least Papa viewed that as an aristocratic pastime, too.

Lucy examined the ancient tools, evidence of a civilization gone for three thousand years at least. Probably longer, but she couldn't read the card.

She'd tried to evade Papa's rules by spending as much time as possible in the stables, learning bookkeeping and balancing the stablemaster's ledgers with him. True, George, one of the grooms, also tried to teach her how to kiss, but she much preferred balancing a row of numbers.

In the end, Papa had discovered what they were doing. He'd sent George away and begun arranging her marriage contract immediately. Her protests had been futile.

She insisted she didn't want an aristocratic alliance; she wanted to inherit Papa's business. But fathers chose for their children.

As she wandered through the exhibits, Lucy tried to fight the accumulating feelings of hopelessness and helplessness. Things felt beyond her reach. Papa hadn't listened. Walter abandoned her, and she might not ever find him. If she did, he seemed unlikely to ever love her the way she wanted to be cherished. She should resign herself to a marriage of convenience, like so many others.

She couldn't look for Walter forever. He might have already left Mainz, and how would she ever know where he'd gone? She couldn't chase him around the entire Continent. She either had to return home in a few weeks when Eleanor moved on to Italy, or she had to actually stay and attend nursing school for the remainder of the six months.

She had never traveled and began to wonder what she'd undertaken when she embraced this venture. She'd never last six months. It had been hard enough the last six days. Lost in thought, she bumped into an elderly man. He spoke angrily to her and moved away.

She didn't understand anything anyone said to her anyway.

And Papa wanted to use her marriage as a means to join the aristocracy. He wanted a title for her, even if she did not want one, and now she was betrothed to a man who had fled from her. All the money in the world couldn't make Chelmsford marry her, even if it paid for train tickets and lodging and new clothes.

She would never be good enough for a viscount. She sat on a bench to study the exhibits. Was it even worth trying? Why was she doing this? Perhaps she should go home now.

She tried to fight the overwhelming feelings crowding her mind and recapture Eleanor's enthusiasm from yesterday. She determined to stop wallowing in self-pity and moved over toward another exhibit. She leaned over the glass to study the prehistoric tools.

A man bumped into her. She braced herself for another tirade in a language she couldn't understand.

But he turned toward her. He wasn't an elderly man, stooped over with age. He was young. Tall. Familiar. Apologetic. A confused voice asked, "Lucy?"

Dark hair. Deep brown eyes. Eyebrows furrowed together. That dimpled chin. So much like his brother. Except when he smiled. A single dimple in one cheek.

Peter.

Surely her heart would stop beating. She had found them. Or they had found her.

CHAPTER 4

Lucy.

What was she doing here, of all places? Were his eyes playing tricks? Surely, she was an illusion. Peter blinked. No. She was still there.

"Sit, Peter. Join me." Lucy walked over to a bench and sat.

He stared at her.

Lucy patted the bench beside her.

He looked around. Who else was here? Lucy couldn't be alone.

"Are you traveling with your father?" Peter asked. He felt awkward. Guilty. Caught.

Lucy shifted to make room for him. "Please, Peter." She smiled. Her blond curls bounced as she tilted her head toward him.

Peter reluctantly walked to the center of the exhibit room. He squeezed himself sideways onto the small bench, acutely aware that his large frame barely fit. His leg brushed against Lucy's, but there was nowhere to go. It twitched, and Peter stood back up again, tripping backwards. He righted himself and smoothed his vest and coat.

"I'm surprised to see you here," Peter said. *What a stupid thing to say*, he thought to himself.

"We were enjoying the Roman coin exhibit," Lucy said. "And the prehistoric hoards. Did you know there was such a thing?"

"I did. I didn't know that you knew." Peter wanted to kick himself. First, he said something stupid, and now he insulted her. He sounded almost as condescending as Walter. He needed to try again.

"Why are you here in Mainz?" Peter asked. That sounded too abrupt and rude. What was wrong with him? Why couldn't he have a normal conversation? This was just Lucy.

"I'm training as a nurse with Rachel at the Mainz Institute," Lucy said.

Peter tried to take it in. Lucy. In Germany. Walter was not going to like this. Perhaps if he didn't say anything? He turned and pretended to examine another exhibit.

She didn't move. He looked back at her.

Lucy was watching him intently. "I've been hoping to find Walter. Since we're in the same area."

Now he had to say something again. She expected him to talk.

"Yes, he's here, too," Peter said. *Obviously! We go everywhere together.* He wanted to leave. This was all going wrong.

"Are you sure you won't sit?" Lucy asked. "We have so much to discuss."

Peter blew out a deep breath. "No, I was just leaving."

"No!" Lucy stood. She grabbed his arm. Her face was close to his. Too close.

"Don't go yet." She smiled and spoke sweetly, but her fierce glare gave her away, as well as the fingernails sinking into his forearm.

Lucy threaded her arm through his. Her grip was like iron. Hard as steel. "I'll leave with you. Which way did you come?" She motioned to an older woman in one corner. "Mrs. Glenn? I'm finished with the exhibit."

There was no way out of this. Peter knew how angry Walter would be if he brought Lucy home. How could he put her off for a few days?

"The afternoon is so beautiful. Will you walk along the river with me?" Peter asked.

Lucy's iron grip tightened even further. "I'm in no rush. Is that agreeable, Mrs. Glenn?"

"Certainly." Mrs. Glenn gave Peter a curious look. "Will you introduce me, Miss Maldon?"

"Oh, of course. Mrs. Glenn, this is Mr. Peter Chelmsford, from my neighborhood in Essex. My fiancé's brother."

She's engaged. Peter couldn't escape, with Lucy holding on as if he were a skittish horse about to bolt.

Which was exactly how he felt.

Standing with Lucy on his arm, he couldn't help but notice that she fit perfectly into his side. She felt good, and she smelled even better, like the rose garden in spring. It made him as itchy as springtime did, too.

Yes, he needed to find a way to end this conversation, then get himself back to their cottage and away to Vienna as quickly as possible.

Peter guided Lucy out of the museum and across the street to a walking path. The sky was clear. The August breeze gently ruffled Lucy's hair, and the Rhine flowed quietly beside them. Mrs. Glenn followed discretely behind them.

Peter had no idea what to say. "I wanted to examine the difference between medieval artifacts I had seen at the British Museum and the display here."

"What did you decide?" Lucy asked.

"Fascinating collection," Peter said. "I've been to that museum several times."

Lucy turned her head toward him. "Do you live nearby?"

So, she was not going to be deterred.

"No."

They continued along the river path.

"Peter, where is Walter?" Lucy asked. She stopped and faced him. "Why is he avoiding me?"

"He's not avoiding you. He doesn't even know you're here." He knew it was a lie. Of course Walter was avoiding her. But this is what he always did. Lie for his brother. He hated doing it, but Walter left him no choice.

"Well, now that you know I'm here, we can get together," Lucy said. "In the evenings after my nursing classes." She started walking again.

Really, the weather was perfect. Peter could even hear a few birds. He wanted to stop and try to identify which bird call it was. Was it in that bush ahead? Or over in that clump of trees bending low over the water?

"So?" Lucy said.

"We were about to leave for Vienna," Peter said. "I'm sorry."

"I want to speak with Walter."

Peter tried to listen for the bird again. He couldn't hear it.

"Peter Chelmsford. Are you going to give me your address?"

Peter swallowed. "Will you allow me to call on you this evening? I don't believe you told me who you are traveling with."

"What are you hiding?" Lucy asked.

Peter tried to find something to distract Lucy. Anything. But there wasn't a cloud in the sky. "Nothing. You know I was always terrible at hide and seek. I recall that you were an excellent seeker. Case in point: today."

Lucy waited. "And your dimple is more pronounced when you worry, like right now." She touched his chin. "There."

Even through his carefully clipped beard, the contact seared his skin. Peter blinked and took a step backward. "I would simply like to call on you tonight."

"I am not letting go of your arm until you give me your address." Lucy's fingers dug into his arm. She pulled him around and stared up at him, grinning.

They stood close. Her face was tilted toward him, and her blue eyes flashed with irritation, even while she smiled sweetly. She looked slightly flushed from walking. Her creamy white skin high-lighted the perfect redness of her mouth. He felt a pull like he'd never felt toward any other woman.

This isn't fair. She's going to be my brother's wife.

But she was within reach. So close. He had to get rid of her. Quickly.

The words tumbled out of Peter's mouth. "I promise I will call on you tonight. Will you give me your address?"

Lucy hesitated. True, Walter had not kept his promise. Why should she trust Peter?

"This was my father's ring. A keepsake he passed on to me." Peter held up his fingers. "Take it as ransom that I shall return."

He extended his hand, and Lucy fit her own around it. He didn't know what to do. Her small fingers nestled inside his perfectly. The shock of her touch, and the feel of her hand in his, paralyzed him. Lucy wrestled the ring off his smallest finger.

The ring, Peter reminded himself. *That's why she's holding your hand.*

"You are an excellent negotiator." She slipped it onto her middle finger. "My papa would be proud of you."

Peter cleared his throat. Finally, they were done, and he could leave.

She smiled up at him. "When you bring me Walter, you can have your ring back."

Walter. That unfroze him. He had always admired Lucy's audacity, but this was too much.

"That ring belonged to my father," Peter said. "It's one of the few tokens I have left to remember him. I only meant it as a promise that I would return."

"Then I will keep it safe," Lucy said softly, "until tonight when you bring Walter."

Peter rode toward their rented dwelling as quickly as his horse could go. Trees, the river, cottages. It was all a blur. He had to tell Walter. There was so much he didn't know and didn't understand. The sound of hooves landing on the soft soil of the trail beat time with his thoughts. Why was Lucy here? How had she found him? How would his brother react?

He stabled his horse and washed up. He only had an hour to change, find Lucy's address, and explain that the woman Walter had left England to avoid had just found him.

He took a deep breath and pushed open the door to the drawing room. Walter paced back and forth between the ornate pieces of furniture. Somehow Walter always seemed to select the most gaudy and uncomfortable furnishings everywhere they went.

"Finally," Walter said. "You took a long time at the museum."

Peter removed his mud-splattered boots. No dirt in the drawing room. He brushed off his trousers and lowered himself onto a sofa. Better get it over with. "You should have come with me. I met Lucy Maldon there. We walked along the river together."

"What!" Walter stormed over. "Not possible."

"Possible, I assure you," Peter said. "She's looking for you. Wanted our address. I didn't give it to her."

"Thank you." Walter started pacing again.

"But I promised to call on her tonight. She's expecting you."

Walter's face was a dark cloud. "She'll be disappointed, then."

"Were you able to meet with the widow?" Peter asked.

The scowl on Walter's face deepened. "Her father turned me away. I offered him five times her normal fee and gave him my address. Five times. And her normal fee is not inexpensive."

Peter hated double negatives or anything close to them. Why couldn't people speak clearly and precisely? Why not say exactly how much it cost?

"I'm sorry," Peter said. "I told Lucy we were leaving for Vienna. If you want to avoid her, we could leave tomorrow."

"No!" Walter rubbed his forehead with his hand. "I gave Mrs. Smith's father one week to consider my offer. I'm not leaving until I hear back. A real séance. Think of it. Just like in London. What if I could talk to Father? He could send me a message."

Peter sighed. Walter believed the strangest things. Parlor magic tricks. Table-tilting. Anything that couldn't be proven by science. "What will I tell Lucy?"

"Keep her away from me. Tell her anything. Give me a week. Promise me."

"It's that important to you?" Peter asked.

Walter collapsed into a hideous chair. Orange and purple stripes and too stiff to ever get comfortable. "Being the viscount. Trying to walk in Father's footsteps. He left me burdens I cannot carry. I need his guidance. This woman can do that."

Peter felt a strange sense of pity. He studied Walter's face. "It must be a lot of responsibility."

"Too much," Walter said. "It has tested me in ways I never imagined. Father prepared me my whole life, but when he died, I wasn't ready. Give me some time. Please."

Peter shifted on the sofa. He hated lying. How did he always get into these situations? Walter always had a reason, and the pocket-book. "Yes. I promise, Walter."

"Whatever it takes. Lucy likes you. Just distract her until my séance."

But Peter was more worried about the way Lucy distracted *him*. What lies would he have to tell her? And how long could he keep her away?

CHAPTER 5

Peter arrived for dinner barely on time. He smelled like leather. Lucy loved the smell of leather. His closely tailored clothes fit perfectly. He seemed slightly taller than Walter. Was he taller than Walter? All of the Chelmsford brothers were so athletic. Broad shoulders, muscled arms.

Colonel Loughton cleared his throat. Lucy felt her cheeks warm. She realized she was standing quite close to Peter and stepped away. "Mr. Kempton, Miss Loughton, Colonel, this is a friend from home."

Colonel Loughton grinned at her.

She knew she was blushing, but continued the introduction in a steady voice. "This is Mr. Peter Chelmsford." She turned to him. "We last saw you at Easter, did we not? How are your brothers?"

She studiously avoided Colonel Loughton's scrutiny and attempted to sound like an old childhood friend. That's exactly what she was. This was perfectly ordinary, as normal as the easy friendship between Miss Loughton and Mr. Kempton.

"They are well. Arthur and Benjamin are both at Cambridge this year," Peter said.

"Yes," Lucy said. "I remember they mentioned their courses

when we spoke at *Christmas*." She emphasized the holiday for the colonel's sake. Their families spent all the holidays together. It was perfectly normal that she should be staring at the snug fit of Peter's vest coat across his muscled chest.

Perhaps not.

What had she been thinking this afternoon? Throwing herself at him? Wearing his ring? She and Rachel had spent so many years swooning over all four of the Chelmsford brothers. They looked so much alike. Except Peter. He was the only one with that adorable cheek dimple.

Still, it wouldn't do to confuse Peter with his brother. The one she was going to marry. The one who hadn't shown up tonight. They were complete opposites in personality.

"You're here with all of them?" Peter asked. "Why didn't you warn me? I thought it was merely your father and Rachel."

"Eleanor is on her wedding trip," Lucy said. "They are stopping here on the way to Italy. Where is Walter?"

Peter didn't respond.

She had expected Walter all afternoon. Imagined several scenarios. Heartbroken, contrite Walter. Apologetic Walter. Bashful, embarrassed Walter. Grateful, lovesick Walter. Reluctant, but resigned Walter. Eager Walter, who heard the news and rushed to her side as quickly as possible.

She'd never expected Absent Walter. Unavailable, unapologetic Walter.

"Nice accommodations you have here," Peter finally answered. "We're over in the Mombach neighborhood."

Lucy glanced at Eleanor and Lord Shelford. Did they know where that was? How much did that narrow down his location?

Lord Shelford glared at Peter.

"We expected Walter to come with you," Lady Shelford said. "I had a place set for him."

Peter shifted uncomfortably. "Yes. I'm sorry he couldn't come. We were recently made aware of a widow, and he wanted to make sure she was cared for."

"Oh, how kind," Lucy said. She had never seen a generous impulse from Walter. Perhaps she had misjudged him. What a wonderful thing to learn about him. But still. This widow was more important than her? He hadn't seen her in three months. She felt uneasy. Perhaps the poor widow was ill, and it was urgent. How old was the widow?

"How unexpected," Lord Shelford muttered.

"Shall we proceed in to dinner?" Lady Shelford asked. "Peter, if you'll accompany Rachel? And Colonel Loughton, if you'll accompany Lucy, that is, Miss Maldon? Mr. Kempton, if you'll accompany Miss Loughton? Mrs. Glenn, I am so sorry to find us without an even number." She looked at Peter meaningfully.

He left Lucy's side to offer his arm to Rachel, who glowed. She'd always had a preference for Peter.

Lucy glanced sideways at the colonel. He grinned back at her and lowered his voice as they walked in to dinner. "Once an army man, always a soldier, Miss Maldon. I have my own strategy, so long as you approve. Do you prefer your old friend for her or yourself? Should I worry?"

Lucy was grateful for a distraction. Anything to take her mind off Walter. "The only thing you have to worry about is Rachel's preference," she whispered back. "All the strategy in the world won't win that war. She's stubborn."

"But I am an exceedingly patient man," Colonel Loughton said.

"The doctor is patient?" Lucy asked.

"Precisely."

Lucy watched Peter settling himself beside Rachel. It would be a good match for both of them. It made sense. Something made her stomach suddenly feel unsettled. A match with Colonel Loughton made more sense for Rachel.

"I am enlisted in your cause," Lucy said quietly. "Give me a call to action when I am needed."

Colonel Loughton's smile covered his face. "Right now I need you to be an excellent dinner companion. Step one. Never let your opponent know your battle plans."

"Who's your opponent? Peter or Rachel?"

"Both," the colonel said. "May I serve you?"

The dinner passed agreeably. Colonel Loughton was charming and witty. Across the table, Peter sat quietly next to Rachel. They hardly spoke while Lucy and the colonel laughed and enjoyed themselves.

Lucy felt a strange sense of freedom being engaged. The men knew it was safe to talk with her. She was not trying to entrap them. She was already betrothed. It was remarkable how much more comfortable Mr. Kempton and the colonel were with her than men usually were. Than Walter was.

On the other side of the table, Rachel looked awkward and embarrassed. She kept her head down, staring at the napkin in her lap, or ate to avoid talking. Miss Loughton spoke with Mr. Kempton easily, as old friends.

Rachel and Peter should have spoken comfortably like that. It was remarkable how a little attraction could ruin a perfectly good friendship.

She didn't have a friendship to ruin with Walter. She knew him as an acquaintance more than a friend, really. He could be so aloof, so much more so than his younger brothers. Long rides with the brothers, walks in the parks around their estate, games as children —somehow, she and Rachel ended up talking with Peter and Arthur more often than Walter.

All she had to do was make Walter fall in love with her. They would have the most remarkable, romantic story to tell their children someday about how they fell in love in Germany. Once she saw him.

After dinner, they gathered in the drawing room. Mrs. Glenn read in the corner while the others talked amiably.

Peter waited near the door. "I'm afraid I must leave while there's still enough light to ride home."

"You can stay with us tonight," Lord Shelford said. "We have plenty of extra rooms."

Eleanor moved past Peter to leave the room. "I'm telling them to prepare a room right now. Yes, stay for parlor games. I'll be right back."

Peter looked lost. Rachel could hardly meet his gaze. Lucy hoped he would stay, so she could talk to him and get more information. Perhaps he would let something else slip. She caught his eye.

"Who will you partner with?" Lucy asked. "If you leave, we'll have an odd number of players. Four women and three men."

Colonel Loughton waved for Peter to join him. "That will never do. We need equal forces."

Peter moved into the room. "Perhaps one round."

Lucy smiled at him and relaxed in her chair. "We have to make sure the teams are fair, Colonel."

He shrugged. "Shelford, I leave that entirely to your discretion, but Kempton cheats. Be warned."

"Hey now!" Mr. Kempton said. "Only to level the playing field."

"You admit it?" Lucy asked.

"Of course," Mr. Kempton said. "Loughton is a regular bully at these games. One has to cheat to have any sort of chance at all."

Rachel glanced between them. "Do you cheat at cards as well?"

"Anything at all," Mr. Kempton said. "Until he catches me. That's the fun of it."

"How about Move All?" Eleanor asked as she swept back into the room. "I like games with forfeits."

"Or the laughing game?" Mr. Kempton said. "Loughton can never keep a straight face."

Lucy wondered what kind of games Walter liked. Would they have a merry household? Did he like to laugh as much as she did? Or was he as somber as he often appeared?

But she didn't want to play any parlor games with forfeits, not without Walter here. If she had to pay a penalty, who would she kiss?

They waited while the footmen rearranged the furniture to form a circle. After they found chairs, Shelford began a laughing game.

He looked directly in Lady Shelford's eyes and said, "Ha."

Lady Shelford responded serenely. "Ha. Ha."

The colonel had seated himself beside Rachel. He leaned over, then stopped. His face twitched. He bit his lip.

Rachel raised an eyebrow. His face twitched again.

"He never wins," Miss Loughton said.

Loughton straightened as Rachel tilted her head, batted her eyelashes, and smiled at him. "Ha. Ha. Ha." He began laughing in earnest.

"You're out!" Mr. Kempton shouted triumphantly. He turned toward Miss Loughton. "I'll start the next round. Ha."

"Ha. Ha," Miss Loughton continued.

Peter turned toward Lucy. His dark eyes held a hint of mischief. "Ha. Ha. Ha." He smirked at her, challenging her. Peter. She'd known him her whole life and never seen him act like this. That look—it was almost flirtatious.

"Ha. Ha. Ha. Ha," Lucy said and began giggling. "I'm out as well, Colonel. I think I'll be terrible at this game." She could not erase the image of Peter, eyes sparkling.

The game went around and around until only Mr. Kempton and Peter remained.

"Ha."

"Ha. Ha."

"Ha. Ha. Ha."

It went on and on. "This will take forever," the colonel said. He began waving his arms in Mr. Kempton's face, and Mr. Kempton laughed.

"Now who's cheating?" Mr. Kempton asked between gasps. "Well done, Chelmsford."

Lord Shelford waited in the center of the drawing room. "As winner of the last game, you can begin the next game. Stand in the center of the circle and remove one chair. You know the rules. When Chelmsford calls 'Move all,' if you cannot find a chair, you owe him a forfeit. Gentlemen, I suggest we try exceedingly hard to oust him and take over his position."

Lucy watched Rachel. Did her friend want to kiss Peter or the colonel? Lucy would try to slip into a chair quickly and avoid having to give a forfeit, so Rachel could. These games would be a lot more fun if Walter were here.

Peter shouted, "Move all," before Lucy had a chance to gather her wits. Mr. Kempton elbowed her and lunged for a chair. Colonel Loughton somehow managed to push Rachel onto a chair, which left Lucy standing in the middle of the circle.

Lucy's heart began to beat faster. She remembered this afternoon near the river, when she had talked to Peter. She hadn't meant to stand so close to him.

"Forfeit!" Colonel Loughton yelled.

Lucy advanced to the center of the circle. She blew a kiss toward Peter. That should be enough.

"Boo!" Mr. Kempton yelled.

"Don't give the other women ideas," the colonel agreed.

Lucy went up on her tiptoes. A small peck should suffice. Enough to satisfy the others, but nothing inappropriate from a future sister-in-law.

Peter still smelled like leather. She couldn't reach. She put one hand on his shoulder to steady herself, then tilted his jaw away from her. She kissed his cheek. Right on the dimple.

Warmth filled her, and something else. A desire for more.

He turned toward her, a look of surprise covering his face. His eyes darted to Lucy's lips. They stood still a moment, gazing at each other.

"Out you go! Lucy's in the middle now," Eleanor said.

Peter blinked and straightened. Lucy pulled away quickly and hastily dropped her hands.

"Move all!" she called quickly.

Everyone else shuffled around, and Peter was left standing right where he'd been. He hadn't moved.

They stared at each other. Peter advanced, a half-smile on his face. She waited, her heart pounding wildly. He kissed her on the cheek, as she had kissed him, but not as lightly. A little more.

"Boo!" Mr. Kempton yelled again! "No more cheek kisses!"

"Hear, hear," Colonel Loughton said. "Let's oust them from the middle." He stood up.

"Move all!" Peter called.

Lucy scrambled, knocking Rachel into the center. She landed on something soft. Not a chair. A lap. She looked up. Peter's lap. He'd left the center. She started to fall, and his arm reached out to catch her.

Her eyes widened at the same time his did. He let go, and she slid onto the empty chair next to her.

Colonel Loughton and Mr. Kempton both stood in the middle of the circle.

"Forfeit!" Lord Shelford cried out. "You must both pay a penalty. What shall we make them do?"

"Now who's cheating?" Kempton asked.

"At least we ousted him," the colonel said.

Lucy needed to get away from Peter and these unwelcome, distracting feelings.

"I'll sit with Mrs. Glenn," she said. "Go ahead and play without me." She stood and began to cross the circle.

"I'll join you," Peter said.

They walked side by side without talking, Peter so close that she could feel him beside her. She glanced at Rachel as she passed. Rachel was watching her closely. When Lucy caught her eye, Rachel turned away.

She had left the game to give Rachel a chance with Peter. It wasn't her fault that he followed her. She was trying to get away from him.

Over in the corner, Mrs. Glenn seemed completely absorbed in her book.

Lucy's heart had still not returned to normal. She searched for something to say. Something to restore her focus and take her mind off the feel of Peter's arm around her. "Does Walter like parlor games?"

Peter tried to fit onto the sofa. He shifted this way and that, but his large frame wasn't meant for delicate furniture. "No, we never played them much."

"But you're so good at them," Lucy said. "At not laughing."

Peter laughed. His eyes lit up, and his single dimple appeared. "I learned at Cambridge and on holidays with friends."

Lucy studied him. Who was this man? This light-hearted, yet serious, gentleman who made her pulse race. She had lived near him her whole life, and she thought of him only as a neighborhood acquaintance. A comfortable friend she saw on holidays and during the summer. She'd come to know and love his mother over the last few months, but Peter had been gone to University.

She needed to remind herself that she was marrying his brother. She needed to stop thinking about him and focus on Walter. "Will you help me? Before you leave for Vienna? I know you only have a few days. But I came all the way from England to see your brother. He signed a marriage contract with my father, and I intend to marry him, whether it's here or in England. I don't care."

Peter stared at her. The light left his eyes. "You want to marry him here?"

"Why not? I can come to Vienna with you. I need you to help me convince Walter to marry me." It was rash, but the words tumbled out of her mouth before she thought.

"It will not happen this week," he said. "I'm sorry Walter didn't come tonight. But a wedding so quickly? Something so rushed would be disappointing for both of you, and for my mother."

Peter's kind face and gentle tone almost undid her. His mention of Lady Chelmsford choked her throat, and she couldn't respond for a moment. For the first time in ten years, she had a mother again.

"I would never hurt your mother, but Walter keeps putting it off," Lucy said. "I need him to fall in love with me."

He blinked. "You want me to help you make Walter fall in love?"

"Yes."

Peter leaned his head back on the sofa and closed his eyes. He blew out a deep breath. "Lucy. You're asking a lot."

"I don't know what else to do," she said. "Papa's already paid the settlement money."

He sighed. "Will you give me one week? We aren't leaving for at least that long. I can help you prepare. Get you ready before you see Walter. Would that work?"

Lucy couldn't decide whether to accept his offer or to push him for a better answer. She wanted to see Walter and get away from Peter. Spending more time with Peter seemed like a bad idea, especially after that kiss. *That kiss.*

"No," she said. "Why can't I see him before then?"

"Walter doesn't like surprises," he said. "Give him a week to get used to the idea that you're in town."

Lucy stared at him. "I'm a surprise? An unwelcome one?" Anger got the better of her. "Why does he need a week to accustom himself to my presence? He's had months to accept the idea of our engagement. No, Peter. I should not speak of my marriage in terms of reconciliation. He negotiated with my father, not me."

"A week," he repeated. "You won't get the reaction you want if you push him into meeting you any earlier. Trust me."

His grim face worried her. What was Walter's temperament? Papa laughed so often. Even when they disagreed, Papa was gentle. He never yelled or lost his temper. He simply said "no" and held his ground. Lucy couldn't imagine marriage with an austere or angry man.

But Peter refused to tell her anything more. If she wished to know why Walter still avoided her, she'd have to win his trust.

"A week," she agreed. She would need every moment to understand exactly what kind of marriage she was getting herself into and how to distance herself from Peter while trying to grow closer to his brother.

CHAPTER 6

The sound of Walter's knock reverberated through the clearing. The cottage was a humble dwelling, not too far from their own, but much smaller. Evidently, the widow and her father wanted to stay away from the main part of the city, too, or they couldn't afford a large rent.

Peter hoped no one would answer. When he'd come home from the Shelfords' apartments this morning, his brother had been waiting. The widow's father had sent back a reply. For that much money, the widow would make an exception.

So here he was, middle of the afternoon, attending a séance with Walter, then riding back into the Old City to visit Lucy tonight.

Maybe Walter would come with him. He could try. Maybe he could suggest that to the medium.

A kindly-looking gentleman opened the door. "Come in, come in," he said. "Mrs. Smith requires perfect silence."

Walter glared at him, even though he hadn't made a sound. The creaking of the door hinges was the only noise.

"Before you enter our sanctuary, the spirits require proof of your dedication," the man said.

Ah. Payment.

Walter hefted a large bag of coins and handed it over.

The man opened the bag and counted the coins. "I don't believe we've been introduced. I forget myself. You may speak solely to answer my questions."

They entered the cramped hallway. It was sparsely furnished with only a writing desk and chair shoved up against one wall. The surroundings did not inspire confidence.

A slight creak distracted him. He glanced over. Someone had barely opened the side door. He could see an ear pressed against the wall.

But Walter's attention was entirely on the man.

"What is your name?" the gentleman asked.

"I am Lord Chelmsford."

The man set the payments carefully in the writing desk and closed the lid. "Your full name, location from which you are traveling, and your companion's name."

"Walter Richard Abraham Chelmsford, traveling from my estate in Essex. This is my brother, Mr. Peter Andrew Michael Chelmsford, who is training to take orders and be a vicar." Walter pursed his lips tightly, as though he wanted to make sure no extra sound escaped him. He shot a warning look at Peter.

Peter wondered why he had included the information about him preparing to take orders. Did he think it would impress the medium? That he was supposedly religious too?

"Very good. I am Mrs. Smith's father, Mr. Ford." He put a finger to his lips. "Can you feel that?"

Peter felt nothing. Walter nodded vigorously.

"The harmonic vibrations. You have brought such goodness with you. I feel it. Come, let us see whether Mrs. Smith is ready for you." Mr. Ford ushered them into the small sitting room.

For one moment, when the door opened, Peter could see inside. A round, rough wooden table occupied the center of the parlor. The tiny woman waited with her eyes closed. An enormous shawl wrapped around her and the chair on which she sat. Every curtain in the room was drawn.

Mr. Ford gestured toward the chairs, then closed the door.

Peter blinked. It was nearly as dark as midnight. He stumbled on the uneven floorboards, then caught himself on the table. He felt his way along the edge of the round surface and squeezed into one of the chairs on the far side across from Mrs. Smith.

Walter nudged him and jerked his head, indicating that he wanted to sit in the middle of the table, with the best view of the séance.

Peter switched to a chair on the side. Mr. Ford settled on Mrs. Smith's other side.

They waited in silence for a minute. His eyes gradually adjusted to the darkness.

Finally, Mrs. Smith spoke. Her voice was as pure and angelic as it had sounded in the cathedral. "Join hands."

Peter held her hand with one and took Walter's hand with his other. Walter was probably regretting his seating choice now.

"The circle is unbroken," she said and paused.

He hated this already.

Mrs. Smith glanced sideways. "The spirits need your faith. Speak and tell us your belief."

Perhaps she could sense his antagonism.

"I've always wanted to consult a medium," Walter said. "The moment I saw you in the cathedral, I knew you were an angel sent from God."

Silence.

Peter thought desperately. He had seen Professor Anderson perform false séances in London to disprove them last year at Christmastime. He couldn't very well say that.

"I have attended a séance before," Peter said. That was enough of the truth.

The widow squeezed his hand gently. "Let us pray. Vicar? Will you lead our prayer?"

He wanted to protest, but he knew the strict rules. No words, just answers. This meant everything to Walter. Peter couldn't explain that he wasn't a vicar yet. He prayed.

"Amen," Mr. Ford and Mrs. Smith murmured.

"Now let us sing." The widow began, "Nearer, my God to thee…"

Walter gasped. "That's one of my favorites! How did you know?"

Mrs. Smith continued to sing as though she had not heard him.

It's everyone's favorite, Peter thought. He joined in the hymn.

Five verses later, it finally ended. Suddenly, a loud rap sounded on the floor. Another. And another.

The widow let go of Peter's hand. "Place your hands flat on the table. The spirits are pleased and wish to enter the room."

They flattened their palms, fingers spread out. His eyes had definitely adjusted to the darkened room now. He could see the outline of each person. Together, their hands nearly covered the entire surface.

Peter and Walter barely fit, their knees pressed up against the top of the table. Mr. Ford's knees must do the same. He remembered the demonstration by Professor Anderson in London. If he wasn't mistaken, they were due for some table-tilting soon.

Mrs. Smith's eyes were closed again. The fraud. How many other people had she been cheating?

"The spirits have entered," she said.

"My father," Walter said. "Is he here? Is it him?"

"Yes."

Of course it was. Now that his brother had told her who it should be.

More knocks on the floor. They certainly knew how to create a spectacle.

"He wishes to greet you from beyond the grave." Her voice had grown gentle and misty.

Peter had to give her credit. She was a remarkable actress. Even through his skepticism, he felt a thrill.

The knocking grew loud and insistent.

The widow cried out. Her delicate features contorted. "Oh. He is in pain. He senses worry. He cannot rest. His peace is disturbed. He has come back from the grave for you. Only for you, Walter."

Did she not realize Peter was his son, too?

"How does she know my name?" Walter whispered to me. "It must be Father speaking."

"I am sensing nobility. He was a fine man. Many duties. A lord."

Walter leaned across the table. "Yes, yes. Why is he restless?"

"His name is floating." She waved her arms in the air. "I can nearly sense it. Is it Richard?"

"Yes!" Walter shouted. "He's here. It's him. Father, speak to me."

The table began to lift and tilt. Peter thought Mr. Ford had pushed it up with his knees and that Mrs. Smith had sent it back with hers. He tried to repress his incredulity for Walter's sake.

Walter was oblivious to their tricks. "Father! Tell me how to manage the estate and care for the family. The burden is too heavy."

The table stilled and touched back down to the ground. Mrs. Smith produced a slate in front of her.

"Your father sends a message," she said. "Read the slate."

Walter grabbed the slate eagerly. "It's blank." He turned it over. "Both sides."

"Patience," the widow said. Her voice was smooth and reassuring. "It requires much effort."

Peter saw a bulge under her shawl. While she was moaning and waving one hand, she reached behind her back and quickly swapped the blank slate with another. Yes, a complete fraud.

Mrs. Smith replaced the slate on the table with the new one quickly. She shoved the old slate behind her back and covered it with her mounds of shawls. She put both hands to her head and swayed back and forth.

He glanced to make sure Walter saw this sham. Of course not. Walter was searching the rafters for Father's specter.

She cried out. "Oh, the vibrations are strong. Your father wishes you to receive this message."

Peter wondered, idly, why Father hadn't spoken to him. If he were really there. But he hadn't paid, after all. Only Walter had. Still, he thought the medium should try a little harder to include both of them in her act.

Mrs. Smith moaned and held her head. She put her hand over her heart. She seemed nearly ready to faint.

"I cannot allow this to continue. It takes so much from her," Mr. Ford said.

Walter pointed at the slate. "But the message! We haven't read the message!"

Mr. Ford picked it up and gasped dramatically. "It's here." He handed the slate to Walter. Clearly, he and his daughter conspired together.

Mrs. Smith collapsed backward in her chair, her eyes closed, her hand on her forehead. Peter heard a slight crunch as her back hit the hidden slate.

"Peter! It says, 'Return to England.' Father wants me to assume his duties." Walter put down the slate. "That is exactly what he would say. Father, can you hear me?"

Of course he couldn't. And of course the slate said that. They threatened her livelihood. Mrs. Smith and her father wanted them gone as quickly as possible, so they could continue to prey on the naive local inhabitants. The people in this neighborhood had probably never heard of the séances in London. They didn't know how the parlor tricks operated, like Peter did. He could expose her and put an end to her lucrative occupation.

"He has left the room. Mrs. Smith can no longer hold the spiritual vibrations of the other world," Mr. Ford said. "I must ask you to depart and let my daughter recover now."

"Yes, thank you. But he didn't finish his message. I must return. Promise me. I will pay the same. Double."

He saw Mrs. Smith peek an eye open. Mr. Ford glanced at her. She gave a slight nod, then closed her eyes. She held up two fingers by the edge of the table.

"In two days. If you pay double. This has exhausted her

endurance and she will need to regain her strength. The same time. Mid-afternoon is best for her." He led them out of the dark parlor and back into the entrance. The bright light assaulted Peter's eyes.

"May I take the slate?" Walter asked. "As a memento?"

Mr. Ford laughed. "Oh no. The writing would vanish in the sun. The spirits cannot linger in our world. Come back again and I'm sure your father will have more to tell you about your worries. You have worries?"

He laughed to himself. The old man was trying to get information to use for their next visit. How could Walter fall for this? And pay for it, too? Then again, even Charles Dickens belonged to the Ghost Club in London.

"Why does my father wish me to return to England without completing a Grand Tour? Does he feel I am shirking my responsibilities? I know I am running away from…so many things, but can I not have a few more months before I take up his mantle?"

Mr. Ford put a hand on Walter's shoulder. "I am a father, too. I worry greatly about my daughter and have many cares pressing on me. I understand a little of how you must feel with so many responsibilities as the baron? Earl?"

"Viscount."

"Ah, yes."

They walked to their waiting horses and untied them from the post in front of the house. It was all so obvious. Peter didn't dare say anything to Walter, though. The sooner they finished with the séances, the sooner Peter would be done with Lucy.

And the medium had told Walter to go home. This could be useful.

"What did you think of Father's message to you?" Peter asked.

"She was remarkable. She knew his name. She knew my name. She knew my worries. Only a true medium could do that. I felt Father and the spirits in the air." Walter shook his head. "Why didn't you tell me that you'd already attended a séance?"

"It was in London last year. When I went for the Christmas science lectures," he said, "at the Royal Institution."

"Ah," Walter said. "No wonder I missed it."

"Was the medium as miraculous as this angel?" Walter asked.

"It was a man demonstrating with his young daughters. A little different," Peter said. "They disproved the veracity of the medium's claims. He was able to fake a séance."

Walter glared at him.

They rode along a tree-covered path. The sunlight filtered through the leaves. "I'm going back into the Old Town to visit Lucy tonight. She made me promise to return when I saw her."

"I don't know what to do about Lucy," Walter said. "I'm trapped."

Peter debated what to say. "We played parlor games. She kissed me." He waited for a reaction. None. "On the cheek."

Was Walter even listening?

"I kissed her, too." Peter glanced to check. He didn't add anything about the cheek this time.

Walter was staring straight ahead. "Good, good," he said. "She needs a distraction." He urged his horse forward and left Peter behind.

So, Walter wouldn't come with him. He would have to face Lucy alone tonight. Again.

And Walter didn't mind that Peter had kissed her.

CHAPTER 7

Lucy collapsed into a chair. Her head felt like it would explode. One week of classes and things weren't any easier.

The second week of classes had begun today, and she'd hoped that the break over the last couple of days would help. It hadn't.

She still didn't understand German. She still didn't know anything about bones or bodies or herbs. Rachel still knew more than she did. Miss Loughton, who seemed to dislike classes as much as Lucy did, knew more than Rachel.

And Peter was coming again tonight. Lucy didn't know whether that should make her headache worse or better. There were so many complex emotions to address, and she couldn't think with the pounding in her temples.

She could at least rest for a few minutes before she had to face everyone.

But there was a knock at the door.

"The colonel and Miss Loughton to see you," her butler announced.

Lucy straightened in her chair.

"Miss Maldon," the colonel said. "Just the person. I need to speak with you and Miss Wickford before dinner. May I accompany you to the Shelfords'?"

"Of course." Lucy smiled. It was going to be a long night of pretending to be well with this pounding headache.

"But you seem like you're in pain." Colonel Loughton sat beside her. "How are you?"

She couldn't fool him. "The classes are exhausting," she said.

He leaned over her and felt her forehead.

Rachel entered the room. She looked at the colonel bending over Lucy.

"Do you have a lavender compress?" the colonel asked. "Or some oil?"

"Yes. I grow it myself back home. I brought some dried lavender with me. I have a sachet somewhere," Rachel said.

Colonel Loughton nodded. "Could you bring it?"

Rachel nodded. "I'll look for the oil as well."

They waited in silence together. Lucy wondered whether she should try to start a polite conversation. "How did you enjoy classes today, Miss Loughton? Are you understanding the lectures?"

The colonel took her hand and put two fingers on her wrist. "Your pulse is fine, but I'd like to monitor it for a few minutes. You need rest. Lie back and close your eyes. Pretend we're not here."

Lucy couldn't bring herself to ignore guests. "But who will talk to you?"

"Doctor's orders," the colonel said. "Alice can carry a conversation single-handedly. Go ahead."

Lucy leaned back. Miss Loughton arranged cushions behind her and draped a light blanket over her lap.

"I feel a bit ridiculous," Lucy admitted, and she sat back up. "Do the classes wear on you, too, Miss Loughton?"

"In an entirely different way, I assure you." Miss Loughton glared at her brother playfully. "But I am familiar with the subject matter."

"I'm not allowed to be sick. I'm a nurse now," Lucy protested.

"Now you *are* being ridiculous," Rachel said as she entered the room. She pressed a cool compress over Lucy's eyes. "If you'll excuse me, Colonel."

"What?"

"I need to sit by Lucy."

"I am attending to her," he said.

"I cannot help her with you in the way," Rachel said.

"And I cannot ascertain her condition if you get in my way."

Lucy couldn't see anything with the compress over her eyes. She could only hear the deadly silence between them. She knew Rachel was intractable, and she wondered how patient the colonel really was.

A chair scraped across the floor.

"Will that do, Miss Wickford?"

"That will do, Colonel Loughton," Rachel said coolly.

Someone's fingers began to massage oil on her temples. Lucy breathed in the relaxing smell of lavender.

"Oh, Rachel, thank you." The worries of the last few hours, the last few days, the last few months, all pounded in her skull. Rachel kneaded her temples with expert skill and the tension began to ease.

"Lie back in your chair," Rachel ordered.

She allowed her head to drop onto the cushion of her chair. Rachel continued to rub her temples, then her head.

"I'm not doing very well with classes," she said. "I don't under-stand anything, and you and Miss Loughton understand everything."

"Mmm," Rachel said.

The massage stopped for one moment. Lucy heard the sound of a hand being slapped.

"Wait until I'm done," Rachel said. "You're holding her hand. Check her pulse. That's enough."

"Who is the doctor?" Colonel Loughton asked.

No response. Rachel applied a few more drops of lavender oil. Lucy sighed.

"And you and Miss Loughton get along so well. You're great friends already. I don't blame you, Miss Loughton. I'm glad."

"And I've been delighted with your friendship, Miss Maldon," Miss Loughton said. "Will you and Miss Wickford call me Alice?"

She nodded ever so slightly, so the compress wouldn't slip. "Please, call me Lucy."

Despite her brother's teasing, Alice was soft-spoken and rarely interjected herself into the conversation. They rested comfortably in silence for a long moment.

"I may have work for the three of you," the colonel said. "A distraction. We've had a request come in late this afternoon."

"More work?" Lucy said. She felt the tension returning.

"Work that *Herr* Fliedner believes only you, Alice, and Miss Wickford can do," he said. "An Englishwoman has found her way to us. She will give birth soon and needs someone to assist. Since you are the only nurses who speak English, he says it falls to you, although I am not sure if that is wise."

"No, Curtis," Alice said. "Let Miss Wickford and Miss Maldon assist. You know how I feel about that."

Colonel Loughton's voice was commanding. She could imagine he was used to giving orders and being obeyed without question. "You can assist in the kitchen, preparing things, not in the birthing room."

"We'll talk later," Alice said. "Let Miss Maldon and Miss Wickford do this together."

"Well, that's the thing. I'm not sure Miss Wickford or Miss Maldon is ready. They've only been in classes for one week. It will be only two or three weeks. A month at the most when the woman delivers her child." The colonel sounded as though he'd already made up his mind.

Rachel's hands stopped massaging her temples. "I can assist."

Colonel Loughton let go of her hands and wrist, where he must have been taking her pulse. "You're a surgical assistant already?"

"I am a gentleman's daughter," Rachel said.

"What training have you had? I told *Herr* Fliedner we may need to have my sister come or bring one of the nurse instructors, even if she speaks German."

Lucy tried to hold the compress to her eyes and sit up. "Rachel knows enough. Ask her anything."

"Here?" Colonel Loughton asked.

"I'm not embarrassed to discuss medical matters in the drawing room. We're attending school together," Lucy said. She took the compress off her eyes. She couldn't relax right now. Colonel Loughton thought Rachel unqualified, but Lucy knew otherwise. No one was better prepared than her dearest friend.

The colonel paced over to the fireplace. He stood with his feet wide apart and put his arms behind his back. "Miss Wickford, have you attended any births?"

"Seventeen," Rachel said, "in the last two years."

"How? I thought you were a gentleman's daughter."

Rachel crossed the room and faced him. "And so I am. But he has passed away. And my mother is frequently ill."

Colonel Loughton's face was incredulous. "And you attend births with her permission?"

"No. Mostly by leaving the house when my mother does not notice. Or when she believes I am with Lucy."

"It's true," Lucy said. She knew what to say when Rachel's mother inquired after her. They had worked it out together years ago.

The colonel stared at Rachel. "It can take hours. Or days, even."

"My mother sleeps a lot," Rachel said.

The colonel folded his arms over his chest and leaned against the fireplace mantle. "Very well. And what was the extent of your assistance? Standing by? Washing a forehead? Holding the mother's hand?"

Rachel folded her arms. "I have guided the child through the birth canal, delivered the baby when the doctor was asleep, and seen a mother die."

Alice covered her mouth. The action drew Lucy's attention.

Alice's face looked pale, and Lucy wondered why her brother insisted Alice attend the medical lectures.

Lucy felt a little faint herself. Talking about the death of a mother always made her miss her own mama. She lay back again.

"You are very matter of fact about it," Colonel Loughton said.

"What use is emotion in the sickroom?" Rachel asked.

The colonel took a step toward Rachel. "Great use, when you're comforting a dying man. Or mother."

Rachel advanced toward the colonel. "It doesn't help the birth come faster. Or help me do what is necessary. And this woman who needs our help will not die."

"It can ease the mother's pain," the colonel said. "This woman claims to be a widow, but she is as young as any of you. The school tells me that many unwed women come to them and claim to be widows to hide their true position."

"Then I am not here to ease her pain. I am here to ease her embarrassment and hide her predicament," Rachel said. "An Englishwoman living alone in Germany, with no funds, and expecting a child? Of course, her situation is unfortunate, and I do not wish her to be uncomfortable. But my primary concern is the cleanliness of the room and those involved."

Lucy watched the two of them. So alike. Neither wanted to yield and both had the best interests of the patient in mind. She wondered whether this conversation would improve the colonel's opinion of Rachel or dampen his enthusiasm.

The colonel studied Rachel. "Have you heard Semmelweis's germ theory? It is popular here, though many call him a quack. Miss Nightingale was stringent in her requirements in the Crimea."

"I have read the theory," Rachel said. "No one with filthy hands will enter her house when she is birthing. You included."

"You are a tyrant," the colonel said, a note of grudging admiration in his voice. He stepped closer to her. They stood a breath apart. "But I will be in charge, Miss Wickford."

Rachel didn't back away, but she raised an eyebrow. "We can discuss that when the time comes, Colonel Loughton. It is my experience that doctors say many things but fail to appear when they are needed. Although they always send their bill."

"There will be no bill," Colonel Loughton said stiffly. "The school receives a small pittance, and I will sleep in the stable, if need be, to stay at hand when her time is near."

Rachel stared at him. "No dirt in my birthing room. Boots included."

Lucy saw the terrifying look on Rachel's face and laughed. "I hate to cross her. You best do as she says. If Rachel is going, then I will gladly assist one of my fellow countrywomen. The poor thing. Alone in Germany and expecting a child. She must be frightened."

The colonel laughed and tipped his hat to Rachel. "I am at your command. So long as we agree on methods." He tipped his hat to Lucy. "And I thank you, Miss Maldon. If you are recovered enough, shall we join the Shelfords?"

Rachel dipped her chin and affected the smallest curtsey she could. "Colonel."

He held out his arm to her and smiled irresistibly. "May I escort you to dinner?"

Rachel huffed.

Evidently, the colonel respected insurrection and insubordination. Or, he tolerated it, when it came from Rachel.

"Truce?" he asked.

Rachel took his arm. Lucy threaded her arm through Alice's, and they made their way upstairs to Eleanor's apartments, where Peter no doubt waited with the dinner party. Lucy's headache returned, full strength.

All this talk of pregnancy and mothers had only made her wonder when she would be a mother herself. How quickly would Walter expect her to produce an heir? Would her children have her blond, curly hair, or Walter's thick, dark hair?

She yearned for children, for family. But no matter how hard she tried, the only image that came to mind was a tiny baby with a dimple in one cheek.

CHAPTER 8

Peter waited in the spacious drawing room with the Shelfords and Kempton. Shelford had engaged apartments in the nicest part of the Old City. Lady Shelford's drawing room was nearly as large as her parents' at Barrington Hall. The furniture was tasteful and understated. Nothing orange or purple here.

Lucy and Rachel lived one floor beneath them in their own set of apartments, while the colonel and Mr. Kempton lived one floor above. Well, Lucy could always afford anything she wanted.

What was taking her so long? Dinner yesterday had been an awkward affair. He was in no hurry to repeat it, but sitting with Shelford and Kempton staring him down was not enjoyable, either.

"Tell me again where Walter is tonight," Lady Shelford said.

"Attending to business letters."

Shelford pushed his glasses up his nose. "I have similar business back home, and yet I take time to eat dinner."

Lady Shelford took her husband's hand and pulled him closer to her on their shared sofa. "Be polite, Percy. You're staying here again tonight, Peter. Any night you visit. I won't have you riding home in the dark. That room is yours. You may stay as our house guest."

Peter looked at Shelford's glower and Lady Shelford's determined face. He didn't want to ride home in the dark, but neither did he want to stay where he was unwelcome.

Lady Shelford nudged her husband.

"You are welcome here," Shelford said. "It's your brother who raises my ire. Not you."

Lady Shelford looked at him intently. "Bring your things over tomorrow. How long will you be here in Mainz?"

Peter squirmed under the scrutiny. The Barringtons had always been intimidating, and Lady Shelford was no different now that she was married. "It's uncertain."

"Where will you go next? We plan to visit Berlin."

"Vienna," Peter said.

Shelford smiled. "We loved Vienna."

"When are the Duxfords coming to dinner?" Lady Shelford asked. "We met them in Vienna. I would love to visit with them before we leave."

"I haven't been able to arrange a time yet," Shelford said.

The butler opened the door of the drawing room to announce the other dinner guests. Finally.

Rachel entered on Loughton's arm. Interesting. As soon as she noticed Peter watching her, she dropped the colonel's arm.

Lucy and Miss Loughton joined the others. Lucy looked pale.

Peter went over to her. "How are you tonight?"

Lucy turned her head toward him. My, but she was small. The top of her head barely came to his shoulders. He resisted an urge to wrap her in his arms. She looked so worn.

"Thank you for your concern. The colonel and Rachel have been extremely solicitous as well." Lucy's voice was quiet.

Peter could barely hear her over the other conversations. He felt unsettled. Lucy's usual affability had given way to melancholy, like his mother's so often did. When Mother felt unwell, he brought her favorite pet to her room and listened to her talk. Father and Walter liked dogs. Mother favored cats.

"Shall we find a quiet corner to wait for dinner?" Peter asked. He guided her toward a pair of oversized chairs.

Once they rested comfortably, he smiled at her. "Tell me about your day."

Lucy began to talk slowly, almost painfully. He nodded. She kept talking and talking. Classes were hard. She didn't understand the language. She missed her papa. She moved forward in her chair. Her feet barely touched the ground.

Her voice grew stronger. She kept talking, telling him all her worries. She was imposing on Eleanor. She wanted to help, but she was a burden. Rachel understood the lectures, and she did not. Peter did what he did best—listened.

Finally, Lucy paused. "You're right," she said. "I'll be fine tomorrow. My friends love me. Papa misses me as much as I miss him. I'm glad we had a chance to talk. I feel my headache clearing. I really can't think straight unless I'm talking. Do you understand?"

It was the first time she had stopped or asked his opinion.

"Not at all," he said. "That is, I understand there are people like you, but I cannot relate one bit."

Lucy laughed, a genuine, bubbly sound.

Peter hoped he could sit by her during dinner tonight. He wasn't any good at starting conversations, and neither was Rachel. Last night had been painful. He'd much rather let Lucy do the talking.

Even though he didn't believe in luck, it was on his side. Lady Shelford paired him with Lucy, and instead of worrying about what to say, he got to spend two hours laughing and listening to Lucy entertain the others with stories.

After dinner, Peter waited with dread to learn what parlor games Lady Shelford would come up with. But Lucy had a plan.

"Let's play chess," she said. "I haven't been able to talk to you about Walter all night."

They pulled up chairs. He began to arrange pieces on a chess board.

"I don't care for this game," Lucy leaned across the small chess table and whispered. "But if we sit here, will they leave us alone?"

Peter studied the room. Everyone else seemed occupied. Lady Shelford caught his eye. She winked.

"I assume so," Peter said. What had that been about? What did Lady Shelford think was happening?

Her looked down at the chessboard and saw Lucy's delicate hand hovering over a pawn. His ring fit perfectly on her middle finger. She still wore it. It felt strange to see his keepsake on Lucy's hand.

"May I have my ring? I have kept my word. I came back." He finished setting up the chess pieces.

Lucy stopped, her hand on a pawn. "No. You haven't brought Walter."

Peter wanted to reach out and take it back, but he didn't want to touch her. He didn't trust himself.

"I'll move first and then is that enough?" she asked. "Can we talk?"

He moved his pawn across from hers. "Just match my moves. But pretend to think a long time between moves."

"Tell me about Walter." Lucy moved another pawn.

He moved his knight. "You've known him your whole life."

She tilted her head. "Tell me things I don't already know, then."

Peter tapped his chin and pretended to think.

She laughed. "Your cheek dimples when you do that."

He looked at the board. "Did you know that it is your move, and that Walter has no cheek dimple?"

Lucy picked up her knight. "I know both of those things. It is your turn now, and your cheek dimples only on one side."

Peter considered her move. She had been paying more attention to the game than he realized. She'd also paid more attention to him than he'd realized. Did she like his dimple or prefer that Walter didn't have one? She had kissed him yesterday during the parlor games—right on that dimpled cheek.

"Walter likes music very much. He often sings in the music room with my mother or alone, when he thinks no one can hear him. He's got an excellent voice." Peter smiled, just to make his dimple appear.

She grimaced and placed her knight on the board. "I don't sing very well. I abhor piano lessons and only sing with Eleanor. You've heard me."

He pondered his next move. "You sing beautifully, even if you don't enjoy it. I love your voice. Let's see." He slid his bishop up four squares. "Walter is very superstitious. He believes in Spiritualism, séances and the like."

Lucy's bishop moved along the board. "But they're ridiculous. You would never countenance such nonsense."

"I agree," Peter said. He moved his other knight.

"He rides well and has excellent taste in animals. I do know that," Lucy said. She moved her knight. "He must be generous, if he wanted to go help a poor, old widow."

Peter's hand paused on a pawn. He hadn't said the age of the widow. But he couldn't let her think the widow was old. That would almost be a direct lie.

"I don't know how old the widow is, but Walter is usually very careful with money."

Lucy looked up from the chess pieces. "Oh. Is he generous in his allowance to you?"

He hesitated. He stared down at the board. What kind of husband would Walter be? "I will have to take orders as a vicar to supplement my allowance. Walter has three brothers and a mother to support. My allowance varies, depending on Walter's mood."

"I wonder what kind of pin money they specified in the marriage contract. Was your father generous with your mother?" Lucy had given up on the game, it seemed to Peter.

He moved a piece without thinking. He'd rather not answer that question. "I couldn't say. Walter is much like my father."

"Papa spoiled Mama before she died, after the mines began to produce, and the fountain pens sold well." She moved a pawn and took his knight.

"I thought you didn't like this game," he said.

"That doesn't mean I don't play well." Lucy smiled, then studied the board. "None of this is going to help me make Walter fall in love with me."

Peter blew out a long breath and rested his head in his hand. He looked at the chess pieces, then selected one. He picked it up, put it back down, then selected another. "But I am enjoying the challenge." He met her gaze and held it.

A pink blush spread over her cheeks. He'd never seen her flustered before.

She moved a piece. "Clearly, we need to do something different. Are you free tomorrow? Could you meet me at the Institute?" Lucy asked.

"Yes."

"If you'll accompany me home instead of the colonel or Mr. Kempton, I'll have more time to talk to you. We won't have to whisper and pretend to play chess. We could stop for coffee or tea at a café. Your turn again, by the way."

Peter had rarely played against someone with whom he was so evenly matched in chess. Was it because he had shown her his strategy? Was she that good? Or was he that distracted?

Lucy looked radiant in the candlelight. Her dress fit her perfectly. If her father let her buy anything she wanted, she used the money well. She had exquisite taste. Her hair was pulled back from her face in a chignon, leaving nothing but porcelain skin and the graceful curve of her neck and shoulders.

How could any man play chess when a woman looked like that? It was all he could do to keep his mind on the game. All thought of strategy flew out the window.

Peter watched her turning back and forth to study the board. How did Walter end up betrothed to Lucy? Peter could see his own ring on her finger, over her gloves, as she moved a piece. Her small hands were as dainty as the rest of her. Would she someday wear Walter's ring instead?

Lady Shelford appeared at the table. "How is the game?" She did a quick appraisal of the chess pieces. "I believe Lucy will win. If you'd like to concede, Peter, we are going to play charades and do some puzzles."

"Oh! I love riddles," Lucy said. She stood and held out her hand. "Let's join them."

He stared at the chess pieces. Yes, Lucy was winning. How could he avoid taking her hand without being rude? He couldn't.

He took her hand and let her drag him over near the others. It fit perfectly, just as it had yesterday when she tugged off his ring. It felt so natural and easy, just like talking with Lucy. Their conversations were effortless and so much less awkward than he usually felt with women. All he had to do was listen, smile, and ask her questions.

She pulled him onto a sofa with her. They didn't fit. He felt guilty, as though Walter could see him sitting so close to her and enjoying her fragrance.

Shelford watched him settling onto the sofa. He looked between Lucy and Peter and raised an eyebrow. He tried to push himself further back on the sofa, away from Lucy, but there was no room. Their legs touched, and the more he shifted, the closer it seemed to bring them.

Finally, he rested an arm on the back of the sofa and tried to look nonchalant. He was sure it wasn't working. Colonel Loughton was smirking at him.

Rachel pushed a set of letters across the table.

Lucy was already digging through a pile of letters. "Help me. What word is this?" She leaned across him, trying to arrange the alphabet tiles.

Peter tried to focus his mind. Concentrate on the riddle, not on Lucy.

Meeting her in Mainz sounded like a good idea now. A really good idea. Sunlight instead of candlelight. Plenty of space between them instead of crowding together on a sofa. He could leave anytime instead of being trapped and obliged to stay all evening.

"You know, Lucy, I think I will meet you at your nursing school."

Lady Shelford and Rachel stopped working on their tiles to watch him.

"If it's agreeable to you, Kempton and Loughton, I'd like to escort Miss Maldon home tomorrow afternoon." A short walk, and he would fulfill his obligation for the day.

He gritted his teeth, sat as far away from Lucy as he could, and tried to spell out the word Rachel had given them to decipher. It was "E-N-G-A-G-E-D."

CHAPTER 9

Lucy approached the small building with Rachel and the colonel.

Oak trees lined the clearing outside the entrance. She could hear the river not far away. Crickets chirped and birds sang in the crisp morning air. Tall grasses grew along the sandy trail.

Their patient lived near the outskirts of town. Nearer to Mombach, the neighborhood where Peter lived.

The modest cottage would require perhaps two servants or three at most. The dilapidated stables were empty. No groomsmen worked here. Clearly, the woman could barely afford the small fee charged by the Institute.

"This is where she lives?" Lucy asked. What a difference from her luxurious apartments. What a comedown for a nobleman. She felt almost ashamed of her own abundance.

Colonel Loughton knocked. "A brief visit before we go to classes," he said.

A short man opened the door and peered cautiously around. "Hello?"

"We're from the Institute. Here to meet your daughter."

"Come in, come in," he said.

They entered a small drawing room. A round table filled most of it, with the other furniture pushed to the side.

"Come and meet Cecelia," he said. "I'm her father."

Lucy felt a pang of homesickness again, but forgot in her surprise. The tiny woman who came into the room was an elegant gentlewoman. She moved with grace, almost floating across the floor. Her fair hair was perfectly coiffed, and her brilliant blue eyes shone with intelligence.

"We're here to help with your birth," Rachel said before the colonel could speak. "I'm Rachel, and this is Lucy. That's the colonel. He's here to assist."

"Supervise."

"You'll have everything you need," Rachel said, ignoring the colonel.

The woman's eyes filled with tears. Lucy loved her already. What a difficult and overwhelming situation. Lucy rushed forward and hugged the stranger.

She dragged the woman to a sofa. "Sit. Did your papa say your name is Cecelia?"

The woman nodded.

"May we call you that?"

"Yes, please. I am a gentlewoman, like yourselves. I'm aware of the honor you do me by asking me to call you by your Christian names."

She spoke in a pure and refined accent. It was the most beautiful voice Lucy had ever heard.

"Oh, Cecelia." Lucy settled beside her on the sofa. The two of them fit easily, since they were both so small. "We are here for you. You must feel so alone and frightened."

More tears filled her eyes.

Rachel and Colonel Loughton waited across the room.

"Please, sit down," Cecelia said. "I apologize for the unconventional seating arrangements."

She didn't explain. Lucy wondered what this young widow was hiding.

Rachel came over and knelt beside her.

"Thank you so much for coming," Cecelia said.

"Yes," her father said. "We are glad we found the Deaconess Institute."

The colonel crossed the room and hovered nearby. "May I check her heart rate, Miss Wickford?"

"One moment, if you please," Rachel said.

The colonel folded his arms behind his back and exhaled a long, loud breath.

"Stop sulking," Rachel said without turning to look at him. "You'll get your turn." She considered Cecelia with a practiced eye.

Lucy had seen Rachel scrutinize many women in the neighborhood over the last few years, always giving Lucy her private assessment after a surreptitious appointment when she and Rachel were supposed to be having "tea," but instead had gone to visit someone with Dr. Morrow.

"It's such a relief to know I'll have help." Cecelia closed her eyes.

"May I?" Rachel took her hand. Her tone was gentle. "When do you think the child was conceived?"

Cecelia sighed. She turned toward Rachel. The silence stretched, as if Cecelia were gathering her strength.

Lucy put her arm around her. "Is it difficult to discuss this? I'm sorry. We are trying to ascertain your progress and the child's arrival."

"Is it completely necessary?" Cecelia's father asked. "She's been through so much already."

Cecelia smiled sadly. "Thank you, Papa. They are right. The child's health and safe delivery are important now, not the past. I'm certain it was sometime in December."

Lucy wondered when her husband had died, if she'd had a husband, or what made the topic so painful to discuss. Possibilities occurred to her, most too awful to consider. She gave Cecelia another squeeze with her arm. "Thank you."

Rachel looked around the drawing room. "May we inspect your

kitchen and bedroom? We'd like to see what supplies you have, so we will know what to bring next time we visit."

Cecelia began to stand.

"No, you stay here with the colonel." Rachel pressed her hand. "He'll be impossible if I don't let him fuss over you. Your father can help us. If you would, please, sir?"

"I don't fuss," the colonel said. "Let's put your feet up. May I feel your forehead? Have you felt any unusual movements from the child? How is your heart rate?" He swooped down on her, rearranging pillows and nearly knocking Cecelia off the sofa.

"Well enough," Cecelia said, and laughed. "Please, go upstairs. Papa, will you please show them the cottage?"

Lucy and Rachel followed Cecelia's father up a rickety set of stairs to a narrow bedchamber.

"How many changes of linen do you have?" Rachel asked.

"Two. A housekeeper comes in regularly," Cecelia's father said.

Lucy looked around. There was only one chair with a few shawls draped over it and a small end table with a candlestick. If Cecelia was indeed a gentlewoman, they had fallen on hard times.

Her heart went out to Cecelia. Lucy started to compose a list in her head. She would buy new linens. More candles. A chair for Cecelia to rock the baby after it was born.

Where would she shop? If only she were home, she would know where to go.

Peter could take her shopping today. He could translate.

They returned downstairs. The kitchen wasn't much better than the bedroom had been.

"Do you have a cook?" Lucy asked.

Cecelia's father shut the door to the kitchen. "Ah. No. We are saving funds for after the birth."

More things went on Lucy's list in her head. New pots. More spoons. A footman could go to the market by the cathedral and deliver fresh fruits and vegetables.

Lucy joined Cecelia on the couch.

"We'll leave our calling cards, all our information," Colonel Loughton said. "You must send word at a moment's notice."

"Do not hesitate," Rachel said. "Is this your first?" She looked around the room.

"Yes."

"Many women are uncertain whether the birth is beginning. They do not wish to disturb me. Or the pains begin and then stop." Rachel knelt in front of Cecelia. "I want to know. Everything."

"Oh, yes," Lucy said. "We don't mind."

"It will take you some time to send for us, and it will take us some time to arrive. You must not wait one minute nor doubt yourself." Rachel stared at Cecelia and smiled gently. "We will spend hours and hours with you once we arrive. We do not wish to miss one minute of it."

Lucy took Cecelia's hand. This brave woman, in a foreign country, with only her father. "You have friends now, Cecelia. Rachel and me. We will sleep here if need be. You will not do this alone."

"Where is your water source, sir? How much firewood do you have?" Colonel Loughton drew Cecelia's father aside. "Will you show me your woodpile?"

The men left, and it was just the three women in the room. "You have no idea how humiliating this is," Cecelia whispered. "I never imagined myself in this position. No one to care for myself or my child."

"We care for you," Lucy said.

Cecelia did not respond. Lucy's heart ached for her. She knew what it was like to be on the edge of society, always looked down on and never quite accepted. Cecelia was hiding away, alone, clearly ashamed.

"You never have to confide anything in us," Rachel said. "We are here to aid you and preserve your dignity, Cecelia. Not to judge you."

Cecelia's eyes filled with tears once again. "I will send for you as soon I as feel any pains."

Rachel took Cecelia's other hand. "Never mind the colonel. He acts stiff and starched, but he is very kind and knowledgeable. I'm sure he will insist we return again soon."

Lucy glanced aside at Rachel. She bristled anytime the colonel showed her kindness or a marked preference, yet she must respect him. Lucy smiled to herself. Of course, Rachel would only praise the colonel behind his back.

"Thank you. I have been without friends for months," Cecelia said. "You cannot imagine what this means."

"We will check on you again in a few days," Rachel said. "Perhaps Thursday afternoon?"

Cecelia hesitated. "I sometimes rest in the early afternoon. Morning or late afternoon would be best."

Rachel smiled. "Of course. Many women in their confinement rest or do not feel their best at certain times of day. We shall avoid the early afternoon. Thursday then? You will send for us earlier, if needed?"

Cecelia nodded.

Lucy rose to leave. She was tired of thinking about herself and her own problems. She was glad to have someone else to worry about. It would help distract her until this week was over. "I shall send our footmen with some supplies to prepare for the birth. We will see you again soon, Cecelia. I'm certain we will be dear friends."

CHAPTER 10

Walter paced around the apartments. Peter couldn't concentrate on the treatise about Johannes Gutenberg he had acquired from the University of Mainz. Walter kept sitting down, standing up, leaving for other parts of the house, and rejoining him in the drawing room.

The widow had said to return in two days. Evidently, he wanted to see her today.

"Let's go," Walter finally said. "I'll ask the grooms to saddle our horses. I need to ride."

Peter set down his book. "But I'm heading into the Old Town this afternoon. Could you go alone? I often ride without you."

Walter never went anywhere without him. It would have been endearing, if it weren't annoying. With only a year and a half between their births, they had always been either the best of friends or the worst of enemies, but never apart for long.

Walter slapped his gloves against his legs. "We can ride to Mrs. Smith's house first."

"It's in the opposite direction." Peter wanted a day to recover from the nonstop socializing. After weeks with no one but Walter for company, the constant requirement for polite conversation exhausted him.

Walter gestured over his shoulder. "It is just a short ride away, not too far out of your way. Please?"

Peter groaned and stood up. Walter was right. It wasn't too far in the opposite direction.

His brother grinned. "Thank you!" He rushed out the door.

Peter checked his pocket watch, the only other memento left from his father. The engraving read "To PC From RC." He rubbed the surface until it shone and replaced it in his vest pocket.

He had plenty of time, if Walter didn't spend too long with Mrs. Smith. She would probably turn them away. He hoped she would.

Why did it feel disloyal to Lucy to visit the widow? Walter only wanted reassurance from his father. Or did he?

They tethered their horses to a post outside the home's entrance. The stable doors hung from their hinges, and the empty stalls lacked any brushes or feed. The cottage didn't have a butler, footman, or groom. He didn't understand how Walter, who prided himself on his connections, who surrounded himself with well-placed friends, would want to associate with the occupants.

Mr. Ford answered the door.

"I know I have come early," Walter said, "but I could not wait."

Mr. Ford began to close the door.

"Please." Walter put a hand on the door. "The spirits urged me here today. They want me to visit you."

"Do they?" Mr. Ford asked. He hesitated.

"Yes. I cannot stop thinking about the plight of your young daughter," Walter said.

Peter's heart sank. If Walter was obsessed with any woman, it should be Lucy.

Walter held out a sack of coins. Peter had never known his parsimonious brother to be willing to part with so large a sum.

"I will see if the spirits are in harmony this afternoon," Mr. Ford said. "Ah. How much?"

Walter shook the heavy bag.

"Yes," Mr. Ford said. "The spirits are probably available." He disappeared.

Walter leaned over and spoke in a low voice. "Let me sit by her this time."

Peter didn't bother to keep his voice quiet. "It was your idea to make me sit there last time."

"Stop arguing with me," Walter said. "The spirits dislike it."

Peter wanted to punch the spirits.

Finally, Mr. Ford opened the door. "Come in."

They followed him into the small parlor where Mrs. Smith waited, wrapped in shawls. Walter quickly situated himself beside the widow.

As soon as she asked them to close the circle, Peter watched his brother grab her hand. They prayed and sang again. The table tilted and the floor rattled and banged. No new tricks.

Except Walter didn't seem as eager to receive his message this time. Perhaps he knew that would bring an end to the séance. "How about another hymn? You sing like an angel, Mrs. Smith."

"The spirits are ready to communicate," she said.

Walter reached for Mrs. Smith's hand. "Can you receive their message as a song?"

She pulled it away. "No. They write."

"But it is so burdensome for you," Walter said. "I would like to stay and talk with you afterward."

"You're disrupting the vibrations," Mr. Ford warned.

Mrs. Smith put a hand to her forehead. "Oh!" The slate had appeared on the table.

Walter grabbed at it eagerly. "There's nothing on it yet."

"Because you have been talking," Mrs. Smith said. She closed her eyes and began waving one arm over the table.

Mr. Ford took the slate from Walter and replaced it on the table's surface.

Peter sat across from her. He watched her move the other arm behind her back, then switch the blank slate with a new one. How had Walter missed it? She wasn't particularly subtle, but Walter desperately wanted to believe.

"I feel the spirit of your father," Mrs. Smith said. "He is not pleased you ignored his first message."

The sound of knocking reverberated in the small room as the table tilted and swayed.

"He wants to know why you disobeyed him and did not return to England," Mrs. Smith said. "Why did you seek a second message?"

"Father," Walter said. "Can I not wait a few months?"

"Read the slate," Peter said. Clearly Mrs. Smith didn't mind taking advantage of Walter one last time, but she seemed eager to be rid of them both. She would give birth any day, and she would not be able to hold séances with a newborn baby.

Walter grabbed for it and read out loud. "Leave now."

"Pretty clear message," Peter said. "Thank you, spirits."

Mrs. Smith fake-fainted.

"Leave? That can't be right. Is there more to the message?" Walter held onto the slate.

"You've already had two readings," Mr. Ford said. "That's more than most."

"Mrs. Smith?" Walter asked. "Can you hear me?"

Mr. Ford opened the door of the parlor. "She's in a deep trance, communing with the spirit world. Can't hear you."

Walter watched her. "I can't leave like this. I must see her again."

Peter walked out of the room. For once, he was in perfect accord with the spirits. He was happy to depart and never return. Mrs. Smith's parlor tricks were limited. No wonder she usually insisted on a single séance for each participant. It was hard enough to fool people the first time. If they came again, they might notice her swapping out the slates or knocking wooden blocks on the floor with her feet. She couldn't risk her reputation and her livelihood.

Walter followed reluctantly.

"I wish you both well." Mr. Ford waited for them to leave.

"May I speak with your daughter?" Walter frowned and clasped his hands behind his back. "Not a séance, a social call."

"I do not believe she wants to visit with you," Peter said, trying to move around Walter.

"Sir?" Walter asked. "May I call on your daughter tomorrow?"

Mr. Ford studied Walter. "Why?"

"I wish to know her better."

Mr. Ford studied Walter. "I'm going to ask you to leave."

"Please," Walter said, his voice rising a little. "I am asking for a chance to pay my respects."

Peter knew Walter was used to having his way, but he suspected this father had good reasons to want to protect his daughter. "Let's go, Walter."

Peter heard a sound behind them. The side door slid open, and Mrs. Smith appeared. Peter wished they had left quickly when they had the chance.

"Papa."

"Go back in the parlor."

"It is all right." She moved slowly. She really did look drained.

Walter turned toward her. "Are you well? That must have been taxing. I am sorry if we disturbed you."

"My father is protective of me, but we get so few visitors from England." She glanced between them. "Please, won't you join us for tea?"

Peter tried to move to the door. Walter needed to finish here and fulfill his obligation to Lucy. No distractions.

"What are you doing?" Mr. Ford asked. "The spirits told him to leave."

"Did they? I was in a trance. They speak through me, and I remember nothing myself when I awaken."

The father and daughter stared at each other.

"It will be well enough," Mrs. Smith said. "If you will make the tea, Papa, I will pour it."

Walter looked around. "No housekeeper? Mrs. Smith, you must allow me to bring you more supplies."

She smiled. "No, that's not necessary."

"I insist. We are going into town this afternoon. Allow us to shop for you and find some cakes."

"How kind." Mrs. Smith's smile, directed at Walter, lit up the room. Even Peter, who knew her act was a complete sham, could see how luminous the widow was. It was the kind of smile that made a man want to do anything, just to have it bestowed on him again.

"But we have overstayed our welcome. May we return tomorrow, rather than impose on such short notice?" Walter asked.

Peter could tell he was sincere. Walter wanted to ride into Mainz and make the purchases himself. He was worried about her health. Perhaps this was more than a passing fancy, like the others. It was more urgent than ever that he persuade his brother to see Lucy this afternoon.

"Yes, Mrs. Smith. It would be our privilege. We will stop by tonight on our way home," Peter said. "Do you favor chocolate cake or fruit tarts?"

Mrs. Smith's smile was directed at Peter now. It felt so genuine. She was absolutely stunning when she wasn't acting. If she wasn't acting. "Fruit would be lovely. Thank you."

She beamed at Walter. "I shall look forward to your visit tomorrow, Lord Chelmsford. Mr. Chelmsford. Thank you." Even her curtsey was perfection. Just low enough, but as graceful as anything Peter had ever seen, even though Mrs. Smith was expecting a child.

Peter worried as they began a slow trot toward Mainz. Mrs. Smith was beautiful. Almost as beautiful as Lucy. She was gracious and had a kind of otherworldly appeal that he knew had already drawn Walter in. He could see it, even if he didn't feel the same attraction as Walter. Something about Mrs. Smith put him off.

Walter was far more interested in her than his fiancée, but what could Peter do? He knew how Walter would react if he said anything. It didn't seem right to let Walter pursue one woman while he was already engaged to another. Especially to one like Lucy, who had real depth beneath the veneer of charm.

That was it. Mrs. Smith felt insubstantial, as though the surface were the entire essence. Lucy could chatter in a deceptively shallow manner, but, as he learned during chess last night, her mind never stopped working. He was beginning to suspect that she might be more intelligent than himself, although she took great pains to hide it.

Lucy also took pains to hide her heart. She had begun to trust him, but Peter knew what it was like to have stronger emotions than one could give voice to. Her glib explanations and over-confident assertions that she could make Walter love her must hide a deep yearning.

She was no counterfeit or hoax, like Mrs. Smith. She was a loyal friend to Rachel and Lady Shelford, and she fiercely loved her papa, even though he'd betrothed her to Walter.

She deserved an equally loyal husband who loved her fiercely in return. Walter had no more reasons to evade Lucy. They had attended two séances, and there would not be any more.

Walter accompanied him all the way into the Old Town. As they neared the Institute, Walter said, "Which way to the bakery?"

They pulled to a stop at a corner.

Peter held his horse's reins. "Aren't you coming to Lucy's school?"

"I'm going to the marketplace and bakery," Walter said.

"So am I." Peter's bay was restless, as if she could sense Peter's anxiety. "I'll just stop and collect Lucy first. You have to face her at some point."

Walter jostled his reins. "I know."

"You've had your séance. You've had two. She beat me at chess last night. She's as beautiful and delicate as Mrs. Smith, with a brilliant mind for strategy." Peter could praise Lucy's qualities all day. If Walter couldn't see them, Peter would help him.

"I am unmoved by your eloquence," Walter said, then laughed. "Yes, she's a fine woman. I have always thought so, but she is destined for someone else." He sighed. "I have met my other half, and everything changed that instant. Will you keep Lucy away from the bakery for half an hour?"

Peter pointed. "The shops are down that street."

Walter nodded and turned his horse around. He had chosen his course.

Peter continued toward Lucy's school. He would choose his own course, as well.

Their father had spent a lot of time in London without them. As he grew older, he wondered why their mother remained at Chelmsford Hall. Then, as he grew even older, he had visited London before Christmas with his father or gone during holiday breaks from Cambridge. He'd seen enough to understand why his mother remained at home.

Their father had never been faithful to his wife. His beautiful, young, vibrant wife. When his parents married, his mother had been the loveliest debutante of the Season. Yet his father dallied.

And here was Walter, engaged, already pursuing other women. It made his stomach turn to feel like he was a part of it. He had to warn Lucy. Convince her not to marry his brother. Change her mind before it was too late, before she grew as quiet and sad as his mother had in recent years.

Lucy deserved better.

She deserved someone else.

He would keep his word to Walter. He would keep Lucy away from him. But he had never promised how.

CHAPTER 11

Lucy tapped her foot as she watched for a familiar face in the crowd. Carriages passed each other in the street. Women walked beneath parasols, and men wore top hats. Nearly everyone looked identical from this vantage point.

"Why is Peter coming?" Rachel asked.

"To talk about Walter," Lucy said.

Rachel squinted into the sun. "You seem really comfortable with each other."

Lucy looked around. Colonel Loughton, Alice, and Mr. Kempton stood behind her on the front steps of the Institute. She couldn't say what she thought. Rachel was jealous.

"We are old friends," Lucy said.

"I like him," Colonel Loughton said. "Good man. Doesn't cheat at parlor games." He glared at Mr. Kempton, who grinned.

"And yet he manages to win," Alice said. "Unlike either of you."

Mr. Kempton sighed. "Touché."

"Is he coming to dinner?" Colonel Loughton asked. "I'd like to see more of him."

"I don't know," Lucy said. "I don't think so."

"Perhaps this weekend," Mr. Kempton said. "We could go shooting."

"Does he box?" Colonel Loughton asked. "Or fence?"

"Ask him yourselves." Lucy could see Peter's dark hair through the crowd. He was nearly there.

She felt a burst of excitement. Even though it had been less than a day since she'd seen him, she had been looking forward to this all day. It had given her something to anticipate during the confusing and tedious lectures.

Lucy waved to him and watched him climbing the steps of the Institute. Those strong legs. He must box. He hardly fit on a piece of furniture. Last night she'd had a hard time concentrating when he sat beside her. She'd tried to imagine it was Walter instead.

Peter greeted the others, who left quickly—Rachel especially. "Aren't they coming?" Peter asked.

"I no longer require a chaperone to spend time with you," Lucy said. "One of the advantages of an engagement."

They made their way along the path. "You enjoy being betrothed to Walter?" Peter asked.

"Yes. I don't have to worry anymore. I know I'll marry. I know I'll live in the same neighborhood as Papa. Men aren't afraid of me anymore. Look at us. We've never been better friends." She threaded her arm through his. "I'm completely safe. The colonel and Mr. Kempton know I will not chase them or entrap them, so we are free to enjoy one another's company."

Peter was quiet, so Lucy kept talking. It felt good to explain herself to someone who would understand.

"I admit, I am tired of waiting for Walter, wishing he loved me, wishing I loved him. You know our situation. But marriage will be better. I'll have all of the same advantages of engagement and increased freedom. Consider Eleanor. She's radiant."

"You believe Walter will make you as happy?" Peter steered them away from a spot of mud.

"I choose to be happy," she said. "I always have. A woman never truly belongs to herself, so I content myself with the things I am able to influence." She enjoyed the late summer afternoon. If she could go on walks like this with Walter, they would get along well. She and Peter got along so well.

"The colonel and Mr. Kempton know I will not attempt to influence them, and we are safe to converse with no other apparent motives." Lucy knew she ought to consider Peter in the same manner as the other men, but he was different. He wasn't safe. Every interaction felt laced with underlying tension, especially today.

They walked together, and she wondered if Peter had noticed her omission. If he had, he made no comment. He made no reply at all to her assertion that Walter would make her happy. Again, that uneasiness surfaced.

And the certainty that too much time with Peter was becoming dangerous. It was so easy to talk to him. She could tell him anything, although she probably shouldn't. Hours spent with Peter flooded her mind with doubts and desires that she could not voice to anyone.

She needed to focus on someone or something else, before one of her thoughts betrayed her. "Can we visit some merchants?" Lucy asked. "I would like to send some things to a friend."

"Certainly," Peter said.

He looked across the street. They began to cross, then Peter thew an arm around Lucy's shoulder and pulled her back to the sidewalk. A pair of runaway horses rounded the corner, an empty vehicle chasing the frightened animals. "One moment."

The feel of his arm around her startled her more than the careening carriage. Every time she was with him, she tried to ignore the attraction she felt. This feeling was different. It was protection and something more. Almost—possessiveness.

Her heart pounded wildly as the horses crashed past her. So close. The vehicle tipped on its side. Peter sheltered her, drawing her in as bits of splintered wood flew from the carriage. The wheels ground against the cobblestones. The frightened animals tore down the street, smashing into a second carriage.

He had pulled her away just in time. She couldn't tell whether she was responding more to the thrill and fear of seeing the uncontrolled animals or the warmth and closeness of Peter. His arm lay across her shoulders and she fit into his side, her head barely reaching his shoulder. She moved just a little, so her head lay on his chest, and he held her tight. Safe.

The sound of metal horseshoes striking the cobblestones stopped abruptly, and Peter let go. *I must have imagined it.* He didn't have any feelings for her. He was simply making sure she was safe.

"Those poor animals," Peter said. "I hope they can untangle them safely."

Lucy looked down the street and saw the knot of carriage bits, traces, bridles, and horses. Frantic shouts echoed in the air.

She listened for any echoes in her own heart, any traces of Walter, but found quiet. She tried to remember how she'd felt in the months before Walter left for Europe. He was handsome, certainly, but he didn't see her. It was like he looked right through her.

Peter saw her.

They crossed the street to a row of quaint shops. She felt a little unsteady, still trying to recover, but she was not sure she would ever be the same.

"Can we try the linen draper?" Lucy asked. "I would like to find some muslin."

Peter held open the door. "I would love nothing better."

"I cannot tell whether you are serious," Lucy said. She entered the shop and glanced around. Stacks of fabric and cloth were piled high on shelves behind the counter. A few bolts of cloth lay strewn around, neglected, while the store assistants attended other customers.

He brushed his hand over a bolt of cloth. "What are you seeking?"

"Some plain linen. Good quality. Smooth. Some cloth in simple patterns for a woman who is a friend. Very delicate. But it must be soft."

Peter nodded and moved away.

She watched him. Was he merely waiting for her or was he actually trying to help? She smiled to herself. She had no brothers or sisters, but Eleanor had complained about John and Matthew. They were impatient and detested shopping. Eleanor did all her shopping with Lucy and Rachel when she could.

Lucy studied his clothes. She'd never looked closely at his attire. She had seen Walter's clothing was a little cheap and ill-fitting and promised herself to make him buy new clothes. After talking with Peter last night, she worried that Walter wouldn't allow her to spend enough to make him really look good.

But Peter's clothes were well-made. They fit him perfectly. Clearly, he went to a different tailor, or he was more exacting. The cloth was middle grade, but not poor quality. If Walter didn't give him a large allowance, Peter dressed quite well on the money he had. Especially given his muscular physique.

Peter turned and caught Lucy watching him. She hoped he hadn't noticed which part of him she had been studying.

"I found something," he said and motioned to her. "How is the quality of this muslin? The price is excellent, and the grain is not too defined."

Lucy joined him at the counter. She had to stand uncomfortably close to reach the fabric. Perhaps she should admit to herself that it was too comfortable. She shook her head.

"You don't like it?" Peter asked.

"No. I mean, yes. That will do well. Especially for our purpose. I'll need a few lengths of it." She felt herself flush.

He took her elbow. "Over here." He led her further along the counter to a soft, cotton cloth. White with tiny blue flowers embroidered into it. "A bit pricey, but if you cut the dress pattern carefully, you might be able to use it. What's the design?"

She hated that she loved being near him. He hovered behind her, trapping her between himself and the counter. She swallowed.

"It's perfect. It would suit her." She turned slightly to face him. "Are you a dandy? You don't dress like one."

Peter laughed. "My mother takes me shopping with her. I love to go."

"With four boys, your mother must have little time alone with any of you," Lucy said. She picked up the bolt of fabric and hugged it to her chest. That would put some distance between them.

"Exactly. So, I have become an expert at cloth, hats, and shoes." Peter put one hand down on the edge of the counter and leaned even closer. "Allow me to take it for you. Enough cloth for a woman's dress?"

Their hands brushed as she gave him the fabric.

Lucy sucked in a breath. Maybe he hadn't noticed her reaction. She was only an inch away from the counter and hardly needed his help. She only had to turn around. If it had been anyone else, she would have suspected them of contriving the situation.

Peter was watching her, a blazing heat in his dark brown eyes. His muscled arms still held her trapped. She realized she hadn't let go of the cloth. She relinquished her hold on the bolt and his hand. He straightened.

She searched for something to say to cover her embarrassment. "Yes, enough cloth for a woman about my height," Lucy said. "You must be your mother's favorite."

"I am devoted to her," Peter said. "She is the best mother in all of England. Shopping with her is my way of watching over her." He went back to pick up the bolt of muslin, as well. He carried both to the end of the counter and instructed the proprietor to cut the appropriate lengths.

She let out a deep breath. He had noticed her reaction, and he'd responded with an unspoken invitation of his own. Yes, Peter was dangerous.

But gentle. Now that his mother was a widow, he cared for his mother and watched over her. Why did she need to be protected? Lucy wondered. She had spent months with Lady Chelmsford before leaving for Germany. They had grown close. Spent hours talking, discussing the Chelmsford estate that Lucy would one day help Walter manage. She had learned about the household, so she could run it efficiently when Lady Chelmsford moved into the dower house.

Not once had Lady Chelmsford looked down on her. She and Papa assumed she would, but Lady Chelmsford was gentle and soft-spoken. Shy. Generous. Always caring for others. Trying to make Lucy feel like part of the family and prepare her to become nobility. Lucy had grown to love her. She could understand Peter's dedication.

Lucy had gone shopping with her while Peter was away at Cambridge. She didn't realize it was usually Peter's role. What would happen once she married Walter? Once Lady Chelmsford had a daughter and no longer needed Peter in the same way? Would he resent Lucy's closeness with his mother?

She joined him and counted out several coins. He took the wrapped packages, and they walked back out into the sunshine.

Peter blinked and shifted his weight from one foot to another. Finally, he spoke. "I feel a bit protective of you, too." He turned and quickly opened another door without meeting her eyes.

Lucy felt a dread and an anticipation. What would she see in his eyes, if he would meet her gaze? She wanted it, but feared it entering unsafe territory. One glance could undo their tenuous friendship.

A bell tinkled as they entered the chandlery. Lucy stood in the dim light of the candle shop. The smell of honey and beeswax filled the air. She picked up a candle and twirled it to cover her nervousness. Peter's pronouncement unsettled her. She loved the feeling that he cared about her and wanted to safeguard her. Walter certainly did not.

But how deep did his feelings run? They did not seem brotherly.

Their afternoon outing had grown suddenly serious. She would try to lighten it. Lucy spun the candle in her hand again. "Why? What are you defending me against? Dragons?"

Peter stilled her hand, covering it with his own, and gazed into her eyes. "Are you sure you want to marry Walter?"

The question took her by surprise. *Want* to marry him? That had never been an issue. Her father had decided for her.

She pulled her hand away and moved along the row to examine candlesticks. "It's not my choice. Papa arranged it. Walter signed the contract."

Peter followed her, directly behind her, entirely too close. "If you *could* decide for yourself, what would you choose?"

She stared at the display without seeing anything. She picked up another candle and began twirling it.

He reached around her, his arm brushing her side. "Which candle do you prefer?" He held up the two different candles she had selected. They were nearly identical.

Lucy turned her head. That look; it was there in his eyes again. He was asking her which candles she wanted, and she felt as if her answer determined the fate of her happiness.

How had things gotten so personal? No one had ever asked her what *she* wanted. They made plans without her and she made the best of it. She examined the other candles on the store table without meeting his eyes. "I'm not sure which candles are appropriate for this household."

Peter replaced the candles and took her hands. "Lucy, I'm worried for you."

Lucy loved the feel of her gloved fingers in Peter's and the way he gazed at her.

He searched her face. "I don't think Walter will make you as happy as Lord Shelford makes Eleanor."

Her heart beat faster. "There's nothing I can do. I cannot break my engagement. The scandal would humiliate Papa."

Peter dropped her hands. "Better embarrassment now than heartache later."

She had no response. Why would Walter cause her heartache? True, she had felt nothing but pain and loneliness since their engagement. She had assumed that would change after they wed. "The candles are so similar in appearance," Lucy said. "I'm not certain it matters which I buy. They burn the same."

"Each candle is unique." Peter held up the first and stepped closer to her. "Some candles burn too quickly." Another step. "Others drip because they are uneven. Great skill goes into the making of an excellent light source." Another step closer. "The right wax, the right wick." He stood an inch away, gazing intently at her. The waves in his brown hair were more pronounced today. "Or an oil lamp that smokes and leaves residue on the walls."

She went cold. What did he know about his brother? Was there something he was not telling her? If Walter would just see her, she could fix this. She needed to talk to him in person, without Peter present.

"You were going to help him fall in love with me," Lucy said.

Peter studied her. He walked over to a window and examined a display of matchboxes. "Love can't be forced, Lucy. It can't be planned or scheduled or agreed to. I'm sorry." He turned around. "What else are you shopping for? How many candles do you want? A snuffer, too? Matches?"

She watched him select the best quality candles in a reasonable price range. He didn't wait for the store attendant, but went to work gathering supplies for her.

His coat stretched across his shoulders as he reached up to the highest shelf. He got the right quantity of candles for a small household, a few boxes of matches, a snuffer, a number of candlesticks, and took the items to the counter.

Lucy offered him her reticule, and he drew out a few coins.

Peter completed the transaction as she waited, not understanding a word of the foreign language. As the shop attendant wrapped the packages, Peter turned to face her. Only the length of the store separated them.

And Walter.

Why would he break her heart even more than he already had?

She had assumed marriage would fix her heartache, not increase it.

But what would marriage to Peter be like? A flame of hope flickered, but Lucy quelled the treacherous thought. *She didn't have a choice.*

Peter returned with the wrapped packages and tucked her arm into his side. "Come on, Lucy. Let's buy some cakes."

"How did you know? That's exactly what I need." She welcomed the lighter tone and new topic of conversation.

"Because I've seen that look on my mother's face before. Many times. And we always go for tea and cakes after we shop." The intensity in Peter's eyes deepened. "Please consider what I've said. Ask Lady Shelford. Ask her why she's happy with her husband. I want you to be happy with yours."

CHAPTER 12

The bay mare walked at a gentle pace. No rush to get home tonight. It was just dinner, alone with Walter. Peter had allowed himself to spend the entire afternoon with Lucy, and now it was nearly dusk. It was so easy to lose track of time when he was with her.

After the serious discussion at the chandlery, they'd stopped for tea. Neither of them mentioned Walter again. They had wandered through the marketplace by the cathedral, where he selected fruits for her friend, then gone to a tobacconist for her friend's father. He had quite a stack of gifts for Lucy's friends.

He couldn't erase the image of Lucy in the candle shop. The shock. The fear. The pain.

It was better for her to know now than later. He'd spent years watching his mother's heart break, yet his mother had never said a word. Just like Lucy. Standing there, silent.

He had to do more. She couldn't marry Walter.

He still had more time. Maybe Lucy would realize he was right. He would let her think about what he said, then determine whether to take action.

After all, Walter wasn't in a hurry to marry Lucy.

❦

The next day, Peter watched Walter rush to get to Mrs. Smith's house. His brother had bought an extravagant bouquet of flowers at the marketplace yesterday. Peter wanted to tell him how appalled he felt, but he knew it would only provoke Walter and make him more entrenched in his course of action.

Mr. Ford ushered them into the parlor. Mrs. Smith had set out a tray with tea and sweets.

"Welcome, gentlemen." Mrs. Smith waved them in. "Make yourselves comfortable."

She certainly had a presence, a way of commanding a room, despite her small stature. She managed to move gracefully, even with her impending delivery of a child.

Walter seated himself close to her. Peter took a chair across the room. Mrs. Smith poured the tea and filled the plates with the grace of a queen while her father watched her proudly.

Walter carried Peter's cup and selection of sweets to him, then settled himself at the round table again. Peter looked down and stared. There was a slice of the same fruit tart he'd eaten yesterday in Mainz with Lucy. Blackberries and peaches in an apricot glaze on a pastry crust.

Walter must have stopped at the same bakery. Peter and Lucy had barely missed him. Had Walter walked past the linen draper or chandlery or seen Peter with Lucy? No, he would have ridden directly back to deliver the sweets to Mrs. Smith. Surely.

"Thank you," Walter said. "It is an honor to visit with you."

Peter sipped his tea. He hated being here. Each minute was a betrayal to Lucy and his mother. He couldn't help liking Mrs. Smith and feeling sorry for her, but he didn't want to watch Walter try to woo her.

He'd seen too much of that with Walter at Cambridge.

"Tell me more about yourself," Walter said.

"There is little to tell." Mrs. Smith laughed. "My father and I have lived in Europe for years. I miss dear England. Tell me all about your home. Where do you come from?"

"Essex," Walter said.

"And what is the countryside round about?" Mrs. Smith asked.

Peter wanted to know more about her. "Probably the same as your home. Where did you say you lived before you left England?"

Mrs. Smith cast him a calculating gaze, as if trying to determine how much to disclose. "I hardly remember. Papa and I have spent more time in Vienna than anywhere else. I was so young when we left that Europe has always felt like home to me."

Walter looked at him. "Peter wants to visit Vienna."

"It is a grand city. I miss it, the music especially." Mrs. Smith turned her focus back to Walter. "But what do you miss about home, Lord Chelmsford?"

"I regret that I do not have a piano in my lodgings," Walter said. "It is hard to be without one while on Grand Tour."

Mrs. Smith's smile faded. "I have missed singing more than I can tell. But let us not be melancholy. Tell me about your country-side. Remind me what England looks like."

Walter settled onto his seat. "The country round about is glori-ous. Great oaks. Hazelnut, chestnut, and walnut trees all around. That's one reason I chose this part of town—the trees remind me of Chelmsford Hall. I also have a wide forest of birch to ride my horses, and I've planted rows of laurel bushes to line the approach to our estate. They're coming along well. We've got cherry blos-soms in the spring and great spruce trees and holly bushes for Christmas. Essex truly is the most beautiful part of England."

Peter sat, stunned. He knew his brother loved to ride and spent a lot of time outdoors, but he'd never realized how much Walter loved their lands. Thinking back, they often spent a good deal of time with the gardener. Peter thought he was avoiding other responsibilities when they rode out to view the estate. Perhaps he was, but it seemed that Walter was genuinely knowledgeable and passionate about their land.

Walter had studied botany and zoology at Cambridge, Peter

remembered. They'd shared a few classes, as well as participated in the school's boat races and cricket matches together.

"It sounds magnificent. I can almost see it as you describe it and smell the blossoms on the air. What of your home?" Mrs. Smith took the smallest of sips.

"Chelmsford Hall is magnificent. It has been in the family for generations."

Mrs. Smith tried to lean forward. Her belly got in the way. "I can see it, too. It must be stone. Is it stone? Or is it brick? How many windows are there? Just imagine." She waved her hands dramatically. "I see your laurel bushes lining the approach, the gravel crunching underfoot, the great steps leading up to the entrance."

She could have been an actress. Peter could almost see the portrait she painted in words, her face and voice were so expressive. Her father watched her talking.

Was he a protective father? Or was he part of her scheme, just trying to bilk them out of more funds?

Either Mrs. Smith was homesick for England, or she was trying to ascertain exactly how large the estate was and how much money it brought in. Probably the latter.

Eventually they arrived at Walter's favorite topic: how many horses and dogs they had. Walter began naming the dogs and describing their personalities. It was going to take the entire afternoon.

Mrs. Smith kept smiling. And Walter kept telling her more and more. She looked tired, but completely at ease.

Peter was not.

What was her game? Was she gathering information for a future séance? She had told them not to return. Or was she interested in him for his wealth? No one could possibly be as interested in Walter's hunting dogs as he was.

Peter discretely checked his pocket watch. They had overstayed their welcome and exceeded the polite length for a visit. Surely her father would ask them to leave.

But he did not. Anytime he hinted that Mrs. Smith was overexerting herself, Mr. Ford was quickly reassured by his daughter. She felt fine.

It continued for over an hour. Peter gave up any hope he'd entertained of leaving quickly. Mrs. Smith seemed to like nothing in the world so much as listening to Walter, and Walter loved to hear himself talk. They were perfect with each other.

He loved hunting dogs, and she loved animals. They had common tastes in music, art, poetry, philosophy, and they both abhorred turtle soup. They agreed on every point and shared every dislike in common.

It made Peter sick.

What if Mrs. Smith were genuine? Did she actually care?

After all, he didn't mind listening to Lucy talk.

She would never tolerate a fool like Walter. She was clever. And she had so many ideas to express herself. She wouldn't listen to Walter drone on and on.

"Have we exhausted you?" Peter asked at one point. Perhaps he should try, since her father was obviously concerned for Mrs. Smith. "We should let you rest."

"Oh no, I'm fine," Mrs. Smith said. "Tell me again about your stables. I haven't ridden in so long."

She laughed in all the right places, able to listen indefinitely and prompt Walter with just the right questions at just the right times. They could have gone on forever. Finally, half an hour later, Mr. Ford put an end to the conversation.

"I don't know when I've enjoyed an afternoon more," Walter said. "When can I call on you again?"

"Tomorrow," Mrs. Smith said. "The baby may arrive any day, but you are welcome to visit before then."

Walter's face got serious. "What can I do to assist you, Mrs. Smith?"

"The tart was splendid. Thank you. Perhaps you could bring another next time you come." She smiled at him as though he had brought her the sun, moon, and stars.

They took their leave and rode home in silence. Peter had nothing he felt safe talking about with Walter, and Walter seemed preoccupied with his own thoughts.

Before long, they arrived back at their own rented cottage. It looked like a palace compared to the simple dwelling they had left. Walter and Peter handed their horses to the groomsmen, changed out of their dusty boots, waited for the butler to announce dinner, and began eating a quiet meal.

Peter had promised Lucy that he would see her tomorrow. He wanted to give her a chance to speak with Eleanor and think about Walter. He always needed a full day to consider his own emotions. He couldn't understand how he was feeling without a long time to reflect. Perhaps Lucy required that as well.

Walter and he were similar in at least that way. He was lost in thought, and it was better to let him work out his own emotions than disturb him.

And Peter was exhausted from riding back and forth between his neighborhood and the Old City. Constantly being in the middle between Walter and Lucy was wearing him down, and he wanted a night alone to recover and restore his equilibrium. Silence suited him fine.

Peter's knife scraped against the ceramic plate as he cut another bite of roast pork.

Walter broke the silence. "What does love feel like?"

Oh dear. He was not going to have a break tonight.

He thought of the way he felt when he was with Lucy. "It's comfortable and easy to be with the person. You want to spend time with her, but you don't know where the time goes, because it seems to pass in the blink of an eye. You can see her as she truly is, but you respect her nonetheless."

Walter nodded thoughtfully. "Do you believe in love at first sight?" He pushed back from the table. "Will you talk with me?"

"Of course." Peter set down his knife. He had mostly finished eating anyway.

They settled into the drawing room. Peter stared into the fire while Walter leaned against the fireplace mantle.

"I never understood the idea of love," Walter said. "Father had an arranged marriage. As a viscount, I never expected anything different. Love was not a consideration; only the furtherance of the estate mattered. When Mr. Maldon approached me, it seemed like an excellent arrangement. Others in the neighborhood looked down on their family. I could raise her station, protect her from scorn, and she could infuse the estate with more wealth."

Peter didn't want to hear this, but this was his brother. His closest brother.

"But the moment I saw Mrs. Smith, I knew I had been wrong." Walter picked up a poker and jabbed at the fire. Flames flew from the fireplace. "What am I going to do? I cannot marry Lucy."

Peter waited to hear what else Walter would say. Had he decided to finally undo his engagement?

"I've only got a few days to convince Mrs. Smith. We cannot leave for Vienna now," Walter said. "I'm sorry. I know you wanted to go there, and I said we would."

You cannot marry Mrs. Smith. But Peter's instincts, born of long experience, told him to let Walter talk. Hear him out. Not to contradict him directly, but try to redirect his thinking.

Walter continued. "Do you believe in soul mates? Two parts of one soul, divided asunder? The poets spoke truth. She's my other half. I feel it. She needs me. Her circumstances are dire, and I was sent to help her."

Peter hesitated. How could Walter feel that way toward a widow, and one who would give birth to another man's child? "Do the poets believe that love happens once in a lifetime? What if someone has loved before?"

Walter trained his eyes on Peter. "I am certain she never loved her first husband the same way. This kind of cosmic connection only happens once in an eternity."

First husband? Did Walter intend to be her second husband?

"Perhaps she still mourns for him," Peter said. "Her heart may not be free to give."

Walter dismissed him with a grunt. "You don't understand her the way I do. We sense things without speaking. I know we are connected. We think alike in every way."

"Your heart is not free to give, either," Peter said carefully. "Soul mate or not, you are bound to Lucy." He waited for the explosion.

Walter merely brushed the comment aside. "That's irrelevant. A technicality. I'm talking about something unbreakable—the once-in-a-universe bond between two souls."

There was no way to argue with Walter or make him see reason. He'd always been overly confident, encouraged by Father, and never contradicted. Unless the cosmos or spirits or Mrs. Smith chose to set him right, Walter would believe in destiny, despite the obvious unsuitability of the match.

Peter wondered how he and his brother could be so different. Love wasn't an accident. It didn't happen to people unaware. One was not compelled to love against his will. Love was an attunement of two souls, certainly, but it required effort. Careful selection of a woman who matched and complemented one. Love wasn't an empty chasm to be filled or an incompleteness waiting to be perfected. It was the confluence of two separate and strong individuals who surrendered to each other in order to create a whole, more perfect in its unity.

Walter felt some kind of void that nothing would fill. Peter watched him drink and flirt at Cambridge. He saw Walter struggle for two years after their father died, and then Walter had left England for this Grand Tour. Drink, travel, séances. Now Walter wanted to fill the hollow inside with a mystical belief in love at first sight.

Peter wanted to be practical. He wanted to point out that Walter could hardly break his engagement, then bring home a widow of no social standing and her child from Europe. The scandal would haunt their family and break his mother's heart.

But he didn't want Walter to marry Lucy, either.

He tried to think of a way to make his brother see reason.

"Love takes work," Peter said. "It might start unexpectedly, but it requires effort for it to continue."

Walter jabbed at the fire again. "You're right. I'm not doing enough."

That wasn't what Peter had meant.

"Thanks for understanding," Walter said. "I can always count on you."

He had hardly begun to explain himself, and Walter was ending the conversation. Embers burned red hot beneath the logs.

Peter couldn't let his brother leave without testing Walter's intentions. Was his pursuit of Mrs. Smith just another idle chase before Walter settled down, or did he truly mean to dissolve the marriage contract with Lucy's father? "So, you would not mind if Lucy's heart were engaged elsewhere?"

Walter laughed. "I wish it were! Perhaps you could do the job." He poked at the fire again, and ashes flew out of the grate. The embers flared and then grew dark.

Walter thought the idea too ridiculous. He didn't realize Peter's intentions, so Peter tried again.

"There was a runaway carriage, a pair of spooked horses today. I held Lucy as the carriage passed," Peter began. "To protect her." He should ask Walter directly when he intended to break his engagement. Would Walter allow him to court Lucy after he did?

"Good man," Walter said, stretching. "Well begun is half done." He yawned and left the room.

Peter shook his head. Walter didn't take him seriously. He definitely had to help Lucy call off her engagement to Walter before she found out that Walter thought he was in love with someone else. If only Walter would call it off first, then he would be grateful to find out Peter was falling in love with his fiancée.

CHAPTER 13

Lucy hated embroidery. Since Papa was in England, she refused to even pretend. She picked at the threads in Eleanor's sofa and watched Rachel talking to Alice. Eleanor and Rachel stitched in tiny, even rows, perfectly spaced. Not Lucy.

Nobility was the height of boredom. At home, she and Papa talked about his acquisitions and holdings after dinner. In Germany, she sat with the other women in the Shelfords' drawing room while the men played billiards. Mrs. Glenn read in the corner while Eleanor played piano quietly.

Lucy couldn't concentrate. Peter's words kept running through her head. She wanted to talk to Eleanor, but she didn't want to do it in front of Rachel. Finally, she knew that time was running out. The men would return, and her chance would be gone.

"Eleanor? May I talk to you?" Lucy checked to see whether anyone was paying attention.

Eleanor stopped playing the piano. "What's on your mind? You're quiet tonight," Eleanor said. "Peter isn't here."

Rachel glanced over from the chairs near the fireplace. Alice looked over, too.

Lucy dropped her eyes. She traced the intricate, swirling pattern on the sofa's fabric. "I was thinking about him."

"You must be upset not to see Walter," Eleanor said. "After traveling so far to find him."

Lucy nodded. "Devastated."

Eleanor pushed back the bench and came to sit beside Lucy. "I'm sorry." She took Lucy's hand. "I've enjoyed spending time with Peter. He's rather surprising. Like a bite of lemon tart. Not at all what one expects, but pleasant."

Lucy laughed. "You're beginning to sound like your mother."

Eleanor's eyes grew wide. "That's horrifying. Is it true, Rachel?"

Rachel nodded. "A bit."

"I love your mother," Lucy said.

"But I don't want to be her." Eleanor let go of Lucy's hand. "What did you wish to discuss?"

Lucy glanced around. Rachel and Alice had stopped talking and were watching her. Too late. She'd have to ask anyway, before the men returned. She took a deep breath. "Why did you marry Lord Shelford?" Lucy asked. "Why him? Why not the duke or Alice's brother or Mr. Kempton?"

Eleanor laughed. "Shall I tell you a True Confession? None of the gentlemen are present."

"Yes, please, I'd rather keep this conversation private," Lucy said.

"When did my brother court you?" Alice asked. "How did I miss that?"

"He didn't. We merely danced a few times and talked amiably," Eleanor said. "That's all there is to a London Season."

"So why Lord Shelford?" Lucy persisted. She desperately needed to understand.

"True Confession. The duke is a good, caring man, and your brother, Alice, follows his heart passionately to pursue a good cause and care for the poor. Mr. Kempton has my deepest respect as well. But none of them make me feel the way Percy does. Like no one else in the world exists except me."

Lucy understood. Being seen.

"Why are you asking these serious questions?"

Lucy traced the pattern on the sofa again. "Peter said to ask you."

"Indeed. Why?" Eleanor moved closer. "Why would Peter want you to ask me what love feels like?"

Lucy looked up. When Eleanor phrased it in that manner, the question felt laden with meaning.

Eleanor grinned at her. "I've been watching you with Peter." Her face grew serious. "I'm sorry, Rachel, but Peter is falling in love with Lucy."

Lucy reared back. "No. He's worried. He wanted me to ask you why you're happy with Lord Shelford. He believes Walter will not do the same for me, and he wants me to be careful with my choice of husband."

Rachel turned away. Lucy didn't want to cause her pain, if her dearest friend had feelings for Peter, also, but Eleanor had no qualms about having an honest conversation.

"What else did he say?" Eleanor asked.

"That Walter would only bring me heartache. Instead of letting my father decide, I should determine for myself who I wanted to marry."

Rachel's voice was thick with emotion. "And did he give you an alternative to Walter?"

"No, Rachel," Lucy said. "He's trying to protect me." Or had he intended Lucy to consider him?

"Because he loves you," Eleanor said gently.

"He sounds like a decent sort," Alice said, "whatever his intentions. I haven't met his brother, obviously, but I'm all for Peter."

Eleanor glanced at the drawing room door. So did Lucy. Still closed.

"Rachel, I don't want to hurt you," Eleanor said gently, "but I want to speak freely to Lucy. May I?"

Rachel nodded.

"How do you feel when you're with Peter?" Eleanor asked.

She felt the same way with Peter that Eleanor had described feeling with her husband. "That is irrelevant," Lucy said. "I wish to know more about why *you* are happy with Lord Shelford."

"It is extremely relevant, Lucy." Eleanor leaned in. "But we shall overlook it for now. I am blissfully happy with an extremely irritating man, because he cares about me in a thousand small ways. Because he carries my packages. Because he keeps my secrets and I feel protected. Because we laugh together, and he is ridiculous. Because he smells good and looks incredibly attractive. Because he pays attention to me. Because he apologizes every time he is ridiculous. Because he forgives me when I am equally so, and I can overlook everything else because of that."

Lucy felt more uncomfortable. With every word Eleanor spoke, Lucy was reminded of Peter instead of Walter. His concern for her happiness. His patience and assistance while purchasing goods for the widow. The smell of leather. The look in his eyes when he told her that Walter would bring her heartache. The feel of his lips on her cheek. His complete acceptance of her and lack of judgment, when Walter had always seemed to view her merely as a way to enrich his estate.

Alice leaned in, too. "May I also speak freely?"

"Of course. Quickly, before the men return," Eleanor said.

"I have never experienced love," Alice said, turning to Rachel. "But my brother has fancied himself in love many times because a woman was clever or attractive. I don't think he's aware himself, but I've never known Curtis to be so attentive—until now. The way he looks at you, Rachel, the way he trails behind you everywhere you go. If I didn't already love you so much myself, I would be extremely annoyed with him."

Rachel smiled. Perhaps a little sadly.

Lucy knew it was true. The colonel had confided a passing fancy in her friend, but she believed that Alice had it right, as well. The colonel had no idea how far gone he was.

"Lucy, I will ask you to consider this. If you could choose a husband for yourself, if your father hadn't arranged your marriage, if you weren't engaged to Walter, would he be the man you wanted to marry?" Eleanor stared at her. "Would it be George, the stable hand you once fancied?"

Lucy shifted uncomfortably. Eleanor was fully aware of the answer. Lucy had been heartbroken when George left. She had confided her distress about her father's choice when she was first engaged. She realized with a shock that she had not thought of George for some time. She had long since forgotten him and certainly never loved him, though she had once thought she had.

A vision of dark hair with a slight wave swam before her eyes. If she could have selected a husband for herself, which Chelmsford brother would she have chosen to marry?

Eleanor continued to consider Lucy. "And if the answer is 'No,' then is there any reason you *have* to marry him? Especially if another, better man might be falling in love with you."

Rachel hung her head. Alice took her hand and squeezed it.

Lucy could not afford any scandal. She wasn't a member of the aristocracy. She and Papa were barely considered part of the gentry, and not everyone agreed with that distinction. Plenty of people considered Papa a businessman and nothing more. They ignored his large estate and land holdings, since he had purchased it only twenty-five years ago.

The door to the drawing room opened.

"You're looking for love in the wrong places," Eleanor said quickly. She glanced between Lucy and Rachel. "Both of you."

Lord Shelford made his way across the drawing room and kissed his wife on the cheek. "We're scandalous and improper," he said loudly. "Don't mind us."

Her friends believed Peter had feelings for her. If that were the case, Lucy wished he would stride up to her and kiss her fervently, like Lord Shelford greeted his wife. It would take the guessing out of it.

But relationships were never easy and straightforward, and certainly not with Peter Chelmsford. She wanted someone to love her, cherish her, adore her, the way Lord Shelford doted on Eleanor.

If Peter felt anything for her, it would be up to her to ascertain the truth.

She couldn't make Walter fall in love with her. She couldn't even make him come and visit her. Maybe Peter and Eleanor were right. It was time to consider an alternative.

If only she were not legally bound to marry Walter.

CHAPTER 14

Peter inhaled deeply. The scent of roasting potatoes and roast pork filled the air. The Shelfords had insisted on attending a harvest festival instead of dinner. Walter stubbornly refused to join them. Poor choice. Why sit alone at home when he could be here, eating freshly harvested vegetables and ripe fruits with some of the most pleasant company a man could share?

Peter held a cup of freshly pressed juice. The wine grapes yielded a surprisingly sweet and rich flavor. It was now nearly September. The fields around Mainz were laden with mature crops and waiting to be picked.

The early evening breeze blew in from the Rhine, making the air heavy.

"These tables are available," Shelford said. "We can see the whole valley from here."

Shelford pulled out a chair for his wife. The colonel, always at Rachel's side, quickly seated her beside himself at their table.

That left him with Miss Loughton, Kempton, and Lucy. He made sure to sit with his back to the valley, so Lucy could see the river flowing gently through the farmland and forests. He wanted Lucy to be treated as well as possible while it was in his power.

The tables nestled along the edge of the vineyard rows. A violet hue tinged the pink and amber sky. Someone put a plate of thinly sliced potatoes and onions in front of him with roasted pork and vegetables.

Peter sipped his drink and enjoyed the view: Lucy, and the grapevines beyond her, sloping away up the gentle hill. She looked beautiful tonight, especially in the glow of the setting sun. He couldn't help noticing the way her eyes sparkled or the way the light framed the hair beneath her bonnet like a halo.

Engaged, he reminded himself. *To your brother.*

He turned his attention to Kempton instead. "What do they have set up?"

"Contests," Kempton said. "You going to attempt the hammer toss?"

Peter swallowed his bite. "What's that?"

"Harvest games." Kempton grinned. "I've got a bet with Loughton, if you care to join in."

"What is the wager?" Miss Loughton asked. "You can't cheat with a hammer toss."

"Winner cleans the other's shoes for a week."

"Don't you have a valet?" Lucy asked.

Kempton took a bite. He nodded and finished chewing. "Yes, but I intend to give him a week off, then ride through mud when I win."

Peter loved vying in athletic competitions at Cambridge and with his brothers. "Sure," he said. "Toss a hammer. How heavy is it?"

"Don't know," Kempton said. "But if I bump his arm at precisely the right moment…"

They all laughed.

"The winner deserves a kiss," Kempton said. "If we're playing medieval games, we should get medieval prizes." He raised his eyebrows at Miss Loughton.

Peter blinked. The idea of kissing Lucy held too much appeal to consider. He studied the potatoes on his plate.

"Medieval knights were honorable," Miss Loughton said.

Kempton scoffed. "They poured hot oil on invading armies."

"But they didn't bump each other's arms."

"Which is less honorable?" Kempton asked. "Impaling heads on wooden spikes or bumping arms?"

"I'm eating!" Lucy said. "Perhaps if you'll stop talking about such gruesome details, you'll be more likely to win your case. If it's a kiss you want, contradicting your lady fair will hardly work."

Kempton took a large bite and chewed quickly.

Peter looked at Lucy. Was she only thinking of Kempton and Miss Loughton? Or of himself? He considered the possibility.

"It looks as though they have archery set up, too," Peter said. "You have two chances, Kempton."

Kempton ate even faster.

Miss Loughton laughed. "As do you, Mr. Chelmsford."

Peter studied Lucy. Did she want him to compete? She'd been quiet tonight. They'd spoken so seriously the last time they were together. It was hard to know how to break the tension with her. Perhaps a joke to see whether she were serious.

"Will you give me your handkerchief, Lucy? Is that what the medieval princesses did?

What was he thinking? She was staring at him. *Cover the awkwardness.* Quickly. "I've grown out my beard to look like a knight." He rubbed his jawline. Peter kept his as thin as possible, requiring constant maintenance. His carefully trimmed beard was far from medieval. It barely covered his skin, a feat that required constant effort and precise shaving.

Lucy took out a square of cloth. "I'll give you my favor," she said, "since Alice is cheering for Mr. Kempton and since your whiskers are quite magnificent." She actually smiled at him. His absurdity was working. They could all see how he barely grew a beard in order to stay in fashion.

"No, I want him to lose. I'll put the mud on my brother's boots myself when Curtis wins." But Miss Loughton took out a handkerchief and offered it to Kempton. "But he does have a rather wonderful mustache."

"And I shall redeem your favor for a kiss when I win," Kempton said.

"Bump his elbow," Miss Loughton said to Peter. "Please."

He tucked the handkerchief into his vest pocket. How hard should he try to win? He was accustomed to highly competitive matches and couldn't bear to think of giving anything less than a full effort, but he wasn't sure he dared to win with Lucy's handkerchief searing a hole over his heart.

Peter lined up with the others for the hammer toss. The light was growing dim and they would have to compete quickly.

Loughton threw well. It went reasonably far. The hammer was heavy and curved slightly to the right. Peter made a note to over-correct when he threw it.

Kempton tossed the hammer. Again, it curved slightly to the right, shaving distance off the throw.

Shelford grabbed the hammer. His throw was the best so far.

Peter stepped up. He hoisted the hammer to his shoulder. He ran a few steps, hopped, then threw the hammer to the left. It went perfectly straight, landing farther than the other men.

He turned and smiled at Lucy. Their eyes met. She was watching him. Somehow, he knew she would be, but it still surprised him. He took out her handkerchief and waved it. She laughed. It felt good to make her smile.

Last time he'd seen her, he'd nearly made her cry. He preferred to act the fool and watch her laugh.

He tucked away the handkerchief and joined the others at the archery range. Other men from Mainz were taking turns. Peter studied the bows. There were four targets. The men on the third target consistently got the straightest shots. He queued for a turn to shoot there.

Kempton waited beside him at the fourth target. Shelford was at the first. Loughton was at the second target. Peter blocked out everything else. He notched an arrow, pulled the string next to his cheek, and let the arrow fly. It landed close to the center.

He checked the others. His arrow was more precise than Kempton's or Loughton's. It was nearly the same as Shelford's, but perhaps better by a small amount.

He couldn't help doing anything except playing to win.

Shelford clapped him on the back. "Well done, Chelmsford."

Kempton pumped his hand. "Send your boots my way." He looked down. Peter's boots were covered in hay from the archery target and mud from the river walk. "Oh, I deserve this."

Loughton grimaced. "I owe you, too. Well shot."

"At least there's a harvest dance," Kempton said. "Over there. Rustic sort of event. Wish me better luck with the dancing than the hammer toss." He waggled his eyebrows.

Wooden planks covered part of a meadow. Lanterns were strung along its edge. Rough wooden logs and rickety chairs lined the makeshift dance floor.

Peter caught Lucy's eye and walked over to her. The light had grown dim enough that he could hardly see without the lanterns.

She stood near some grapevines that grew up and around, forming a private bower.

Peter dug in his vest and took out her handkerchief. "Most noble Lucy," he said, and bowed. He offered the square of cloth to her.

Lucy reached out and their hands met. He saw his ring on her gloves. On an impulse, he seized her fingers and raised them to his lips, gazing at Lucy.

She drew in a breath. "I thought it was *my* duty to redeem the favor." She stepped closer to him, their hands still intertwined. "Since you've gone to the trouble of growing a beard noble enough for King Arthur himself."

Peter rubbed the thin layer of stubble and bowed. "My lady fair. I am at your service. Here to protect you from dragons and boiling pots of oil—"

The night hid them. The vineyards. Everyone else had gone to the dancing area. Lucy shivered as a river breeze blew across them.

"And river breezes and crushed grapes that threaten to stain the hem of your dress." Peter let go of her hand and drew Lucy's shawl tighter around her. He left his arms around her shoulders, loosely, as he searched her face.

So many thoughts flew through his head. *Did she talk to Lady Shelford yesterday? Why was she looking at him in that manner? Could he protect her from the greatest threat to her happiness—Walter?*

She put a hand on his cheek. "You won twice, my faithful knight."

Peter waited to see what she would do, wondering if he dared do what he wanted to.

Lucy went up on her tiptoes.

He moved his arms down around her waist. She fit perfectly, so small.

She pulled his head down and drew herself up. But not like in the parlor. Her lips were much closer to his own. It was almost as if she couldn't decide whether she wanted to kiss his mouth or his cheek. If he turned his head ever so slightly, their lips would meet. She kissed his cheek slowly, her hand on his other cheek, and her lips barely missed his own.

Lucy didn't pull away when the kiss ended. She lingered, the palm of her hand still on his face, her eyes upturned toward his. Peter's arm was around her. One slight movement, one shift to the side, and he could kiss her.

But she was engaged to his brother. How did this make him any better than Walter or his father, if he kissed her? He could not do it, in good conscience, no matter how much he wanted to.

He rested his head on top of hers and held her in the dying light.

"Let's join the others," Peter said reluctantly. It took all his self-control to pull away. He let go of Lucy and held out his elbow.

She dropped her hand. She tucked the handkerchief in her pocket without saying anything.

Peter felt frustrated with himself and the situation. He wanted her to feel loved and valued, everything that she deserved, everything that Walter would never give her, but someone had to break her engagement before he could act. Anything else would be dishonorable, worse than what Walter was doing.

If he showed any emotion or affection toward Lucy, he would betray his brother and make Lucy vulnerable to slander, but not doing so felt as though it might cause him physical pain.

But he had to make an attempt. Time was nearly out. This felt like his last chance.

He looped Lucy's arm through his. She held back, trying to walk as far from him as possible. "Lucy," Peter said. "You're betrothed to my brother. In the eyes of the law, you'll be my sister."

He stopped before they left the vineyard. "You said you cannot break your engagement. Once you marry, you're forever out of reach, even if Walter dies. So, I'm asking you, one more time. Are you sure you want to marry Walter?"

He felt an ache, a physical pain in his heart, as he waited for her answer.

"If Papa had given me a choice…"

Peter swallowed. "Don't say it. If you're going to marry my brother, don't say anything we can't live with for the next fifty years."

She looked up at him. "No, I'm not sure I want to marry Walter, but I don't know how to do anything else." She walked toward the dance area, toward Rachel and Miss Loughton, leaving him alone.

Peter shook his head. That was worse than anything he could hear. She didn't want to marry Walter, but she was going to anyway.

She deserved better. He would treat Lucy like a queen.

And Walter would make her miserable, while Peter slowly watched Lucy's spirit die.

CHAPTER 15

Lucy didn't go to the Institute for classes on Thursday. She had a headache before the day even began. She wanted to attend. She wanted to learn how to help others and care for them. She wanted to please the colonel and help Mr. Kempton. She wanted to show Rachel that her interests were important. She wanted to get to know Alice. She wanted to prepare to help Cecelia.

But Rachel forbade her. She perched on the edge of Lucy's bed. "I can tell when you have one of your headaches. You will not be able to concentrate. Please, rest."

Lucy tried to sit up, but Rachel gently pushed her back down on the pillows.

Rachel folded her arms. "Find a horse in an hour or two. Go on a ride. Get some sunshine after the headache subsides. Don't stay inside all day. You've never been one to sit idle." Rachel put her hand on Lucy's forehead. She rubbed her temples and massaged her head. "Dear heart."

Rachel's use of her aunt's name for her was too much. Lucy began to cry. "Peter's mad at me, and you're mad at me, and Walter won't see me."

"There now," Rachel said. "If Peter loves you and you love him, I wish you well. He has two younger brothers who are just as handsome. Why should he be angry with you?"

"And you like Alice better than me, and I've known you longer." Lucy hiccupped.

"Alice and I both understand medicine. I enjoy her friendship, but that will never replace my friendship with you." Rachel ran her fingers through her hair.

"You are the best nurse there will ever be," Lucy said. "You listen to me, and you know exactly what to do, and I never know what to do, and I still can't speak any German. I'm pathetic. Listen to me."

"We've been here but two weeks," Rachel reminded her. "I'm leaving now and expect you to be fully recovered when I return. I love you. Alice loves you. If Peter is angry with you, then you need to discuss the reason with him."

"But you…" Lucy began. How could she ask her friend for permission to fall in love with someone?

"I already told you," Rachel said. "He has two younger brothers. Arthur and Benjamin are equally athletic and handsome." She swept out of the room.

How did she feel about Peter? Lucy closed her eyes. She felt confused. Eleanor was certain that Peter was in love with her. Lucy could always rely on Eleanor for answers.

But when Lucy tried to kiss Peter last night, he turned aside and let her kiss his cheek. How mortifying to be rejected. For the first time in her life, Eleanor was wrong.

Newly married, viewing life through her own haze of happiness, Eleanor wanted everyone else to fall in love, too.

But then Peter asked her if she wanted to marry Walter, with that blazing look in his eyes. The look from the draper shop and the candle shop. Why would he ask unless he cared? Did he mean that he couldn't kiss her while she was still engaged?

If so, she would have to get un-engaged, because she could

never marry Walter now. How could she sit at the Chelmsford dinner table with Peter while married to his brother? It would be excruciating. Whether or not Walter broke her heart, seeing Peter and knowing she was not married to him would cause her enough pain.

But she couldn't break her engagement. The repercussions were too great for their fragile social status. It would break Papa's heart. What if it hurt his business?

She had to choose between her own happiness and her papa's aspirations. Could she be happy with Peter, if she did love him, while it displeased her family, made them social outcasts, and hurt their financial prospects? What if Papa cut her off, and Walter cut off Peter?

Her right temple pounded. How could she sit at the Chelmsford family dinner table, married to Peter, with Walter looking on? What would his mama think? What would Walter think? He didn't want to marry her himself, but that didn't mean that he would allow his younger brother to marry her instead.

And did she love him? How did a woman know when she truly loved one man more than she would ever love any other man in her life?

Rachel came back in the room. "He's downstairs. Sitting across from our apartments."

"Who?"

"Peter."

"But he's not supposed to be here until tonight. If at all."

"Well, he's sitting on a bench, and he looks as bad as you. I told him to come into the drawing room. I'll send in a maid. How quickly can you get dressed?" Rachel rushed back out of the room. Classes started soon, and she was not one to waste words.

Lucy pinched her cheeks as she stumbled out of bed. She tore through her closet. There—the riding habit. Peter would only have to wait a few minutes. Lucy's maid braided her hair, and they pinned it up onto her head.

She changed into the scarlet outfit quickly. The riding habit's midnight black hat would cover her hair. Her maid slipped a pair of black leather gloves onto her hands, and Lucy rushed out of the room.

"Peter!" She held out her hands. "How unexpected."

He stared at her, taking her hands mechanically. "Are we going somewhere?"

Lucy nodded. "Rachel's orders. I am supposed to go riding. Can you help me find a place?" Her head still throbbed, but Rachel was right. Brisk air and sunshine were the best thing for this kind of headache. Lucy often had headaches that needed to avoid light, but this was the other kind. The kind that came from too much crying.

Lucy looked down at her gloved hands, which Peter still held.

"Yes." Peter let go immediately. He cleared his throat. "I know the city well. Is there a horse you can use?"

"Lord Shelford has retained some," Lucy said. She didn't know whether she had the courage to ask Peter why he was angry with her, if he still was. He seemed different today. She needed exercise and fresh air, though, and Peter was willing to accompany her. That would have to be enough.

Lucy rode beside Peter along the crowded streets until they crossed a bridge. They found a quieter path to ride along the river.

"Why were you here so early?" Lucy asked. "I wasn't sure whether I would see you today."

"I wanted to apologize," Peter said. "I hurt your feelings yesterday. I couldn't sleep."

"I did not sleep well, either." She loved the feeling of riding. The smooth, steady stride of a brisk trot. Everything seemed clearer when she was in motion. It was so much easier to feel a sense of control over her life when the only choices were how fast to go or when to turn.

"I'm sorry, Lucy. I have no right to question your decisions." Peter's face was closed.

She sped up. She felt the wind blow across her face as the sun warmed her skin. "You're right, Peter."

He rode silently beside her.

"I don't make my own decisions. I let things happen and make the best of it. My mother died, and I had to comfort my papa. No one comforted me. He spends time in London and leaves me alone. I have to smile and tell him it is well. People I love are taken away from me." Lucy swallowed. "And I am powerless. I don't have an ability to command or choose. I am my father's ward, then I will marry. As an heiress, my assets will belong to my husband."

The rhythm of riding made it easy to talk. Peter was a good listener. "Papa lets me buy anything I want, but that brings me no satisfaction. What good are fancy dresses if I never see anyone? Or beautiful rooms if they are barren? Eleanor has married and moved away. Rachel will stay and finish nursing school, then remain in London. With whom will I associate in Essex? I don't want to embroider and pour tea and sit around with the gossips all day. I'd rather go to London with Papa and learn his trade."

Peter merely nodded.

"No one asks me if I'll be happy. They expect me to be, so I am. All the time," Lucy said. "Have you ever felt that way?"

The horses followed a curve in the path and came to a point. They stopped and watched the two rivers flowing.

"Walter expects a lot of me without asking. He's always been the oldest and known he would take Father's place," Peter said. "He gives orders, and I have little choice or control. My preferences or my happiness is never a question. My monthly allowance, on the other hand, can be negotiated, so, I must be very careful."

He found a rock and dismounted. He tied his horse to a rail and came over to help Lucy. He led her horse to the same rock.

Peter put his hands around her waist and helped her out of the saddle. He paused when she reached the ground, holding onto her a moment longer than necessary. Lucy gazed up at him.

He reached behind her to take the reins from her hand. His

fingers grazed her side. Lucy didn't move but looked him in the eye.

He slowly took the reins, then turned to secure her horse. Lucy let out a breath. Peter had become more than dangerous. Spending time with him endangered her future, a future she had once pursued across the European continent.

Now she stood at a crossroads.

Peter led her along the rest of the path where it narrowed and down some steps to a viewpoint. From there, they could see the entire city of Mainz. The great spires of the cathedral shone, and the city stretched out.

"The two rivers meet here," Peter said. "It's the confluence of the Main and the Rhine."

She looked out over the rivers. The waters swirled together, two colors joining and becoming one river.

She played with Peter's ring on her finger. Lucy had grown accustomed to the feel of it on her hand.

Peter glanced down at her hand.

She should give the ring back to him. Soon.

The Rhine reached the edge of the bank, its water lapping against rocks. Lucy stood still a moment, allowing the soothing sounds to wash over her. Birds called to each other in the bushes around them. The heat of the sun in the mid-morning air warmed Lucy as a gentle breeze blew off the river.

Sometimes she grew weary of behaving properly and managing social expectations.

"How do I change?" she asked. "How do I tell Papa I don't want to do what he expects? What if he requires it of me?"

Peter leaned over to examine the rocks. He selected a few. "Your father does not seem like that kind of man. He loves you."

"But he wants to join the nobility." Lucy twisted the ring on her finger.

Peter bowed with a flourish. "My lady fair. You are noble enough without a title." He straightened and spoke more seriously. "Does it mean that much to you?"

"Not as much as it means to my papa." She shaded her eyes with a hand as she looked over the river. The reflection of the sun on the water dazzled her vision. "Have you ever tried to tell Walter you would not do what he expects?"

Peter scuffed a rock, which tumbled into the river. "He asked me to take orders. I will return home and become the vicar. I cannot imagine risking my future or livelihood by defying him."

"Then you understand my predicament." She gazed at Peter. "My papa has determined my future, and my livelihood depends on acquiescence."

The rivers ran along, indiscriminate and unconcerned. Nothing would alter their course. Perhaps she had been foolish to believe alternatives existed.

Peter threw the rocks one at a time. They skimmed the surface, leaving ripples across the water. He stared at the river and would not meet her eyes. "I find that I have grown attached to you this past week, but I do not wish to endanger your future. I wish to protect it."

Lucy covered her mouth. Eleanor was right.

Peter turned back and searched her face. "Lucy, would your father consider a change in his plans? Would you?" He blinked in the sun. "If I wanted to marry you, would your father allow it? Instead of Walter?" He cleared his throat. "I don't mean to presume that you would wish to, or that your affections are engaged."

Time seemed to still. "I cannot predict my father's course of action, but I can assure you of my own affections. They are engaged only by you."

Peter stared at her a long while, then skipped another rock across the water. "But I don't have a title."

Did he mean it? Did he really love her? "I don't care," Lucy said. "I've had enough of nobility. It's boring."

She watched Peter toss a handful of pebbles nervously in the palm of his hand, then throw them into the river. They sank immediately.

She covered his hand with her own. "Almost as boring as skipping rocks on the river when you could embrace the woman you just proposed to."

Peter dropped the remaining stones, wiped his hands on his trousers, and took a deep breath. Finally, the familiar look returned to his eyes, his gaze intense. He put his hands on her waist. "I want to make you happy. I cannot stand to see you suffer."

"How can I be happy without you?" Lucy whispered.

She slipped an arm around Peter, and he crushed her in a hug. After a long moment, they drew apart, his arm across her shoulders. Peace settled on her as they stood watching the waters coming together.

"Keep my ring," Peter said. "I like the way it looks on your hand."

Lucy turned, put her hand on his chest, and gazed up at him. This was everything she had ever dreamed. A man who adored her. She had hoped to make Walter fall in love, and instead, Peter had found her.

"What will Walter think? Is there any hope that he would release me?" Lucy asked.

Peter rested his head on hers. "I will speak with him. Perhaps he can persuade your father to alter the arrangement in my favor."

She felt hope dawning. "Papa will see reason. He must." Then a wonderful thought occurred to her. "When Walter left, and I thought he would never come back, I was terrified most of losing your mother. Not him. I haven't had a mother for so long, and she has embraced me."

Peter searched her face. "She already loves you."

So did he. Lucy saw it in his eyes. This was love. In all the thousand indescribable ways that Eleanor had said. Peter saw her.

"Why did this happen now, when I've known you all my life?" Lucy asked. "It's like one of Papa's prized stallions has suddenly decided to gallop and take me away with him, when all I expected was our usual walk. I'm not sure which way to turn, but I want to see where this breathless ride will take us."

The fire in Peter's eyes was a smolder, a burning without flame. "Love is not rational."

She dropped her hands from Peter's chest, but he held them and drew her close. "Nevertheless. Stranger things have happened."

She wanted to believe he was sincere. His eyes held a blazing truth, but his words made her feel unsure.

"But you are uncertain?" Lucy asked. "You prize rational thought above all else."

His grip tightened, and Peter pulled her toward him. "I've never felt more lucid or logical. I'm not articulate, Lucy. I don't even understand my own mind. I—" He blew out a breath as he looked over the river. "I know that I wish for you to marry me. My greatest desire is to safeguard you and delight you, all the days of your life. You have a gentle, generous heart, and a brilliant mind, and I could never let Walter trample a soul like yours."

Lucy moved her arms around his neck. He had to lean down. "It makes all the sense in the world to me, Peter Chelmsford. My noble knight, trying to fight my battles. You are kind. You attend to me when no one else is listening. You see past my façade when no one else does. You don't mind that I abhor all the ladylike pursuits. You accept me as an equal, even though I am the daughter of a businessman."

Lucy felt love wash over her. She leaned toward him.

"I can't," Peter said throatily. "Not while you're engaged to my brother."

A heavy silence fell between them. "He is a dragon, you realize," he said. He put a hand on her cheek.

Lucy laughed. "I'm not betrothed. I changed my mind." She knew that she would never marry Walter, regardless of the consequences.

"But your father signed the contract," Peter said.

She ran her fingers through his thick hair. "And I will ask him to break it."

"Slay the contract. Free the princess." His tone was wry.

"The heiress," Lucy said. She could see the indecision on his face. The dimple in his chin was more pronounced when he worried.

She did not know whether Papa would allow her to marry Peter, but she knew she would refuse to marry Walter. She felt as free as though she'd flung the papers into a fire, but Peter hesitated.

"Let's return to Mainz," Lucy said. The euphoria ebbed, and the reality settled. What if Walter would not release her? What if Papa would not agree?

They walked silently back to the horses. Peter untied hers first, then Lucy climbed onto the rock. It put her nearly level with Peter. She was still inches shorter than him.

He put his hands around her waist to help her into the saddle. Tears welled in Lucy's eyes. She felt so cherished and adored when she spent time with Peter, but she did not know if their families would allow them to marry. And what if he did not love her as much as she cared for him?

Any sensible man would want to kiss the woman he professed to love.

She blinked the tears away and prepared to take the horse's reins. Peter was being stupid and noble. She could do with less chivalry and more affection right now. She needed some reassurance. After the rejection by Walter, Lucy wanted Steady Peter. Reliable Peter. Look At Me Like No One Else Exists Peter. Not Honorable, Honest, Not Kissing Me Peter.

What if he walked away like his brother did and never came back?

Peter's hands were still on her waist. He drew her closer, encircling her, glancing down at her lips, then back up at her. She caught her breath.

"Lucy," Peter said in an agonized voice. "Will your father allow you to choose?"

She was afraid her shaking voice would betray her. "My papa will see reason, and Walter will, too."

She waited for him to help her onto the horse. She did not

believe the things she said; she only hoped them. He was probably right to be careful.

"I have let Walter decide my happiness for too long," Peter said. "And you have let your father decide yours. Do we dare attempt this?"

Lucy felt terrified and euphoric and overwhelmed all at once. She closed her eyes to blink back the tears. The river breeze wafted a hint of leather.

She nodded.

Peter didn't lift her into the saddle. He traced a finger down her face and let it rest on her lips, then she felt his lips on her, soft and cautious.

Their lips met, and Lucy closed any gap between them, putting her arms around his neck. His hands at her waist drew her close. Peter's kiss was gentle, as if his uncertainty extended to his lips. Lucy deepened the kiss, losing herself in the emotion.

She felt the moment Peter responded. His hesitation vanished, replaced with confidence. An insistency replaced his caution. He ran his hands along her back, and she felt as though they had become one person, as surely as the two rivers combined and flowed together.

They kissed again and again, the horse whinnying behind her. Finally, they broke apart. Lucy put her head on his shoulder. Peter hugged her tight. They stood that way for several moments before the horse neighed.

"I love you, Lucy," Peter said. He ran a hand across her cheek. "I cannot wait to tell the world."

Hope filled her. Walter and George had never said those words to her. Finally, someone to love and be loved by in return. Not just someone, but Peter.

"I love you," Lucy said. She laughed. Everything was right with the world. The sunshine and the river breeze and the sound of birds. "Can we speak to Walter? I want to be released from my engagement at once."

"Let me tell him," Peter said, "and I will ride over as soon as it is done." He kissed her again. "He is visiting the widow again today, so he may not be at home."

"We will be gone this afternoon as well, visiting our patient from the Institute." Lucy turned her face to the sun. A perfect day. "Perhaps this evening?"

Peter lifted her onto the horse. "I shall await our dinner tonight, my lady fair. I'm off to slay a dragon."

CHAPTER 16

Peter and Lucy enjoyed a sunny ride back to her apartments. He couldn't resist helping Lucy dismount, just to hold her tight, or kissing her when she threw her arms around him one last time before he left.

She watched him climb back into the saddle and offered him her handkerchief. He had to lean down precariously to accept the token.

"My chivalrous nobleman, astride his gallant steed." Lucy blew him a kiss. "I await news of your endeavor." She laughed. "Hurry, Peter. I'll miss you."

He rode as quickly as he could without harming the horse. Riding in and out of Mainz twice in a day. He was going to be saddle-sore tomorrow, but Lucy was worth it. She was worth any effort.

He urged his horse forward. Perhaps he would use Walter's horse for the return journey to give his poor animal a rest.

Walter would be so relieved to hear that Lucy wanted to break her engagement. How did it work? Now that the papers had been signed, Walter would need to contact a lawyer or someone, Peter supposed. How quickly could they get word to Lucy's father? Had the new telegraph line in Germany been connected to the French network? Was the British undersea line currently working?

And when would he begin to draw up his own marriage settlement? He wouldn't take orders for months yet, and he couldn't marry until Walter had given him the living at Chelmsford. Peter hoped Walter wouldn't feel upset that Lucy had chosen him. Would he? He had all but told Peter to marry Lucy.

Perhaps he would keep his part quiet for now. Let Walter feel relieved that the engagement was over. Walter handled things best a little at a time. Let him get used to that idea first.

What reason would he give for Lucy's decision? Walter would not require a reason. He would welcome her decision and turn his attentions to Mrs. Smith.

He could not actually tell Walter that Lucy had given her heart to him. Walter had not been serious when he suggested that. Or had he? Peter mulled over the possibility. How honest could he be? Walter had laughed when he told him that he had kissed Lucy on the cheek and held her.

Peter wanted to tell Walter right away, but could he risk an unpredictable reaction? He never knew which way his brother would respond to something. Would it be uproariously funny or an insult to Walter's honor and dignity?

Their house drew into sight. Peter approached the stable and saw that Walter's horse was already gone. He must have gone to visit Mrs. Smith without him. They'd visited her yesterday, too, and spent hours talking to her. Mrs. Smith must have the patience of a saint.

Again, for hours, Walter and Mrs. Smith had agreed on every particular. The wonder of it was that Peter knew it was all true. His brother really did enjoy those things, but who would want to discuss them in such minute detail? Evidently, Mrs. Smith did. Peter didn't know the difference between an Irish country air or a folk song, but Walter had to discuss the revival of traditional music and debate every piece with Mrs. Smith.

And that was just the first hour.

Then they discussed opera, and piano concertos, and how many pedals a piano should have. Peter's patience was most tested when they revisited the subject of Walter's hounds, listing each one by name, and describing their personalities.

It was the longest afternoon of his life.

Against his better judgment, Peter decided to test his theory and ride to Mrs. Smith's house directly. He had to think of a way to persuade Walter to leave quickly today.

Indeed, Peter recognized Walter's horse in front of Mrs. Smith's home. How many hours had he been here? Peter wondered where this could lead. She was going to give birth. They could not stay in Mainz indefinitely after the widow delivered her child. She would not want to entertain visitors then, nor would it be appropriate. And how would Peter continue his attentions to Lucy, after Walter finally decided to leave for Vienna?

How could Peter protect Lucy's social status, once Walter did cancel his contract? There would be some talk and a bit of scandal.

Peter could begin to court her as soon as they returned from their Grand Tour. By then, Walter's engagement would have been over for a while. It would seem natural for him to spend time with Lucy, a friend of the family. No one need know their courtship had secretly begun in Germany while she was still engaged to his brother.

Peter could court her slowly while he prepared to take orders. Lucy knew his affection was secure. She'd have plenty of time to plan their wedding. He would protect her reputation, quiet any rumors, and restore her social standing.

Peter knocked on the door, and Mr. Ford welcomed him into the parlor to join Mrs. Smith and Walter.

Mrs. Smith's face was soft. She smiled at Walter like he was the whole world to her.

Peter felt a pang. It was the way Lucy had just looked at him.

But there was no hope for Walter and Mrs. Smith. She would give birth, and Walter would continue on his Grand Tour. Would the two of them ever see each other again? Walter wanted desperately to help her, but how could he?

Walter, usually so stiff, leaned forward in his chair, his elbows on his knees, as if he could not sit close enough to her.

Peter settled onto a sofa. They hardly noticed him.

Walter was talking about breeding his dogs. Again. "Her last litter was five pups."

Mrs. Smith's laugh tinkled softly. "And you helped with all of them? Just like you, Papa. He loves animals."

Mr. Ford exchanged a glance with Peter. He looked as uncomfortable with the conversation as Peter felt. "We haven't kept a dog for years. I do miss my hounds."

Walter continued as though they were in the stables at home, not in a gentlewoman's parlor. "Birth is the most natural thing in the world."

"For your pointers, perhaps, Lord Chelmsford," Mrs. Smith replied. She seemed equally at ease.

Walter shook his head. "You'll be the best at anything you do."

Mrs. Smith's smile was heavenly. "Thank you for your confidence. But I cannot take credit for such a natural process. Mr. Chelmsford, I apologize for talking so freely in front of you."

Peter was startled. He had been thinking how vulgar this conversation was. It must have shown on his face. "I'm sure it must occupy a great deal of your thoughts, Mrs. Smith."

"It is far from appropriate drawing room conversation," she said.

Walter shrugged and glanced at Peter. "He helps with the pups. He knows a thing or two about it. I'm more worried about you, Mrs. Smith, than drawing room conventions. Are you ready?"

"Thank you. Your concern is touching." Mrs. Smith did look affected. "I have some new friends coming to help me."

"We'll do well enough," Mr. Ford said. "I can provide for my daughter and grandchild."

"Will you have clothes for the child? Blankets? What can I

purchase in town?" Walter pulled his chair closer to the widow. "You must let me help."

"My friends have sent some linens to make clothes and other supplies. I believe we will be taken care of at first." A cloud passed over her face. "By living prudently, we have set aside funds to supplement my father's income for some time."

Walter moved the chair until he sat directly beside her. "But after that? After the supplies run out? I'm not worried about one week. What about a month from now? A year from now? What is this child's future, Mrs. Smith? What is yours?"

Peter knew Walter could not be involved in her future. He was torturing himself if he thought otherwise.

Mrs. Smith's eyes gleamed with moisture. "You ask difficult questions," she said lightly. "I don't have answers."

"We're doing our best," Mr. Ford said. "We'll manage."

Walter stood and strode over to the fireplace. "But your best isn't enough for a woman like her." He faced Mrs. Smith. "You are a goddess. How can I witness you living in such circumstances, when you were meant to live like a queen?"

"We have not always lived in this manner," Mrs. Smith said quietly. She winced.

"Are you having the pains again?" Mr. Ford asked.

Mrs. Smith nodded and let out a long breath.

Peter's heart went out to her. So vulnerable and brave. She must have a tragic history to have fallen into this poverty and dire circumstance.

Walter returned to her side and knelt. "What is it?"

"My pains come and go."

"I will send for the nurses," Mr. Ford said. "It's been hours now. They will want to know."

"Not yet," Mrs. Smith said. "If it continues, I will send for them."

Mr. Ford looked at Walter. "She insists it is nothing, but I think she does not wish me to leave her."

"I shall leave this instant," Walter said. "Please allow me to go. You are in pain. What is the address?"

"Or your brother?" Mrs. Smith asked, her face pale. "Will you stay with me, and would you go, Mr. Chelmsford?"

Peter agreed with her father. Mrs. Smith would not be easy if she were alone. She needed her father to stay with her, and it seemed she wanted Walter at her side. "Yes, I'm going into Mainz tonight. Walter, may I speak with you privately outside before I go?"

"This is urgent," Walter said. "No time to lose. You must leave now."

"Where is their card?" Mr. Ford asked. "I'll find their address." He left the room in a rush.

"This matter is important, too," Peter said. Imperative, really, but he could not speak of it in front of Mrs. Smith.

Walter glared at Peter. He took Mrs. Smith's hand. "Nothing could be as important as this."

Mrs. Smith studied their hands. "Sir?"

"Mrs. Smith. I cannot see you live in abject poverty while it is in my means to alleviate it."

"We have friends who have sent supplies." Mrs. Smith's face looked flushed. This had been happening for hours? How many?

Peter suspected she was in more pain than she let on. He needed to leave quickly, but he needed to talk to Walter about the engagement first.

"Walter," Peter said. "Let's leave Mrs. Smith to rest for a moment. A quick word."

"I cannot leave her side," Walter said. "Now, or ever."

Peter wasn't sure how to react. He wanted to stop Walter from doing this. He was about to make a serious mistake, but he felt powerless to say or do anything. Whatever Walter felt, he needed to rein in his emotions. Consider the ramifications.

Walter knelt before her.

Mrs. Smith rested a hand on his shoulder. "Lord Chelmsford." Her voice was thick with emotion.

He gazed at her, still kneeling. "From the moment I heard you sing, I knew you were my soul mate. The moment I beheld you, it was as though the heavens parted and God himself had given you to me and sent me for you."

Mrs. Smith smiled tremulously. Walter seized her hands. "Please allow me to care for you and your child and treat you the way a goddess deserves. Come home with me to Chelmsford Hall. We'll marry here, as soon as you're able."

Peter sat in shock. This was too far. Too much. Walter couldn't do that. He was legally bound to another. He'd need to get a lawyer, undo his marriage contract. It would take days. Weeks. How quickly was Walter planning to get married?

"Perhaps we can marry before the child comes," Walter said.

Mr. Ford entered the room. "What's this!"

The woman was in the middle of birthing pains. Peter had helped enough animals to know that Mrs. Smith had only hours before her child came. Not days or weeks.

"Yes," Mrs. Smith. Her radiant happiness made her shine. "Papa, it's all right. I've never met anyone so selfless and unconcerned for himself. His sole worry is for me." She lowered her head and paused. "That has not been my experience with other men."

Mr. Ford gave the card to Peter. "This is the address."

Peter held the card without looking at it. "I'll leave momentarily."

"What's this? Marry my daughter?" Mr. Ford asked.

Mrs. Smith waved her hand at her father. "Why not?"

"Now is not the time," Mr. Ford said. "Are you sure you want him to stay?"

She took Walter's hand in her own. "I have been so lonely these past months, and then he came into my life. He understands me as no one else ever has." She turned toward Walter. "We talk for hours, and I cannot wait until the next time you come. I think of you while you're gone, Lord Chelmsford. I want to know everything about you, and one minute is too long to delay before speaking with you again."

So she was serious. She actually did enjoy those boring conversations with Walter. She actually cared about the details: the hunting dogs, the horses, the stables. The window glazings. The musical arrangements and hymns they discussed.

But then Peter thought about how he'd asked Lucy question after question himself, just this morning on their ride. He smiled, then sobered. Walter had created an impossible situation.

"And your dedication to your departed father. Your unwavering determination to fulfill your duties as viscount. It inspires me." Mrs. Smith took a sharp breath. "I know he is a spiritual man, too."

"Come now," Mr. Ford said. "This is too much excitement."

"Papa has tried to protect me," Mrs. Smith said. "We have been treated ill by dishonest men before." Her face shone. "But you are different."

Peter shifted in his seat. Walter could not keep these promises he had made. What would happen to the widow when she learned the truth? Peter wanted to protect her, but Walter had already made rash assurances. "Walter, I must leave, but it is urgent that we speak."

"In a moment, Peter. I will do anything I can," Walter said, turning to Mr. Ford. "Sir, I request your daughter's hand in marriage. You know my situation. I am the viscount Chelmsford, well able to provide."

"I don't know the first thing about you," Mr. Ford said. "How do I know who you are? If you'll allow me to verify with the Foreign Office, run a telegraph to London, perhaps we can begin to become acquainted."

"All will be in order," Walter said respectfully.

Peter couldn't believe the change. To have anyone doubt his peerage would ordinarily insult and offend Walter, yet here he sat, calm, polite, deferential. He must be in love. He was certainly deluded.

Because all would not be well.

Nothing would change the fact that Walter was legally engaged and had just proposed to an entirely different woman.

And Peter had just glanced at the calling card. It had Colonel Loughton's address on it. The same address as Lucy's and Rachel's. They were Mrs. Smith's nurses.

CHAPTER 17

Lucy changed out of her riding habit and freshened up. She found the most flattering dress she owned. The sapphire silk with ruffles. It brought out the color of her eyes and accentuated her curves. She felt a little daring when she wore that dress. Secretly, she'd been saving it for the day she knew she would see Walter.

It was perfect for today.

She smiled at everything. Everyone. The grooms. The footmen. Her abigail. It was the most beautiful day. The most wonderful tea. Peter was the kindest, most gentle, most wonderful man alive.

She was in love.

Lucy found Mrs. Glenn and allowed her to tell her about the Roman occupation of Germany until Rachel and Alice arrived home from class.

"The 'General' insists we check on our widow," Rachel said. "And Alice insists on staying home."

"I do not attend births," Alice said. "My brother knows I will tolerate everything else. I moved from London to Germany for him. I am training as a nurse. I will help Miss Nightingale establish her school. But I draw the line there. No deliveries."

"And births are my specialty," Rachel said. "So I will train Miss

Nightingale's students in that area. You need not come. I will tell your brother."

"He hates it when you call him 'General' instead of Colonel," Alice said.

Rachel smiled. "And that is why I do it. Lucy? Will you come? Her time must be very close. I've been worrying about her all week."

Lucy felt guilty. She hadn't thought about Cecelia nearly as much as she should have. At least she had sent the linens, the candles, tea, tobacco for her father, fresh fruits, and vegetables from the marketplace. "Of course. I'll leave a note with the footmen."

"For Peter?" Rachel asked.

Lucy nodded. "He is coming this evening. Perhaps this afternoon. What about Eleanor? She would want to meet Cecelia. Shall we invite her as well, since Alice is not coming?"

They met the colonel, who assisted them into a carriage. Mr. Kempton waited beside him.

"Where's Alice?" the colonel asked.

Rachel settled herself onto the carriage seat. "I asked her to stay home, General."

Mr. Kempton laughed. "If she is staying, may I be excused? She may want someone to entertain her." He bowed to them and turned back toward the apartments.

Colonel Loughton's nostrils flared. "We may require her assistance."

"I made other arrangements."

He stared at her. "Pardon?" The colonel climbed into the carriage, then rapped the ceiling.

The vehicle lurched and began to move forward.

"Lord and Lady Shelford are following us in their carriage. I gave them the direction."

The colonel turned to look through the window. "I see."

"The Shelfords are most concerned that a fellow countrywoman is in distress. Lucy told Eleanor, and she insists on coming, too. And anywhere she goes, Lord Shelford goes."

"Am I to have the entire town in my sickroom?" Colonel Loughton's voice was resigned, and Lucy could see admiration for Rachel in his eyes.

"You don't mind," Lucy said. "We may need her, and Alice should not be forced to come."

"You seem recovered," the colonel said. "Now you and Miss Wickford are both ordering me around." His smile belied the stern tone of his voice.

"Has your headache improved?" Rachel asked.

Lucy leaned back against the seat cushions. The carriage gently swayed from side to side. "Yes. I did as instructed and took a ride."

"With Peter?"

Lucy nodded. She wondered how Rachel felt about Peter, really. Had she been honest this morning?

Colonel Loughton studied Rachel, who had schooled her face to give no sign of emotion.

"I'm glad it helped," Rachel said. "I hate to see you suffering."

Lucy took Rachel's hand. "You hate to see anyone in pain. That's why you're a nurse."

"Not yet. In training."

The carriage moved along steadily. When they reached the small clearing, Colonel Loughton assisted them down the steps. Lucy enjoyed the charm afforded by the shady oak trees and vibrant chrysanthemums while they waited for the Shelfords' carriage to arrive.

"There are some horses already here," Rachel said. "She may have visitors."

Colonel Loughton strode around the carriage to join Rachel. Lucy followed him. There were two horses tied to a post in front of the cottage.

"That looks like Peter's horse," Lucy said. "Beautiful creature."

The colonel grimaced. "They'll have to leave, whoever it is. I don't want anything to excite or upset Cecelia right now."

Rachel saluted the colonel and smiled at him.

"You've got an insurrection on your hands," Lucy said quietly.

"And the battle hasn't even started," Colonel Loughton muttered in response.

She smiled at him. He had already lost the war. Not just the battle. He really had no idea.

Lord Shelford and Eleanor joined them.

"This is the place?" Eleanor asked. "You're right, Lucy. For a gentlewoman, it would be quite an alteration in circumstances to live like this. Even if it is charming."

Lord Shelford glanced around the crowded space. "What did you do with the carriages last time?" he asked.

"They waited here," Colonel Loughton answered. "But two carriages will fill the entire clearing. Should we send them down the road?"

Lord Shelford nodded. "Come back in fifteen minutes," he instructed his driver. "The home doesn't look much larger. I can wait out here."

"Thank you," Colonel Loughton said. "We'll keep the visit short. I may ask the rest of you to step out and give me time alone with her."

"But I will stay," Rachel said.

"And I," Lucy said.

"I will, as well," Eleanor said. "Of course."

"Good heavens." Lucy laughed. "Full scale mutiny, General."

"Don't turn on me," the colonel warned. "I need one person on my side."

"I'm loyal to you," Lord Shelford said. "I've already agreed to stay outside."

"Knew I liked you." The colonel clapped Lord Shelford on the back, then rapped smartly on the door. "Very well. Miss Wickford may stay for the examination, but the others will wait outside.

Shelford, I charge you with coming in to clear the room, if they haven't left in five minutes."

Lucy, Rachel, and Eleanor saluted him. Colonel Loughton shook his head. Lord Shelford doubled over with laughter.

Cecelia's father opened the door. "Ah. The nurses. Come in. We'll be a bit tight, but Cecelia's in some pain. It's well that you came."

"They never send for me," Rachel said. "Every time. I tell them, and they wait too long. What did I tell you, General?"

Lucy loved seeing this lighter side of Rachel. Her friend was usually so serious, quiet, and reserved. The fact that she had adopted a nickname for the colonel during classes today, that she teased him and flouted his attempt to enforce regulations, boded well.

Lucy followed Rachel into the parlor. Cecelia's father filed in behind her.

Rachel stopped abruptly, then turned around. "Maybe we should go, dear heart." She put a hand on Lucy's arm, as if to turn her around as well.

Why was Rachel using her aunt's special name for her? The one she only used when Lucy was in the depths of despair? Something was wrong.

Cecelia was in pain. This was important.

"What's wrong?" Lucy pushed her way forward. Rachel was trying to protect her, but she wanted to help, even if Cecelia was in pain.

Walter knelt on the floor near Cecelia. Peter sat across the room, his eyes wide open, as if in shock. Walter stood and put his hand on Cecelia's chair. Protectively.

Lucy's heart began to beat fast. What was happening? She felt faint. Rachel took her arm and helped her onto the only place left to sit, a sofa next to Cecelia. Walter was caught, almost in the arms of another woman. A woman expecting a child. Had he been in Germany long enough to be the father? She did some quick calculations. Impossible.

But the idea sickened her. Who was the father of Cecelia's child? And why was Walter so affectionate? Had he known her before this, then sent her away to Germany with his child? Was this why Walter left so suddenly in May?

Eleanor pushed her way into the crowded room. "Cecelia!"

Colonel Loughton looked between them. "You are acquainted?"

Eleanor stared. "Excuse me. Percy is here, outside, and will wish to greet you as well." She turned and exited the room.

Cecelia's father, Rachel, and the colonel seated themselves at the round table.

Lucy could hardly take in the crowded room. What was Peter doing here with Cecelia? What was Walter doing here? Were Eleanor and Cecelia acquaintances? Friends?

Eleanor returned with her husband. "She's here," she whispered.

"How are you, Cecelia?" Rachel asked. "Your father said you've been having some pains."

Cecelia winced. "Yes. They began some time ago."

"How long?" Rachel demanded.

"This morning, or perhaps last night." She closed her eyes and pressed her lips together.

"I've got to ask everyone to leave," Colonel Loughton said.

"Yes, it's crowded. Chelmsford, come back tomorrow," Cecelia's father said.

So, he did know them. The widow that Walter had been visiting was Cecelia. Lucy collapsed against the sofa. How long had they known each other?

"One moment, if you please, Mr. Duxford?" Eleanor asked.

Cecelia's father looked around the room. "One minute. That is all."

"I want to know why Walter is here," Eleanor said.

Walter crossed the room to stand beside Peter. He folded his arms across his chest. "Why are *you* here? What do you mean, calling this man 'Duxford?'"

"Keep a civil tone, Chelmsford," Lord Shelford said.

Lucy didn't know what to think or feel. Too much was happening at once. Peter. Walter. Cecelia. Peter. Why hadn't he told her? Lucy picked up a pillow and hugged it to her chest. She didn't care whether it was ladylike.

"Can this conversation happen outside?" Rachel asked. "I must attend to Cecelia."

Eleanor glared at Walter. "I want an answer before he disappears."

"Make it quick." Colonel Loughton shoved Walter aside. He began to take Cecelia's pulse. "Miss Wickford, you can begin to cut the muslin into strips as we discussed. You sent muslin, Miss Maldon?"

"She did," Cecelia said. "It's in the kitchen, in the brown paper package. I did not know where it would be needed. Papa, will you please help?" She shifted uncomfortably. The strain in her voice scared Lucy.

The colonel studied the fire. "Will you check the fireplaces upstairs, in the kitchen, and bring in more wood? I'll need water drawn from their well. We must move quickly." He glanced at Cecelia.

"Follow me." Cecelia's father led Rachel out of the parlor. "I want this room clear when I return."

"Are you acquainted?" Cecelia asked, then took a deep breath. "You married Mr. Hauxton, Eleanor. Congratulations."

"Lord Shelford now," Eleanor said. "It's been an age since we saw you in Vienna. I suppose I saw you last right here in Germany with—" Eleanor's eyes grew wide.

Cecelia nodded her head ever so slightly and cast her eyes to the floor.

"So, you do know each other," the colonel said.

Eleanor glared across the room. "Explain yourself, Walter."

Lucy followed Eleanor's gaze to the corner of the room. She felt sick, just catching a glimpse of Walter's duplicitous face.

She forced herself to put down the pillow. She took a deep

breath and pulled her shawl around herself. This was the man she had pursued? He hardly seemed worth the effort.

"I don't need to justify my actions to anyone," Walter said. He tried to draw himself up to his full height, but he was wedged into the corner of the room where the roof met the ceiling.

Lord Shelford's chair scraped the floor as it pushed back from the table. "I gave you one warning. That's all you get." He flexed his fists at his side.

Lucy looked across the room at Peter. She wanted to hear his explanation. At the very least, something did not add up, or something could be very, very wrong. Peter met her gaze, but she could not read the look.

"You're upsetting my patient," Colonel Loughton said. Cecelia's face was flushed.

"Please, stop," Cecelia said. "I don't know how you know each other, or why you should be upset to find him here. But you needn't worry on my account. Lord Chelmsford and I have visited and grown attached while he's lived in Mainz. We just got engaged."

Lucy went cold. Walter—engaged to someone else? And Peter knew, but did not warn her or explain or tell her? He *had* warned her that Walter would break her heart, but she had asked him to make Walter fall in love with her anyway. The humiliation. It was too much to take in.

"That's why I'm upset, Cecelia," Eleanor said. "He's already engaged to Lucy."

Lucy picked up the pillow and hugged it again. She felt suddenly alone in the world.

Peter had lied to her.

CHAPTER 18

Peter stared at Lucy. This couldn't be happening. He needed a chance to explain. He had to talk to Walter alone. To talk to Lucy alone. There were too many people in the crowded parlor. Everything was happening too fast, and he couldn't think. Walter hovered behind him, making it even harder.

"How can he be engaged to Lucy?" Cecelia asked tremulously. She glanced around the room. "I don't understand. Are you acquainted?"

"Outside. Now," Shelford said. "I want a word with you." Peter wasn't sure who he meant. Him? Walter? Had Lucy told anyone she was engaged to him instead of his brother? Were they engaged?

Peter pushed out of the chair, but Walter stepped around Peter and moved to the middle of the room. He faced Shelford. "I'm not leaving."

Loughton dropped Cecelia's wrist. He joined Shelford. "Yes, you are."

"I'm Lord Chelmsford. You're not going to tell me what to do," Walter said, pushing out his chest. He drew himself up to his full height now.

The colonel still towered over him. "Your title means nothing in the sickroom, man. I decide who stays and goes. Don't suppose I am at all impressed. I fought alongside men of every rank in Crimea, and my grandfather is a duke. I'll not back down to you."

Walter glanced back at Peter. No. He would not join this fight.

"If you care about this woman, as you claim you do, then do what's best for her. Go. Now." The colonel and Shelford formed a massive wall hiding Lucy and Cecelia from the brothers' view. Shelford crossed his arms.

Peter yearned to see Lucy's face, to know how she felt. He considered the two men. It would be a fair fight, even, but he had no intention of helping Walter. Still, he couldn't see Lucy.

"No." Walter tried to advance across the room, but the colonel and Shelford would not relinquish an inch.

"Are you engaged to her?" Cecelia's gentle voice asked.

The men moved aside. Peter could see Cecelia's soft face, stained with tears. She looked even more beautiful when she cried. If Walter truly thought he loved her, his heart must be breaking.

"He signed a settlement," Peter said, when no one else spoke.

"A marriage contract?" Cecelia asked. She looked at Walter. "With Lucy?"

The whole room seemed to hold its breath.

"Yes," Walter said. He crossed the room and knelt down beside Cecelia. She struggled to breathe.

"I suppose I am legally betrothed, but it doesn't mean anything, Cecelia. I swear. I never loved her. I only want to marry you." He tried to take her hands, but she would not let him have them.

Peter wanted to run to Lucy and hold her in his arms. This humiliation was worse than he had imagined: seeing him with Cecelia and hearing Walter say these things in front of other people, in front of another woman he professed to love instead of her.

That it never meant anything. That Lucy meant nothing.

He wanted to wrestle Walter to the ground, as he had when they were boys, and make him forfeit the prize. He might throw in a kick for good measure.

"How can you talk to Lucy that way?" Peter asked, rising to his feet. "Lord Shelford, Colonel Loughton, I will not stand for this. Help my brother see reason."

"I'll see him outside. He's not going to marry Miss Maldon or Miss Duxford while I'm around. I have ten reasons right here." Shelford cracked his knuckles.

Peter crossed the room, daring the colonel with one look to stop him. Colonel Loughton stepped aside.

Peter dug inside his vest and pulled Lucy's handkerchief out of his pocket. When she did not move to take it, he wiped her cheeks and tucked her handkerchief back into his vest. He covered her motionless hands, holding them tight. She would not return the gesture.

"Lucy," Peter said. "I would marry you."

Her dull, lifeless eyes met his for a brief moment. No warmth or understanding or agreement or joy. Just pain.

Peter knew she hurt right now. He smiled at her, trying to let her know she meant the world to him, trying to tell her how beautiful she looked today, with her vibrant sapphire eyes and that dress that accentuated her natural silhouette. He gazed at her, longing to hold her.

He brought her hands to his lips, then set them down gently.

She stared at him as though he were the one who had betrayed her, and he had. He had withheld the truth from her.

Cecelia took a sharp breath. A wave of pain passed over her.

"Your time is up," Colonel Loughton said.

Peter returned across the room, sat on a sofa, and crossed his arms. He would not leave.

Lucy watched him with blank eyes, and then something changed. Her gaze darted to his brother. "Did you know I was here in Mainz, Walter?"

"I'm sorry, Lucy. Peter's right. I spoke to you disrespectfully. Let me be clear and honest with you now. That would have shown more courtesy. I cannot marry you. I'll cancel the engagement," Walter said. He turned to Cecelia. "As soon as I saw Mrs. Smith, I knew we were destined for each other."

Lucy sat up. "This is why you wouldn't let me see him, Peter. Because he was with her."

Anger flashed in her eyes. The spark stung him across the room.

"I was trying to spare you," Peter said. "But I should have told you."

Walter crossed the room and sank into the chair where Peter had been. "I should have cancelled our contract months ago. It was wrong to send Peter in my place. Mrs. Smith needs me."

Lucy tried to stand, but collapsed back onto her seat. "You were distracting me, so he could marry someone else. I asked you to help me marry Walter, and you helped him marry someone else."

Eleanor came and sat beside Lucy. She put her arm around her, and Lucy laid her head on her shoulder.

"There, dear heart," Eleanor said. "Clear the room, Percy."

Lucy held up a hand. "He made me promise to stay away from Walter," Lucy said. "He was only trying to distract me. I want to hear him tell me the truth."

"No, Lucy." Peter scrambled for the right words. "It's not like that." What could he say to convince her? He felt something precious slipping away, and he was desperate. Like a man on the edge of a cliff, about to fall off, grasping at tufts of grass. "I wanted to spend time with you. Everything I said was true, especially today."

Lucy's quiet voice pierced him. "Did Walter ask you to keep me away from him?"

Peter squirmed on the sofa. "Yes." He could imagine his grip on the grass slacken.

Lucy wiped her eyes. "Did you know he was spending time with Cecelia?"

Peter blew out a breath. "Yes." He was sliding, falling fast, and there was no way to stop. The grass was slippery, and he could not hold on.

"While you spent time with me?" Lucy asked. Her voice had nearly dropped to a whisper.

"Yes." In his mind, the other hand let go at last. He imagined himself crashing over the cliff to land on rocks below. Lucy would never forgive him. He felt shattered.

Lucy crumpled onto Eleanor's shoulder. Her body shook with sobs.

On the other side, Cecelia looked at Walter. In a strained voice, she said, "You were engaged to her the entire time we conversed?" Cecelia watched Lucy. "You could do this to her and expect me to accept you?"

Cecelia began to shake. The colonel rushed over to her. Her breathing had grown ragged.

"You're leaving. Now. All of you," Loughton said.

Shelford grabbed Walter by the arm and began to drag him from the room.

Peter stood. He had to speak to Lucy before he left. "Lucy," Peter said. "Let me explain and apologize." She had become his whole world.

She turned toward him. Her large eyes were filled with hurt and betrayal, far deeper than anything he had seen earlier. Tears streamed down her delicate cheeks. She was the most beautiful woman he had ever seen, and he had caused her the most exquisite pain.

Lucy slowly took Peter's ring off her hand. She brought it over to him and placed it back in his palm. Her tiny fingers barely fit around his hand as she closed his fingers into a fist.

"Peter," Lucy whispered. She gazed at him. "Please go."

He knew that look. The look of intense suffering caused when the person who you think loves you has betrayed you. He'd seen it on his mother's face so many times. The look he'd sworn Lucy would never have if she married him instead of Walter.

But he had caused that pain. He'd hurt and betrayed her. Not Walter. Walter's unfaithfulness was nothing compared to his lies. Peter had wounded the woman he loved just as deeply as his brother had, and perhaps more.

In that moment, his world shattered.

Peter slipped his father's ring back onto his smallest finger. *How appropriate.* He was like his father after all. Lying, breaking hearts, kissing women engaged to someone else. Yes, he took after his father more than he had ever dreamed. Peter felt sick and ashamed. He followed Shelford out of the cottage, but he couldn't help taking one last, long glance back at Lucy.

She had crumpled into a ball, her head on Eleanor's shoulder, her body wracked with silent sobs. Beside her, Cecelia strained through a birthing pain. Rachel met his gaze.

"I'm sorry," Peter said intently. "Deeply and truly." He turned and left.

CHAPTER 19

Lucy buried her head in Eleanor's shoulder. Peter didn't love her. He'd played her false. He seemed so genuine, yet everything had been an insincere act. His time with her, his attentiveness, his kindness, and those meaningful glances. Even their shared kisses didn't mean anything, just like George, the stable hand. He hadn't truly cared for her either, though she'd believed his declarations of love, too.

Peter was trying to convince her not to marry Walter and give her a reason to break her engagement. Perhaps they had planned it this way, so she would be the one to end the marriage contract. Was there a clause allowing the estate to keep her dowry, if she broke the agreement? Would Walter give Peter a portion as compensation for his work?

One thing was certain: Peter and Walter were in this together. They had planned to keep her and Walter apart. Had Peter rushed home, triumphant, to tell Walter that their scheme was accomplished?

Peter never intended to marry her. He'd said those things at the river today in order to convince her to break her engagement with Walter.

And Walter refused to marry her. Publicly. She would be ruined socially. She couldn't stand any more humiliation. All the strength drained out of her. Breathing was a chore.

Eleanor's arms crushed her. "I am always here for you, Lucy Maldon. Your friends love you. Your papa and Aunt Ellen love you. Never doubt us."

Papa. Poor Papa. She felt almost as bad for him as she did for herself. He'd wanted to join the aristocracy, and she hadn't. He'd feel this disappointment keenly.

"Miss Cecelia, may we move you upstairs?" the colonel asked. "Will you assist me, Lady Shelford?"

Lucy looked over. Everyone else had left. Cecelia's father was helping Mr. Kempton and Rachel prepare the fires and bedroom for the birth.

"No." A fierceness she didn't know she possessed overcame Lucy. "No, Colonel. I will help Cecelia." She found her strength and pushed her way up. She put one of Cecelia's arms around her waist. They were the same slight stature and their arms fit easily across one another's shoulders. "Let me help you up the stairs."

Cecelia stared at her.

"You may rely on me," Lucy said. "I am here for you. Please." She felt close to tears.

Cecelia seemed to make up her mind. She accepted Lucy's arm. They began to slowly make their way through the parlor. Lucy felt Cecelia shaking. Or was it her own shaking? She could not tell.

Lucy steered their way around the table and weaved between the pieces of furniture crowding the room. "I will bring her up. You prepare her chamber."

"Rest," Eleanor said. "I will attend the birth."

Lucy shook her head. "The Chelmsfords took so much already. They will not take my friend from me, too. Cecelia needs me, and I need her. Come, let us attempt the stairs."

She paused. The colonel waited at the base of the stairs. He watched helplessly. "I'll just…Well." He cleared his throat. Clearly, he was not used to seeing things spiral out of his control.

"Ensure the men have left," Eleanor said. "Could you do that, please, Colonel?"

He marched toward the front of the house.

Eleanor hovered behind Lucy. Gradually, with Eleanor's assistance, Cecelia and Lucy made their way to the bedchamber.

Lucy and Eleanor changed Cecelia into a shift and settled her on her bed.

Rachel entered with warm rags and began to scour the room. "It's going to be a long night. Your father is pumping water, Cecelia. We'll need some dinner."

"I can cook," Eleanor said. "Mama taught me a few things before we left on Grand Tour." She disappeared down the stairs.

Lucy took Cecelia's hand. She propped pillows behind her and wiped her forehead with a cool cloth. "We are here with you, Cecelia."

"Why?" Her voice was tiny. "Your engagement is broken because of me."

"I don't want to marry him," Lucy said. "I never will, and I never loved him."

"Nor will I," Cecelia said, and began to cry. "Though I fear I began to fall in love. We were alike in every way. Was I wrong? Why am I always deceived by men?"

Lucy hugged her. They held each other tight while tears streamed down both of their faces.

"We both lost the man we love tonight," Lucy whispered. "I fell in love with his brother. I'd known Peter as long as I can remember, and then something just changed. Rest assured, Cecelia, I never felt that way about Walter. Ever. They deceived us both."

Rachel stopped cleaning. She joined Lucy on the bed and put her arms around them.

"I never felt the way you do about Peter," Rachel whispered. "A passing fancy, a childhood admiration, nothing more. I have never felt your pain or deep attachment."

Lucy reached around and squeezed Rachel's hand. It didn't matter anymore, but she felt relieved anyway. She would have hated to have hurt Rachel's tender heart, the heart she hid so carefully.

The three of them held each other for a moment until Eleanor entered the room. "Oh, I am glad I didn't miss this."

She walked around the bed to the other side. "How can you possibly breathe, Cecelia?" Eleanor squeezed all of them. "What a mess. I love you all. The soup is started." She released them and went back downstairs.

Lucy laughed, and Rachel resumed scouring every surface in the room.

Cecelia closed her eyes against a wave of pain. After it passed, she spoke. "Eleanor and Lord Shelford knew me in Vienna. My father told me they were here in Mainz, but we've been avoiding them and declining their invitations." She took a handkerchief offered by Rachel. "I couldn't let Eleanor see me like this."

Lucy dabbed at her eyes. She wished she had her handkerchief back. Peter did not deserve it. There was nothing gallant in his behavior this week. She remembered the look in Peter's eyes when he'd shown it to her downstairs, still tucked in his vest pocket, with his hand over his heart. What an actor. She wiped a stray tear with the back of her hand.

Cecelia wrapped her arms around Lucy again. She spoke to the bedsheets, without meeting Lucy's eyes. "Thank you. I don't understand why you don't hate me right now. Eleanor hasn't said an unkind word to me since her arrival. You are remarkable, all of you, and I do not deserve such friends."

Lucy pulled back. She took Cecelia's hands and looked her in the eye. She paused a long moment before speaking. "Friendship is freely given, not deserved or undeserved. You are as innocent as I am or as your unborn child. Did you know?"

Cecelia bit her lip. More tears formed in her eyes. Her face registered shock as another pain seized her.

Lucy waited for the wave of birthing pain to pass, then spoke. "No, you did not. You would not have grown attached to Walter, if you had. That is why I still love you, and you must know that Eleanor is as loyal a friend as you'll ever find."

"Thank you," Cecelia said in a ragged voice. Her breathing had grown more difficult.

"You've had enough loss and betrayal," Lucy said. "You do not need to lose your friends as well, and I need you right now." Her voice shook. With Papa in England and Auntie Ellen far away, she needed her friends around her, especially ones who understood her heartache.

Cecelia's face contorted in pain.

Rachel dropped her rags. "Get the colonel, please, Lucy. The baby is coming."

CHAPTER 20

Lucy stoked the fire in Cecelia's room. She could throw these gloves away. The sapphire dress, her best silk, would be ruined, too. She was glad. She never wanted to wear it again. "Is it warm enough, Rachel?"

"Far too hot. Open a window. No, I will. Could you please braid her hair instead? Can you see how it's getting damp? We'll want it out of our way."

Lucy picked up Cecelia's brush and began to untangle her hair.

Cecelia lay sweating in her bed. Colonel Loughton hovered over her. "Most midwives favor heat."

Rachel fanned Cecelia. "More recent research suggests ventilation is crucial."

"What kind of doctor do you have in your neighborhood?" Colonel Loughton asked.

Rachel cracked open the window. The late August air brought the river breeze with it. "One who is well-informed. Has Eleanor made the caudle? You've both washed your hands again?"

Lucy looked around the bare room. "Yes, Rachel, I've washed them several times. I don't see any glasses or cups. Will you check, please, Colonel?"

"My hands are clean, of course. Am I the errand boy or the attending doctor?"

"Both," Lucy and Rachel said at the same time.

"I'll go," he said. "What do you require?"

Rachel checked Cecelia. "Time. Her labour is progressing too quickly."

The colonel left.

Lucy smoothed Cecelia's forehead as another pain took hold. She waited until it ended. "You're handling it well. If you'll shift to your side a little, I can braid your hair and move it out of your way."

"Some mothers are naturals. You're doing fine," Rachel said.

Cecelia tried to sit. "My mother always said pregnancy was comfortable for her, and that giving birth wasn't nearly as hard as other women said. I never believed her. I believed she said it to make me feel special, as her only child. She could not have any more children after me."

"How have you felt while you were in the family way?" Lucy asked.

Cecelia smiled. "Wonderful. Sick, too, of course, and tired. But I felt ashamed I did not require a confinement. This is so much more difficult for others. I've been able to work—" She stopped herself.

"What kind of work?" Lucy asked as she wove an expert set of braids in Cecelia's hair.

"I'm so ashamed." Cecelia bowed her head, then winced as another wave of pain moved across her face. "A medium. Giving false readings."

Rachel laughed. "That's wonderful. I wish I'd seen one."

"I'm a trained opera singer and actress, but I could not perform or let my condition be known. It would be disastrous for my repu-tation." Cecelia said. "I felt desperate to accumulate funds for the child while I could, so I never stopped giving readings. I always felt well enough. We left all our belongings in Vienna, believing we would return after the concert tour. I never expected to live for a year from the contents of one trunk."

Cecelia stiffened in pain, then the contraction passed. The pains continued to come closer and closer. Soon, Cecelia was not able to speak. Lucy tied her braids off and pinned them into a neat bun. Her hair would stay untangled for days. Lucy held her hand and sponged her forehead while Rachel observed her closely.

The colonel returned. "Lady Shelford will bring the caudle directly. I wish I'd brought some chloroform. I should have slipped some in my bag. How is your pain?"

Cecelia couldn't respond. The colonel moved to the lone chair in the corner and waited. Lucy worried what would happen if the baby came too quickly.

Rachel guided Cecelia through the pain. In, out. Deep breaths. Lucy held Cecelia's hand and wiped her forehead. She lost track of time. She did not know whether minutes or hours passed. Nothing mattered except this moment, this room, and Cecelia. Peter, her own pain, everything else vanished.

Rachel spoke in soothing tones, encouraging Cecelia and instructing her. An infant's cries pierced the night air, as Cecelia collapsed against the pillows. Rachel caught the infant and gently delivered her into Cecelia's arms.

Rachel whispered instructions to Lucy and the two of them worked feverishly to clean the child. Rachel knew exactly what to do, while the colonel watched.

"What can I do?" he asked. "You seem to have things well in hand."

"Get Eleanor, if you please," Rachel said over her shoulder.

Colonel Loughton immediately turned and exited the room.

Cecelia cradled her daughter as Rachel gently sponged the child clean. The child quieted as she held her close.

"She's precious," Cecelia whispered. Sweat matted her hair to her forehead.

"Her eyes are as blue as yours," Lucy said. She accepted a cloth from Rachel and began to clean the child, too. It felt like a privilege, not a responsibility, to be allowed to attend a birth, to witness the creation of a new life. Her eyes met Rachel's. For the first time, she understood her friend's passion for nursing.

Rachel turned her gaze to the infant. "She looks just like you." She patted Cecelia's forehead with a clean cloth. "Are you comfortable?"

"I'm grateful," Cecelia said. "Thank you. Yes. I was scared I would have a boy or that she would remind me of her father every time I looked at her."

Rachel and Lucy finished cleaning the baby. Rachel wrapped her in a soft blanket and handed her back to Cecelia.

Eleanor came into the room with a mug. She pressed it into Cecelia's hands. "Warm caudle for the new mother."

"Oh, Eleanor. No one's called me that." Cecelia accepted the drink with one hand and tried to hold the baby with the other.

"May I?" Eleanor held the infant. "I'm in love. What will you call her?"

"I don't know," Cecelia said. "Perhaps Sarah, after my mother."

A harsh sound came from the corner. A sob. More crying. The women turned. Colonel Loughton's head was bowed.

"Are you well?" Rachel asked. She crossed the small room and put a hand on his shoulder. She inclined her face to peer at him. "What is it?"

Colonel Loughton waved her off with one hand. He struggled to control his emotions. She maintained her grip. "Colonel?"

"You should be worrying about Cecelia, not me," he said roughly.

"What is the matter?" Eleanor said. "Tell us."

The colonel took a deep breath. He rubbed his eyes and ran a hand through his hair. "I served in the Crimean War. I watched men die countless times. But I've never seen a birth." He heaved another sob. "I had no idea what it was like."

Rachel guided him to Cecelia's bed. "The experience is different from the textbooks, isn't it, General?"

Colonel Loughton smiled weakly at her.

"*Herr* Fliedner assigned the colonel to attend your birth,

Cecelia," Rachel said. "Might he have a moment to hold the infant? We're training him." Rachel's mouth twitched, as if hiding her own smile.

He straightened. "It would be an honor, Cecelia. I'll be the director of a hospital, and I cannot have only theoretical knowledge. Only surgeons and country physicians practice medicine, not gentlemen doctors. Outside of the army, I'm not supposed to get involved in any actual sickrooms, just philosophical studies."

Cecelia nodded at the colonel. Rachel folded his arms into a cradle. Eleanor placed Sarah into the colonel's arms.

Rachel supported his arms with one of her own. "Rock her gently." She put another arm around the colonel and led him back to the chair.

The colonel traced the features on the tiny child's face. "She's perfect. I thought that I performed miracles. I saved lives on the battlefield and in the hospitals." He held the child close to his heart, then stood and placed Sarah in Lucy's arms. "But I salute womankind." He put a hand over his heart. "Thank you for allowing me to stay, Miss Wickford, and watch you work."

"We needed the firewood, General," Rachel said, and truly smiled. "Let Cecelia rest, and we will clean up in the kitchen."

Lucy held the precious bundle as Eleanor gathered the soiled linens and cloths. The colonel took the rags and buckets of water. Eleanor returned the mug downstairs and promised to bring soup.

Love flowed through Lucy, powerful and calm. Tranquility as she'd never known settled on her heart. "Your daughter is the height of perfection," Lucy said. Sarah wrapped her tiny fingers around one of Lucy's. "I agree with Eleanor. I am in love with her already."

Cecelia could not speak. Finally, she took a deep breath. "I was afraid I would not love her, after all that I've been through."

"She is the remedy I needed to ease my grief," Lucy said. "Thank you for allowing me to attend her birth." Lucy nestled the small baby beside Cecelia.

"I love her, too, more than anything," Cecelia said. Her eyes met

Lucy's, and an unspoken understanding passed between them. They had both been hurt, yes, but they would heal in time, together. Their new friendship was unshakeable.

"Cecelia requires rest," Rachel said. "I'll watch her and Sarah. I don't believe you've had dinner, Lucy."

Lucy knew the complications that sometimes arose after a birth. Rachel had told her stories. She was glad someone with experience was there to ensure Cecelia and Sarah would be well cared for. They needed to sleep and recover from the birthing.

Night had fallen, and they had sent one of the carriages back to Mainz with instructions to bring provisions. Lord Shelford guarded the cottage entrance with Cecelia's father and the other footmen.

Lucy and the colonel joined Eleanor in the kitchen. "Shall I tell the others?" Eleanor asked. The colonel nodded.

Lord Shelford joined them in the tiny kitchen. They made plates with bread and cheese and moved into the small parlor. Eleanor served bowls of piping hot stew she had made earlier.

"She's a perfect image of her mother," Eleanor said.

"What will I put in the birth record?" Colonel Loughton asked. "Advise me, Shelford. You know the ramifications for your friend. I haven't asked her name. She's still the Widow Smith to me, and that's what I'll put. But part of me wonders how many times I'll be asked to sign 'Smith' as the last name for a baby."

"If you're going to seek out the women who cannot afford care for themselves, Loughton, they're all going to give you that name," Lord Shelford said. "It's not dishonest for you to sign a birth record with the name they give you."

"Or don't give you," Eleanor said. "I doubt you'll hear many fathers' names."

"What will she do?" Lucy asked. The stew was delicious. She needed the strength and warmth it gave. "Where will she go next?"

Then it hit Lucy. What would *she* do? She had come to Germany to find Walter and, perhaps, marry him. She had found him. But she would not marry him. So, now what? Her circumstances were remarkably similar to Cecelia's.

They had both lost men they were beginning to love. Neither knew what to do.

"She's coming with us," Lord Shelford said.

"To Berlin? Eleanor asked.

Lord Shelford looked at her. "Given the circumstances, perhaps it's best to go home."

"No. You already missed your Grand Tour once. Absolutely not." Eleanor rose from the table.

"The child needs an adequate income to be raised as a gentlewoman. We can provide that."

She collected the used bowls from the table. "What are you suggesting?"

Lord Shelford pushed his chair back and took the bowls from Eleanor. "An annuity."

Eleanor nodded. "Of course. Clearly, they've been trying to save money for the future. How much does the Foreign Office pay?"

Shelford looked around the cottage. "Mr. Duxford has never achieved a prominent position because he moves so often. I am certain his pay is not as high as others. He will need a supplement to support both Cecelia and his granddaughter's upbringing."

Colonel Loughton cleared his throat. "If I may, Shelford. Promise not to punch me?"

"No," Lord Shelford replied. "I enjoy boxing, and I've already let Chelmsford go. Take your chances. What is it?"

"When word travels through London that Lord Shelford is paying an annuity to a woman, people will talk."

Eleanor paled. "He's right, Percy. We knew her in Vienna, and then if she appeared with a child, people would talk."

"And the timing? May I ask?" Colonel Loughton peered at Lord Shelford.

"Watch it. I don't like your tone," Lord Shelford said. "I was nowhere near our friend at the time. Elle, explain."

Eleanor glanced upstairs, as though Cecelia could hear them. "It's her business, not ours."

"He thinks I'm the father. Either you tell him, or I punch him. I prefer the latter option." Lord Shelford flexed his fist.

"Percy left Vienna nearly a year before Cecelia would have been with the father. I visited Cecelia in Munich last December, around the time the child was conceived. She spent time there in the company of Mr. Felsted, an acquaintance of ours."

"The lowest scum on earth." Lord Shelford practically growled. "Now I really want to hit someone."

"I feel certain he forced his advances on her," Eleanor said. "I knew both of them well enough to guess the circumstances. Mr. Felsted controlled all the financial resources for the orchestra's tour of Europe, and she trusted him with her career's success. I fear he betrayed her trust."

Lucy felt sick. Cecelia seemed ashamed, but it sounded as though the orchestra director had taken advantage of her.

Lord Shelford spoke loudly. "We'll deal with him later and help her another way. If we take Cecelia and her child home right now, no one can suggest the infant is ours. We were only married one month ago."

"Nearly two," Eleanor said.

Lord Shelford brushed the comment aside. "Loughton, would anyone in London think my wife had given birth in Germany? When she did not appear to be increasing at our wedding in July?"

"No, and I attended the birth personally. Kempton is here to witness as well," Colonel Loughton said.

"We'll bring Cecelia as the baby's nurse. We'll hire her as governess when she grows older. She will never leave Sarah's side. Would they think she was my mistress, or would they accept our story?" Lord Shelford took Eleanor's hands and led her to the small sofa.

"I don't know," the colonel said. "You're in difficult territory. I won't advise you, since I have heard tales of your right hook from others at the boxing club."

"You want to adopt the child. We have barely been married a

month," Eleanor said. "I thought you wanted to give her an annuity."

Lord Shelford grinned. "Almost two. We've been married almost two months."

Lucy began to clear the used cups and napkins. If Eleanor and Lord Shelford went home, she would go home. She would not stay and finish the six-month course of training at the Institute. But how could she face her papa and the entire neighborhood?

And when would Walter and Peter return? How would she live the rest of her life next-door to them?

She would insist that Papa allow her to live in London. He would understand.

Eleanor talked quietly with Lord Shelford while Lucy cleaned the table. She imagined how hard it had been for Cecelia, a gentlewoman, to cook and clean for herself for the last few months when most women would have been lying down in a confinement.

"But what about Cecelia?" Lucy asked. "Can she assume a false name to work as a nurse?"

"She's lived abroad for so long, that not many people will recall her name or her visage," Lord Shelford said.

Eleanor shook her head. "She's famous. She sang in concerts and operas all over Europe."

Lord Shelford nodded. "And Mr. Duxford works for the Foreign Office. People know him."

Colonel Loughton grimaced. "I fear she could not keep her identity secret. She would have to say that she'd fallen on hard times. That would be the reason for her employment. Any attempt to hide her true identity would cause the rumors you seek to avoid."

"It's true enough," Lord Shelford said. "Sound advice. I still need to hit something. Do you fence? We should spar sometime. I've missed it."

Eleanor was wringing her hands. "Don't fall for it, Colonel. Percy cheats. Now, how can we bring the child into the same neighborhood as Walter?"

"You live in Cambridgeshire now, Elle," Lord Shelford said. "You married me. Remember?"

Eleanor blushed. "We went straight from the church to the train station."

"Did you think you were going back to Essex after Italy?" Lord Shelford snuggled himself closer to Eleanor.

Lucy looked away. She could hear them talking as she straightened the chairs. Eleanor married before her. Would she also become a mother before her? She could not imagine Cecelia giving up her child.

"It's hours away. We will not tell the Chelmsfords when we visit your parents," Lord Shelford said. "Or we will leave Cecelia and the child behind at first with her father. Your parents can visit us."

"But how can I ask Cecelia to do this?" Eleanor asked. "I cannot ask it of her. How will we explain her father's presence in our household?"

"I'm connected with the Foreign Office, as is he. It's natural. This is the only way we can protect her and help her child," Lord Shelford said. "Even so, the social risks are great for all of us, Loughton included, if he vouches for us."

Lucy gathered some dishes and took the cups to the kitchen. She loved to see Eleanor's devotion to her friend. She felt the same and ached to help Cecelia.

Eleanor entered the kitchen. "Oh, Lucy. What shall we do? Will you come with me? I've got a hard question to ask Cecelia. We must care for her and Sarah. I cannot abandon her, but my heart aches to even broach this topic. It is too painful to consider."

"Of course," Lucy said. "Is there any other way?"

Eleanor shook her head. "We cannot think of one, and we cannot leave her." She searched Lucy's face. "How are you? It has been a difficult day, dear heart."

"I'm tired," Lucy said.

Eleanor hugged her. "Don't give up hope," she whispered as she held her. "Peter loves you. He declared himself in front of all of us. Walter came to his senses and has freed you."

"Peter didn't mean any of it," Lucy whispered back. "It was all a lie, and he acted a part. Then he dared to look at me like that in the drawing room, with his brother right there."

"He said he wished to marry you," Eleanor said gently.

The anger returned. Peter gazing at her like a man in love, as if he would sweep her into his arms, ride away on his charger, and make her his queen.

As if nothing had changed.

No. Everything changed as soon as she understood his true intention. He was only keeping her away from his brother.

"He meant it," Eleanor said. "I know what love looks like. I doubted Percy often enough in the beginning, but I know now that he was always sincere. Give him time. And trust his eyes."

Eleanor took Lucy by the hand, and they climbed the stairs to speak with Cecelia. Lucy felt exhausted and empty. Maybe tomorrow she could make sense of today, after she slept, after the pain subsided.

She didn't even know where she would be tomorrow. Packing her trunks. Purchasing a ticket. Traveling somewhere. Returning home without Rachel, without Walter, without a husband or hope.

Lucy pushed open the door to the bedroom and rested her head against the doorway. A peaceful scene greeted her. Rachel rested in a chair, eyes closed, holding Sarah against her chest, as Cecelia slept.

No matter what happened tomorrow, she knew Eleanor would not abandon Cecelia, and neither would she. They would make certain that Sarah was cared for, one way or another, before they left.

Lucy knew what it felt like to be abandoned and discarded. She had money enough. She would not allow any gentlewoman of her acquaintance, now or in the future, ever to be alone or live in poverty.

CHAPTER 21

Peter waited on the cobblestone street outside their rented home. The early morning fog blew in from the river, reminding him of the forest fairy tales and stories about spirits that wandered in the mist.

It had been an unpleasant night. After Walter raged against Shelford and Loughton, he sank into a quiet despondency for a while, furious with himself and desperate to know about Cecelia. Later, he paced through the house, imagining every scenario, interrupting Peter over and over with his fears.

Walter knew someone had taken advantage of Cecelia, and the thought sparked another torrent of anger as he plotted revenge.

Walter's wild highs and lows were so different from Peter's own way of processing emotion. Walter had to talk to understand how he felt, which meant that Peter had to listen as his brother poured out all the reasons Cecelia had captured his heart.

Perhaps Peter would make a good vicar, after all. The thought depressed him—a lifetime of listening to other people's woes and sins. It would be a heavy burden to carry. He could imagine weeks and years of listening to all the worries of every practitioner in his parish.

It was enough to make him want to provoke Walter into disowning him.

Peter needed time to think before he understood his emotions. He was still trying to sort through everything that had happened and how his world had turned upside-down. What could he do next? How would he convince Lucy to give him an opportunity to make amends?

Peter left the quiet street and went around to the stables. It might take a while for Walter to wake and breakfast. He could wait somewhere warmer, away from the fog.

He greeted the grooms, selected a comb, and began to brush his horse. She was a beautiful bay. He'd miss her when they moved on. The comb pulled through the dark brown coat, leaving a trail where the bristles had been. He loved to create a uniform look. He continued to groom the patient mare and hoped it would bring order to his jumbled thoughts.

For a man who wanted to take action, Walter certainly slept a long time. The horse's flank shone. The midnight black mane and tail were completely untangled. There wasn't anything left to do. Peter rubbed the white blaze down her nose, and she nuzzled his shoulder in response.

Animals were so much easier to understand than people.

Like Lucy. Peter wished his attempts to make things right had not gone so terribly wrong. For a brief moment, he'd been brave enough to tell her how he felt. She'd returned his love, and he'd thought that love was enough to insulate her from harm, like a shield against the dragon's fire.

But it was a paper dream that burst into flames at the first test, and he could only watch as the castle crumbled around him.

He had no idea how to make amends, but he wanted to. He loved her. If anything, his desire to care for her had increased, but his ability to do so had vanished, like one of Walter's parlor tricks. She intended to never allow him near her.

He couldn't fault her judgment. She had good reasons. He had to give her equally good reasons to change her mind.

And there was still Walter, who controlled Peter's future, his livelihood, his position as the vicar at Chelmsford, his quarterly allowance, and his ability to wed. Walter would have to agree, as would Lucy's father—if she ever forgave him.

Peter imagined a new fortress with walls almost insurmountable.

The bay nickered, and Peter rubbed her nose again. He recommenced brushing, even if the coat shone to perfection. Why was Lucy so easy to be around and so easy to love, but so hard to woo? Was the path to true love always this thorny and strewn with obstacles? He leaned his head against the horse's neck and rubbed her nose again. Obstacles of his own making.

Well, if he had made them, he could undo them.

Finally, Walter appeared, and they made the short journey to Mrs. Smith's home. "That's not her name," Walter said. "But I still think of her as Mrs. Smith."

"Cecelia," Peter said. "Duxford, I believe it was, but she hasn't given us leave to call her that."

"Then we'll call her Mrs. Smith until she tells us otherwise." Walter's tone brooked no argument.

They dismounted. The clearing was empty. The sun had risen nearly overhead and the trees cast no shadows. It was going to be uncomfortably hot today.

"I wondered if we'd meet Shelford here again," Peter said. "I thought labour took a while."

"How long has it been?" Walter asked.

Peter tried to calculate in his head. "Sixteen or seventeen hours, I suppose. Perhaps eighteen since we arrived at her home yesterday."

"I haven't been able to sleep," Walter said. "I've worried about her all night."

Peter held the reins of his horse. "You slept late enough. It's well into the afternoon."

"I could not fall asleep until the early morning hours. I was in torment," Walter said.

Peter suspected that his brother liked to fancy himself as the hero in a tragic poem, just as Peter couldn't help imagining himself as a medieval hero. That would not serve either of them well. He would speak the truth today. "She doesn't want to see you."

"What if something happened?" Walter asked. "Birthing is painful and difficult. She shouldn't have had to do this alone, with strangers." His voice was agonized.

Peter scoffed. "We cannot intrude."

Walter tossed the reins of his horse to Peter. "I need to apologize to her. I caused her pain and felt it as though it were my own. We are one. I cannot rest until we are reconciled. What if she will not ever see me again?" Walter paced in the clearing. "I've made a mess of things. If she is my other half, I will be incomplete the rest of my life."

"I'm not going in. She should be resting," Peter said. "If she's already delivered her child. If not, she may yet be labouring." It was so crass to discuss this.

Walter knocked on the door. "Then wait here if you will not accompany me. But I mean to apologize and beg forgiveness. I will not live a life of regret and loneliness."

An unfamiliar woman answered the door.

"Peter, translate," Walter yelled. "Quickly, please."

Peter tethered the horses to a post in the yard. He paused to give each an affectionate rub, then approached the door.

"Good day," he said in German. "Is the widow Mrs. Smith here? Cecelia? Or Mr. Duxford?"

"No," the woman said. "She's gone. No more."

"Where to?" Peter asked. "When will she return?"

"She won't return anymore. Excuse me. I must clean." The woman started to close the door.

Walter pushed it open. "What did she say?" He looked inside.

"They're gone. Moved," Peter said.

Walter stormed inside. "Impossible."

But the woman had rearranged the sparse furniture. Peter heard Walter pound up the stairs, then he heard a door slam.

"Peter!"

He climbed the stairs to find Walter.

Walter pointed to a small bedroom. "The closet is empty." He crossed the tiny hallway and pushed open the other door. "This one, too. No clothes in either room."

Peter caught a glimpse of the room over Walter's shoulder. Nothing, except a few candlesticks, a blanket, and a brown-paper package. Peter recognized the bolt of white cloth with blue flowers peeking through the brown wrapping.

He and Lucy purchased the muslin together, yet Lucy must have persuaded her friend to leave the cloth behind. Peter remembered how close they stood at the fabric counter, how he'd allowed himself to hope in that shop. Lucy wanted to forget.

Walter returned to the first room. He got on his knees. "Ha!" He pulled a bundle out from beneath the bed. A tangle of shawls, wooden knockers, yarn, slates, and chalk. He hugged it to his chest.

They descended the stairs and looked around the empty entryway. "She had nothing to pack, just a few clothes. I would have given her the world. I must find her. Eleanor knows where she is. We'll ride into Mainz. She must be with her."

Walter untangled the mess of objects. Two slates fell to the floor. One said, "Return to England," and the other said, "Leave now."

Walter seized them. "The spirits are telling me to leave now to find her. Return to Mainz. It's a message. We have to go, Peter."

It was ridiculous. How could Walter still believe in omens and portends?

Walter kept the slates and left.

Peter picked up the mess of shawls and baubles and placed it on a table. Always cleaning up after Walter. He hesitated, ran up the stairs, took the length of cloth, and returned to the entrance.

He yelled, "*Danke!*" to the housekeeper and followed his brother into the clearing.

Walter was slapping his thigh with his glove. "Do you know any shops?" He mounted his horse and began to ride without waiting for an answer.

Peter followed at a reasonable pace. Walter usually showed more consideration for the animals he rode.

Walter urged his horse to a canter. Peter sped up to match him.

"Slow down," Peter said. "This ride is longer than you realize. We can talk as we go. A trot will suffice for the distance."

"What stores do they have here? Any jewelers?" Walter asked.

Peter slowed down. If Walter wanted an answer, he would have to respect his animal and ride slower. Walter matched his pace.

"Yes," Peter answered. "Why?"

"I've got to make this up to Mrs. Smith."

Walter would not listen to reason. Peter had tried yesterday, but he would attempt again today. "She moved. She does not want you to visit, Walter."

"I cannot let her escape."

"This isn't a hunt," Peter said.

"You don't know what it's like to love deeply," Walter said. "I'm in agony. Take me to a jeweler without delay. Please." Walter sped up to a canter.

Peter refused to treat his mare the same way. He rode behind. Walter didn't know the way to the store. He would have to slow down eventually.

Walter would make a fool of himself and waste more money. Just as he had for the last week. Then it would be over. "Mrs. Smith" would reject him, and they could go home. Or go to Vienna. Whatever Walter wanted to do for Peter's Grand Tour.

Because Walter was the viscount. The oldest brother. He had all the control. It chafed. Was there any part of him that had tried to steal Lucy away just to hurt Walter? He had to confront himself. Had he been trying to humiliate Walter? Or compete with him?

No. He couldn't help but see Lucy's good qualities when he spent time with her. He would never stand by and watch Walter destroy her spirit. Peter would have loved her even if she hadn't been engaged to Walter.

What a strange thing to say.

Walter waited at the crossroads and motioned for Peter to lead the way. His face was a thundercloud, but Peter ignored the look. The only creature in the world who thought well of him right now was the bay below him, and he wanted to stay in her good graces.

They arrived at the storefronts in Mainz. Peter led Walter through the same set of shops he had taken Lucy through a few days earlier. Now he knew who she'd been shopping for.

Peter wondered how Cecelia and Lucy were doing. He wanted to hold Lucy and reassure her that his love was genuine. Would he ever get an opportunity? Certainly not with Walter around. He would have to find a way to visit her alone.

They found a jeweler along the same street as the mercer and tobacconist and entered the shop. A store attendant greeted them immediately.

"What size would Mrs. Smith wear?" Walter asked, his eyes searching the rows of dazzling jewels and strings of pearl necklaces.

Peter took off his ring and gave it to the jeweler. "This would fit her middle finger, so perhaps something smaller."

"How do you know that?" Walter stared at Peter.

"Lucy is about the same stature, and I gave her my ring to wear. She returned it just now." He waited for a reaction. *He'd* given one of Father's few heirloom rings to Walter's fiancée. He left out the reason Lucy had worn it—she'd wanted to see Walter.

Walter shrugged, then turned to the jeweler. "You're right. They are about the same size. Will this help?"

The jeweler selected a gold ring with a small blue stone, and Walter paid him. Peter slipped his ring back onto his finger.

They made their way toward Lucy's apartments.

It was well into mid-afternoon, now, and they were both hungry. Walter would think more rationally after he ate. Perhaps it was wishful thinking. Walter never thought reasonably, but a hungry and desperate man was even more irrational.

"Shall we stop for a luncheon or tea?" Peter asked.

"Perhaps they'll invite us in," Walter said. "When I explain."

Not likely, Peter thought.

When they arrived, three footmen guarded the entry to the building.

"That doesn't bode well," Peter said.

Walter approached the footmen with his shoulders back. "Stand aside."

"No, sir." The footman knocked on the door behind him.

Shelford and Kempton pushed open the doors to the building. Loughton followed.

Had they been standing guard all day? Waiting for them?

"You're not welcome here." Shelford crossed his arms across his chest. "I made that clear yesterday."

They addressed themselves to Walter. Lucy must not have told anyone she had switched her affections to Peter. Instead of feeling relieved, he felt hurt. He'd rather confront Shelford than stand off to the side, irrelevant and useless, unable to fight for the woman he loved. He'd admitted his feeling for her in front of the entire room, and no one considered him a viable candidate for marriage.

They all assumed Lucy would prefer Walter over Peter.

"Where's Mrs. Smith?" Walter demanded.

Loughton exchanged a glance with Shelford. "Passed on."

"To where?" Walter asked.

"Mrs. Smith did not survive the night," Loughton said.

"We're leaving in the morning," Shelford said, "and I'm telling you not to return. There's nothing left for you here." He entered the building, leaving the colonel, Kempton, and the footmen.

Walter collapsed against the stone pillars supporting the stairs. "No. Her child."

"Someone will care for it," Loughton said.

"Who?"

"I cannot tell you."

"An angel rejoined heaven yesterday. She was too pure for this earth." Walter covered his face with his hands. "Cecelia."

Peter blinked. Dead? So many women passed away in childbirth. He had begun to notice some of Mrs. Smith's good qualities, even if she was a fraud. Anyone who could love Walter was a saint, after all. He was sorry for her, for her child, and for Walter.

Her last moments were spent with heartache brought on by him. If Peter had stood up to Walter, tried harder, perhaps he could have prevented the pain she felt when she learned of Walter's betrayal. He should have done more.

Peter set the packages down at Kempton's feet. He included the parcel of cloth. Lucy would see it and know he had brought it back for her. "My brother wanted the child to be well-cared for. He intended to give these to Mrs. Smith. Perhaps someone else at your Institute could use them."

Peter lifted the smallest package off the top. "Do you want to keep the ring, Walter, as a memento?"

He shook his head.

Peter put the tiny brown paper package on top with the others.

"Thank you," Kempton said. He took the packages and went inside with the colonel.

Peter guided his brother down the steps and over to a bench across the street. He listened to the Rhine flowing behind him and watched the building. The footmen remained near the door. Walter leaned over with his head in his hands.

Peter studied the windows. Mrs. Smith, dead. And Lucy was inside that building. She might be leaving tomorrow, too, with Shelford. And he couldn't get inside to talk to her. She was as good as dead to him, unless he could figure out a way to see her.

She had cut him off entirely. How would they explain this to their mother, who loved Lucy as her own daughter? He had to remedy this before she left.

His grief was as deep as Walter's, he felt sure. Walter did not know, and Peter would never tell him. He would not lessen Walter's own pain by asking his brother to console him. He would suffer alone.

Did she know he was outside? Did she know that he had tried? Was she watching him?

But no curtains moved.

They sat for a long time as the sun grew warmer. Hunger gnawed at Peter's stomach.

Finally, Walter spoke. "Let's go to the cathedral where I first saw her."

Peter knew it was unproductive to stay any longer. Lucy wasn't coming out of the building, and the footmen wouldn't let him in. He'd have to think of something else, once Walter returned home.

When they arrived at the cathedral, Walter entered alone. Peter bought an apple from the market and found a bench in the shade. The day had become as hot as he knew it would be. The late August sun scorched him, and his silk topper offered little relief.

After some time inside, Walter emerged, crossed the plaza and dropped onto a nearby chair. Peter offered him the apple, but Walter pushed it aside. "I can't eat."

"How are you?" Peter asked.

"I hardly know," Walter said. "That was the most magnificent week of my life. Thank you for giving me that."

And Lucy hates me because of it, Peter thought.

"What do I do now?" Walter asked. He shifted in his chair. He tugged at the hard slates he'd been carrying. "Maybe I should have listened to Father. I didn't heed his warning. He told me to go home. I would have escaped this pain if I had."

No. Mrs. Smith was trying to get rid of you before you exposed her as a fraud.

Walter held up the slates. "What if I had? Did Father want me to marry Lucy?" He gasped. "Did Mrs. Smith leave me these slates? She's talking to me from the grave. She sent the messages. Leave now. She's telling me to marry Lucy."

Peter felt chilled despite the sun.

"The spirits still reside in her house. She knew she would die and wanted to prevent my pain. Do you understand, Peter? These messages were telling me to take up my responsibilities. To marry Lucy. To assume Father's place."

"No," Peter said. "It was merely a game."

Walter waved the slates in Peter's face. "This is real. How do you explain the writing?"

"She wrote them before you came and switched them while you weren't looking," Peter said. "I told you the séance was a hoax."

Walter shook them in front of Peter. "You don't believe, but I felt the spirits. It was real."

It was no use arguing with Walter. Peter had seen her do it, but Walter would never admit that a dead saint could do anything wrong.

"I have to marry Lucy. Father wants me to do it. Mrs. Smith wants me to do it. I will never love again. It doesn't matter who I marry. No one will ever replace my angel."

"That's not fair to Lucy, to marry someone you can never love."

"What do you know about it? No, Father and my eternal star are guiding me. We have to go back to the Shelfords' apartments. I must call on Lucy."

"She won't see you," Peter said. "You hurt her."

"I'll make it up to her. Give her the ring."

"The one you bought for Mrs. Smith?" Peter asked.

Walter grabbed Peter's arm. "Start walking. Yes. You said they wore the same size."

"You didn't keep the ring. You gave it away," Peter said.

"I'll think of something. Offer to marry her right away. Today."

"No," Peter said. He stopped. "You cannot marry Lucy." If she married anyone, it had to be Peter.

Peter watched him cross the square. Walter continued without him. He reached the horses, without waiting for Peter. He didn't turn around but mounted and rode away.

Did he actually believe the stupid spirits wanted him to marry Lucy because Mrs. Smith had died? He really wanted to punch the spirits now. Or Walter.

Peter ran through the square. He had to stop him. Walter was already gone. He untied his horse and rode as hard as he could.

But the footmen were still there, and his brother was sitting across the street on the bench.

"Won't let me talk to her," Walter said.

Peter was out of breath from riding hard and running. He doubled over, with his hands on his knees, and gasped for air. Lucy would never want to look at either of them again, let alone marry them. They had caused her enough pain. It was time to leave.

Finally, he got his wind. "It's nearly dinner," Peter said. "We haven't eaten all day." He looked up. Which window belonged to Lucy? "Let's go home." He could return without Walter.

"They'll be gone tomorrow," Walter said.

He approached the footmen. Walter counted out some coins and returned with a smug smile.

"Got the address," Walter said. "Did Lucy ever mention Berlin?"

Peter read the slip of paper. "The Shelfords were set to go there."

"I was right." Walter smiled. "They leave at dawn, but I have their address. We can follow them there. Let's pack."

CHAPTER 22

"Am I doing the right thing?" Cecelia asked.

Lucy wrapped her in one of Eleanor's shawls and pulled a hat low over her face. Cecelia was far too short for Eleanor's dress, but Lucy's maid, Jane, worked to pin it up. Anyone who saw Cecelia would not recognize her in the expensive, stylish attire, but assume she was a lady's companion or friend.

They waited in the entrance to her rented rooms. It was a quiet Saturday morning and hardly anything moved on the streets below. The streetlamps still shone.

"This is your choice," Lucy said.

Cecelia looked at her father, Mr. Duxford. He nodded. "The Foreign Office approved an emergency transfer to Florence. I can work there as well as here."

"It's the best for little Sarah." Cecelia nestled the baby against her chest and held her tight. "I've met men like Lord Chelmsford before. They can't be trusted, and I've got to protect my daughter. Papa, I hate to upset your life. You've moved so many times for my singing, for my concerts, and now for this."

Mr. Duxford put his arm around his daughter. "You're my everything."

Lucy's heart ached at the tenderness between father and daughter, between mother and child. Months ago, she thought she would marry. Her papa had not given her a choice. Now she had been publicly humiliated and would be socially ruined when she returned. Would she ever marry? Or would she only watch her friends, one by one, marry and have children while she remained alone?

Rachel could marry before her, if she would stop antagonizing Colonel Loughton. How long would he endure before he moved on to another woman who reciprocated his attentions?

"Are you sure you want to leave, Lucy?" Rachel asked.

Lucy had seen Rachel cry once, when her father passed. Never again. Even now, Rachel's voice barely quivered, but Lucy knew her friend hid deep emotions behind her calm exterior.

"Papa's already paid for six months here," Lucy said. "Someone should use the apartments. I'm so glad Alice and Mrs. Glenn agreed to live with you."

"I'm delighted to be away from Curtis and living with a friend for a few months," Alice said. "Brothers can be quite suffocating."

Neither Lucy nor Rachel would know. They had no brothers, but Lucy could well imagine the colonel could be stifling at times. Alice and Rachel would get along well. She felt no qualms about leaving Rachel behind.

Rachel hugged her. "Thank you. I'll miss you. Write often." She pulled back and examined her face. "I am worried about you."

Alice pulled Lucy into a hug. "Write to both of us, please. Farewell."

"I love you both," Lucy said. "Give my regards and disrespect to the general." Rachel bit her lip. Alice smiled.

Lucy and Cecelia crept down the stairs to the crisp morning air. Fog from the river swirled around, as it often did in the mornings. The carriages stood in a row on the cobblestone street. One of the horses snorted and shook its head. Lucy could see its breath in the early morning air. Another flicked its tail. Their heads were up, ears forward. They stomped the ground, seemingly eager to begin the journey.

Eleanor and Lord Shelford were waiting in the carriage. Cecelia pulled the hat low over her face and carefully made her way down the steps, pressing Sarah to her.

"Wait!" Someone yelled at Cecelia as she climbed into the carriage.

Lucy hurried down the steps, hoping to gain entrance to the conveyance before Peter could stop her.

Because she recognized his voice.

"Stop, please! I beg you." A man approached out of the fog, running toward her.

Lucy picked up her skirts and tried to make her way across the slippery cobblestones.

She'd recognize his form anywhere, even through the morning mist. Peter.

"Don't leave. Lucy!" His voice cracked as he yelled after her.

She rushed into the carriage and pulled her shawl tightly around her. Her heart pounded.

He'd ridden here, looked for her, come running after her.

The carriage jerked and pulled away.

"Who was that?" Eleanor asked.

Lord Shelford turned to look through the carriage's window. "Did Chelmsford come? Do I need to speak with him?" He wiped the glass. "I can't see anything in this fog."

"Peter." Lucy exhaled a breath. "Alone."

Eleanor studied her. "Shall we stop?"

Lucy shook her head. "Please, continue." She didn't want to see him, but she desperately wanted to know what he would have said.

She did want to see him, but nothing could make things right. She still hurt too much to imagine speaking with him. There was no explanation she could imagine that would ever make her trust him again.

Men lied. George lied to her, then Walter lied to her, then Peter lied to her. They lied to Cecelia.

But she still ached for him and missed his quiet presence. Her heart softened when she saw him standing outside her windows yesterday. Seeing him today nearly undid her. She could not trust herself to talk with him.

Because even though she could not ever trust him again, Lucy yearned for the closeness and comfort she'd felt with him. She feared she would believe another lie, if she allowed herself to listen to him.

Worse, she had to ask herself if she had constructed any of the lies she now believed. What had Peter actually said, and what dreams had she built around him? How much was she to blame for letting emotion run away with her?

She and Cecelia would leave with the Shelfords and stay away as long as it took to mend their hearts.

CHAPTER 23

Peter raced after the carriage, even as it departed in a clatter of hooves and clang of metal. Lucy had left him. She knew who it was. Even from a distance he'd seen her hesitation.

The vehicle rounded a corner and vanished in the morning fog. Gone.

She heard him calling and left anyway. He'd risen early, left Walter behind, ridden through dense pillows of river mist, and chased Lucy. So close, only to have her spurn him.

He made his way back over to his bay, which he'd tethered next to a bench, gasping for air. His bench. He'd spent a lot of time here recently. He wrapped his arms around the loyal animal. They'd been through a lot together this last week, but she'd been faithful. He laid his head against hers, and she whinnied in response.

"I've lost her," Peter said. "We'll see about some oats for you when we return."

He began to untie the mare, then glanced up at the windows. A curtain moved. Someone was watching him, but Lucy was gone.

It was cold. The sun hadn't come out yet. Should he leave? Lucy had left. He doubted the footman had given Walter the true address. Shelford wasn't the type to employ witless or disloyal servants.

Peter patted the horse's nose, then settled onto the bench. Perhaps he'd leave his mare tethered, wait a few minutes, and see who had remained behind. It was Saturday, and Peter knew Rachel did not have any classes today.

Five minutes. Ten. The fog began to burn off as the sun rose. Fifteen minutes. Twenty. Someone checked the window regularly. As long as they watched him, he would stay. They would have to leave the building eventually, even if they didn't have classes to attend, and he would be there when they did.

Let Walter wonder where he was. Walter wasn't even awake yet anyway.

Lucy was gone, Walter would require him to go to Berlin needlessly, and he would not see Lucy again until they arrived back at Chelmsford Hall. By then, she would have found somewhere else to live. He might not ever see her again.

Unless he spoke with whoever was behind that window pane.

Half an hour. Rachel, Miss Loughton, and Mrs. Glenn came out of the entrance and hurried down the street.

Peter rose from the bench and ran after them. "Rachel!"

They continued walking. He caught up to them, panting. His horse was securely tethered, and he could pursue them as far as necessary.

Rachel finally stopped. "What are you doing here?"

"She's not going to Berlin," Peter said.

Rachel didn't say anything.

"Where is Lucy going? Home?" Peter asked.

Rachel shivered. "I can't tell you. It's cold for a summer morning."

Peter closed his eyes. "I did everything wrong. I understand. She won't let me apologize or explain." He looked at Rachel. "But I am asking you to give me a second chance anyway."

"She doesn't trust you or Walter," Rachel said. "Neither do I."

Peter fidgeted with the ring on his smallest finger. It felt strange to wear it again. Wrong. "I never expected this to happen."

"You didn't think we would find you with Cecelia?" Rachel asked.

Peter shook his head. He glanced at Miss Loughton, who glared at him. "I never expected to fall in love. I've known Lucy my whole life. But it's as though I never noticed her and then suddenly, I just *saw* her. Everything about her that had been right in front of me."

Rachel drew her shawl around herself. Miss Loughton studied him.

"Now what do I do?" Peter asked.

Rachel shifted her weight, as if impatient to leave. "To win her back?"

"To live without her," Peter said. "To see her in the neighborhood and watch her marry someone else. I cannot do it. Help me, please. There must be a way, and I need her address in order to find it." He looked at Mrs. Glenn. No sympathetic face there, either.

Rachel sniffed. "You want me to help?"

"I don't know where she went, and she won't listen to me. She saw me, but she left anyway." Peter swallowed and motioned for them to keep walking. "I'm sorry. It's damp this morning, and I will not make you late if you have an appointment. May I walk with you?"

"I can't believe I'm doing this," Rachel said.

"What? Talking to me?" He drew alongside her. Miss Loughton and Mrs. Glenn followed them. "I'm sorry, Rachel, for the pain I've caused you and your friends, for betraying your trust, and for not telling you the truth."

"No. I can't believe I actually believe you." Rachel glanced sidelong at him. "You're right. The footmen were instructed to give you a false address. They did not go to Berlin."

"Shelford is smarter than that," Peter said. "He would not allow Walter to follow him."

They turned a corner and continued toward the market and cathedral in the center of town.

Rachel turned toward him. "Why didn't you tell Lucy the truth?"

He stared at the cobblestones. He couldn't meet Rachel's accusing stare. "Everything I told her about my own feelings was true. I neglected to tell her the full and complete truth about Walter, because his actions turn my stomach. I thought I could protect her from pain if I kept her ignorant of his behavior, but I hurt her worse than he did. I'm sorry, Rachel. It was badly done."

Peter steeled himself to meet her gaze. "But I would do anything in the world if I had one more chance. I'm asking you for her address, please. I want to grovel at her feet." He attempted a weak smile.

Rachel looked into his eyes. "You won't hurt her again?"

Peter could sense something deep in her. He returned her gaze. "Her happiness is my sole concern."

She reached out to grasp his hands. "They went to Florence. I didn't tell you."

He squeezed her hands. "Thank you, Rachel."

She turned back to join Miss Loughton and Mrs. Glenn. "Farewell, Peter."

Peter ran back through the streets, back to his bay mare, and rode home, keeping the pace at a mild trot. Should he tell Walter the truth, or let him depart for Berlin on his own?

Walter had insisted on packing all night to be ready to depart for Berlin and hadn't fallen asleep until the early hours of the morning. Peter was ready, and Walter was still asleep. He could leave now, and Walter would never know where Peter had gone.

But Walter had all the money and the train tickets. Peter could not withdraw money from a bank without Walter's consent or knowledge. Even if he managed to talk a bank into giving him an advance, they would notify his brother immediately. Walter would learn his location and be furious.

No, it was better to play things straight.

"It's not Berlin. It's Florence," Peter told Walter, after his brother finally woke and breakfasted. "I spoke with someone after I saw their carriages depart."

"It's certain?" Walter asked.

"The footmen were paid to misdirect us," Peter said.

Walter swore and tore up the tickets for Berlin.

Peter picked up the pieces. "We could have exchanged these."

"I'll buy new ones. We leave tomorrow," Walter said.

For the first time he could remember, Peter and Walter were in agreement. That, however, was a problem. They both wanted to leave for Florence. They both wanted to find Lucy. They both wanted to marry her.

☙❧

Early September 1856

Peter spent the next few days trying to figure out a way to tell Walter that he couldn't marry Lucy, that Walter was deluded and séances were fake, that Cecelia had lied to him and been a hoax, and that Lucy would never forgive him.

But anything he imagined would only strengthen his brother's resolve. He had to find an indirect way that would not raise his ire.

Besides, he had already told him all those things, and Walter had dismissed the ideas. He'd told Walter that he'd kissed Lucy, held her, and wanted to marry her, and Walter had never believed him.

What would happen when he realized Peter was serious?

He thought during the entire train ride from Germany down to Florence as the dense forests and half-timbered cottages gradually gave way to cypress trees and terracotta-colored villas.

Walter didn't speak at all. He was mourning, almost as deeply as if Father had died again. There were circles under his eyes, and Peter suspected that he hardly slept.

Peter didn't know how to begin an uncomfortable conversation when Walter was already in pain and deeply hurt. The void inside his brother seemed to have grown larger, not smaller. He was looking, again, for the wrong solution. Marriage to Lucy would not ease his pain at losing Cecelia but enlarge it and make them both miserable. Peter would never allow it, and Lucy would never agree to it.

He still hadn't found a way to broach the topic by the time they arrived in Florence. Or when they wandered through the dusty streets or walked along the Arno, listening to the river lap against the embankment. Or when they rented rooms in a small *pensione*. Or when they ate their first meal of pasta and tomato sauce. Not when they tasted decadent, chocolate-covered cream puffs for dessert, either.

Not even the next morning when they visited the marble duomo and baptistry in the center of town. Peter still couldn't find the right words to dissuade his brother, to tell him that he himself wanted to marry Lucy, or to assuage Walter's raw grief.

So he waited for inspiration. They bought gelato and watched pigeons in the town square. Still no ideas.

They sat in the afternoon sun. Dark thunderclouds rolled across the sky, threatening rain.

Walter leaned back in his chair. "Peter."

"Walter."

"I've had a lot of time to think, riding on the train. Watching the scenery. Being alone with my thoughts for days."

"As have I," Peter said.

"I don't like what I see inside myself," Walter said. "I've become like our father in his worst ways and shirked my responsibilities."

Peter took a bite of his gelato. He felt the same way. Guilty and afraid that he was destined to be as unfaithful as Father.

"If I'm ashamed of anything, it's the part I asked you to play in Mainz. I did it in Cambridge. I've done it all our lives. But no more. Starting today, I'm a new man."

Peter put down his spoon. Walter seemed serious. He'd never heard his brother engage in self-examination or contemplate his own actions. While Peter constantly worried, Walter never seemed to.

"Do you know what I inherited when Father died?" Walter asked.

Peter leaned forward, so he could see better. A cloud shifted and the sun shone momentarily in his eyes. "A lot. I know it's been hard the last two years. I've been thinking about Father's death these past days, after Mrs. Smith's death. Cecelia's death." There. He introduced the topic, so Walter could broach the subject.

"A bill from the jeweler's in London. Four pocket watches."

Peter remembered. "Our keepsakes from Father. You gave them to us after he died. One for each brother. I treasure it."

"He ordered them when he knew he was dying. But do you know what else he ordered? Sixteen identical bracelets. Trinkets to thank women for dalliances over the years. Fifteen, with their initials, and one for Mother."

Peter pushed his gelato aside. He'd lost his appetite.

"I had to pay the bill and deliver the bracelets. Look the women in the face. See who caused Mother that pain. It was Father's dying wish to give these gifts. I could not deny it. But I was angry."

"I'm sorry," Peter said.

"I didn't want to do what he wanted me to do. I left England with you for so many reasons. To spite him. To avoid becoming the kind of husband he had been, because I could not bear to see Mother's grief. To play and avoid anything to do with responsibility. Lucy was one of those burdens."

"Walter, I've never heard you talk in this manner," Peter said. He began to understand why Walter had left England so quickly and refused to return.

"I'm telling you that I'm a changed man," Walter said. "It was never fair to ask you to keep up appearances for me while I hid behind you. That's not the kind of man I want to be. I'm going to be the best of Father and not the worst of him. The kind of husband that Mrs. Smith would have deserved."

"You have so much good in you," Peter said. He really did.

Their mother had instilled many fine qualities in her sons. She'd poured her heart into raising them.

"But the first thing I did, when I hurt a woman's feelings, was run to a jewelry shop," Walter said. "I thought of Father and hoped that if it worked for him, it would work for me. I despise myself for thinking that I could be the same sort of husband as he."

Peter glanced around the square at the crowds of people. He thought of the secrets he was keeping from Walter. "I've done things I'm ashamed of. Every person here has, too. Look around. You're not alone. How can I take the weight off your shoulders? Can I carry some of the burden?"

Walter rose from the table. "Thanks for supporting me. You've been my closest friend and my brother. That gives me the strength to take up Father's mantle and care for Mother. To face my obligations and bury my pain once more."

Peter hoped Lucy wasn't one of them anymore. Maybe this new, more mature Walter would realize that, but he kept talking about being a husband.

It was such a burden to carry his brother's guilt as well as his own. As a vicar, he would have a lifetime of shouldering other people's pain and problems. What confessions would he have to hear?

What would he be expected to say? He felt tongue-tied at the best of times.

And who did a priest confess to? He had kissed the woman his brother was engaged to, but there was no one to carry the burden for him.

He would have to reassure others. Absolve them. Hold their pain inside regardless of how much it hurt him.

"Would Father be proud of me?" Walter asked. "I still want to please him, even though he's passed on."

Peter pulled him into a hug. He understood the need for approval. Father had so seldom given it. This was the way he could ease Walter's burden. "I'm proud of you."

"I'll never forget this," Walter said. "Let's go light a candle in their church."

Peter laughed. "It's a cathedral."

Walter gestured at the towering structure. "It's a green and white Gothic gingerbread house. Let's go say a prayer for Father."

"We're Anglicans," Peter said.

Walter grabbed his arm and proceeded toward the *duomo*. "God loves Catholics, too, Vicar."

Peter wondered when he'd be able to tell Walter how he felt. He'd wait and see if the changes were real or permanent. By the time they found Lucy, would Walter still want to marry her? Or would he finally be ready to hear the truth?

CHAPTER 24

Late September 1856

Lucy looked over the green rolling hills of Tuscany. Tall Italian cypress trees dotted the landscape. An orchard of olive trees filled the valley below her.

They had driven in a carriage for hours to reach San Gimignano, in order to have a luncheon. Eleanor insisted they had to visit the place famous for its saffron. It was some kind of joke between her and Lord Shelford.

Lucy took a bite of the golden ham. It was worth the ride for this. The region's famous white wine, the delicate flavor of the local saffron, and the salty pork were unforgettable. Trust Eleanor to know where to get a good meal.

They'd wandered through the town's narrow streets and toured the ancient church before having a late luncheon, al fresco. It was hard to imagine anything more wonderful than this, except the man sitting beside her. Papa.

Lord Shelford had asked Mr. Duxford to send an urgent tele-graph through the Foreign Office. Mr. Siemens had connected the new German line to the undersea line in the British Channel. It was finally working.

Papa had packed and brought his lawyer immediately. They had arrived yesterday. Now she was sitting here with the person who loved her most in the world and the two most interesting people in the world. Eleanor had brought Mr. and Mrs. Browning. Lucy was too intimidated to talk to them, but she loved to listen.

Cecelia sat on her other side, near the end of the table where Sarah could sleep undisturbed.

"It's peaceful, is it not?" Lucy asked Cecelia.

Cecelia nodded. "It is exactly what I need."

"Germany feels like a dream, another world." Lucy took a bite of pasta with a cream sauce.

Cecelia looked at her sleeping child. "So does the rest of my life. Temporary. People come and go. Sarah is the only permanent thing now."

"We have our fathers," Lucy said.

Cecelia tore off a piece of roll to dip in the cream sauce. "With my mother gone, he is my strength. When I wanted to sing in operas and concerts, he arranged for an assignment to Vienna. When I went on a tour of Europe, he got reassigned to Germany. He's always directed his affairs around me and my needs. I understand that now. I will do anything for Sarah."

Lucy admired Cecelia. She had matured so quickly and given up so much. Not all women would have made the same choices her friend was making.

Lucy watched Eleanor talking with Mrs. Browning and Mr. Duxford. "Has it been hard?"

Cecelia smiled. "It was easy, once Sarah was born. I can't describe the kind of love that washed over me. A different one. Not the kind I felt with men. Something so overpowering and unbreakable that I knew I would do anything for this child."

"You have my admiration and regard," Lucy said. "I adore your daughter, too. Utterly."

"Why would you admire me?" Cecelia asked. She studied her plate, her cheeks slightly pink. "I'm not one to envy or emulate."

Lucy put down her roll and took Cecelia's hand. "I respect and honor the choices you're making and the way you love Sarah. She is blessed."

"Thank you," Cecelia whispered. "I gave Colonel Loughton my full name. Sarah will carry my name and my father's name. I wanted to be honest with him. I wanted Sarah to have a mother who was proud of her. I spent months hiding away, ashamed of my child. But now that she's here, I feel differently."

The consequences in England would be severe for both Cecelia and Sarah. Cecelia had refused the Shelfords offer to raise Sarah as their own, and Lucy admired that courage.

Lucy hesitated. "How did you feel when the colonel wanted to tell Walter that Mrs. Smith had died?" It was a hard question to ask. Everything about this situation had been hard for Cecelia.

Cecelia hung her head. She dabbed at the edges of her mouth with a napkin. A loud laugh erupted from the middle of the table. Lord Shelford had finished telling a story or joke.

"It's true. She's dead. Mrs. Smith is no longer. I am Miss Cecelia Duxford. I am the mother of Sarah. I appreciated Eleanor's offer, but I will be the mother of this child. She and I will bear any shame from Society together."

"Will you stay in Europe?" Lucy asked.

"Most likely. People are much more forgiving here," Cecelia said. She indicated the Brownings. "If they live here, there's a reason. They're outside Society themselves in some way."

Mr. Browning turned toward them. He was nearly as old as Lucy's papa. Perhaps older. "I can't help but overhear you, dears. You're quite welcome among us, Miss Duxford. As you said, we're quite compassionate and lonely for good company."

"You're very kind," Cecelia said.

"What kind of work does your father do?" Mr. Browning asked.

Cecelia looked down the table. "My father has been with the Foreign Office for his entire career. We've traveled from office to office, so I could sing. We were in Vienna and Germany most recently."

"Ah, so you've talent. We would love to hear you," Mr. Browning said. "My wife will put together an evening sometime."

"I can also perform a séance, if you like that sort of thing," Cecelia said. She put her hands to her head and closed her eyes. "I sense the spirits here." She smiled.

Mr. Browning's face darkened. "Oh no. I'm opposed to that sort of chicanery. Drives people away from proper medical care. No, dear, we'd much rather enjoy your voice."

"Then I shall truly let Mrs. Smith and her ways die forever," Cecelia said. She laughed. "Oh, I feel free. I can simply be Sarah's mother and myself. I never expected this. I thought motherhood would be a burden, but it has freed me. I don't care about so many things that used to trouble me. Now they seem unimportant."

Mr. Browning shook his head. "Naturally. The conversation turns toward philosophy already. If you are a friend of Eleanor's, then you would also be intelligent and thoughtful, as well as talented and beautiful."

"Oh good! Philosophy!" Mrs. Elizabeth Barrett Browning called out. "We do love to argue. Is motherhood a burden or freedom? I would love to take up that debate. He is trying to charm you and trick you into believing he is harmless. Watch him. He has a silver tongue. He means every word, of course." She winked at Lucy and Cecelia. "You are adorable, and you must visit us often. We need more friends who speak English and will oppose him on every point. You will take my side on every argument, won't you, dears?"

Lucy threaded her arm through her father's. They wandered among the grey and green olive trees in the grove. She examined the burnt orange and reddish-brown stone presses that turned the olives to a rich, thick oil.

"Thank you for coming immediately, Papa," Lucy said. He was her rock. Steady and reliable and truthful. Because of him, she knew there were good men in the world, but she wondered how she seemed unable to meet any others.

"Shelford said your heart was breaking." Papa studied her face.

She loved talking to Papa. They could discuss anything with perfect frankness. "What else did he tell you?"

"To bring my lawyer." Papa patted her arm. "Besides, now I can finally buy a few paintings of our own. Acquire a Rembrandt or some such artist."

Lucy felt the soft leaves of an olive tree. "He should have said my engagement was breaking, not my heart."

"You're my concern. I will deal with contracts and clauses later, sweets." Papa turned and enveloped her in a hug. "And art purchases. Tell me the whole story. We have an entire town to see."

"It's a tiny medieval village." She laughed. "This olive grove is nearly larger."

Papa put her hand on his arm. "Then walk slowly and talk quickly. Don't leave anything out."

Lucy's mind skipped quickly over the many things she wanted to say. She had never wanted to marry Walter. The aristocracy held no appeal for her. She'd fallen in love with a man she couldn't trust. Again.

The medieval walls and towers brought back memories of Peter. "Perhaps we should continue our journey to Rome, where you can find that Rembrandt," Lucy said. "There will be plenty of time to talk on the train."

She did not want to tinge her memories of this perfect, peaceful day, by reliving her experience in Mainz. There would be time for that later.

Lucy had travelled with Eleanor and her husband on every part of their wedding trip. She should let them enjoy a honeymoon alone. Cecelia and her father would establish a household here in Florence near the Brownings. She and Papa should move on to Rome where there were fewer reminders of Peter.

CHAPTER 25

Peter had searched everywhere for weeks. "This is what it was like for Lucy," he told Walter. "When she tried to find you in Mainz." He tried to think logically. Where had they not tried?

"What if you have the wrong information?" Walter said. "What if they're in Berlin? I had the house number. Everything was precise."

"Shelford would never be that careless. Why would his footman have that information? He wouldn't hire anyone so disloyal."

Walter paced up and down the small chamber in their rented rooms. "Perhaps I paid him enough. Maybe he felt bad. He liked me."

"No," Peter said. "This is where Lady Shelford always intended to come on her wedding trip. I'm certain they're here." He was beginning to feel desperate, but he never doubted Rachel's sincerity. "You're free to go to Berlin without me. I'll understand if you need to."

Walter narrowed his eyes. "You'd send me alone?"

Peter had to walk a fine line. He could not let Walter know yet that he loved Lucy. Walter could disown him. He had to appease Walter without raising his suspicion and appear supportive, but

Peter would get to Lucy first. He would find the address and speak with her on his own. "Where would you rather spend the winter? Northern Germany or Southern Italy?"

Walter shrugged. "Good point. How did you find Lucy in Mainz?" Walter asked.

"At a museum," Peter said. He still remembered his shock. The image was seared in his memory: her look of concentration as she studied the exhibit, her hat perched at an angle with the fair hair underneath, her form silhouetted perfectly from behind.

"Then go to another museum." Walter left the room, then returned. "I'm sorry. I'm trying not to be Father, but still be the best of Father." He sighed. "It is hard."

"It's a good plan," Peter said. "You're right. I'll try a few museums. That's a natural place to consider. But I would prefer if you ask, rather than order me."

Walter had surprised him the last few days. He'd begun to treat him differently, sometimes. Peter could see the effort.

"I am trying to change," Walter said. "Stick with me. I'll get there in the end."

Peter put a hand on his shoulder. "Perhaps try the Foreign Office. Shelford's connected there."

Walter gripped his hand. "I'll go there, and you try a museum? Excellent notion."

"I will see you tonight at dinner," Peter said. "I've heard something about Florentine steak, and I want to try it."

Walter's spirits seemed to be lifting. The search gave him purpose, rather than allowing him to reflect endlessly on his loss. The train ride had given them both necessary time to reflect, but it felt good to be actively seeking for something.

Peter only wished that something wasn't the woman he loved.

He wondered at the depth of Walter's attachment to Cecelia. How deep was his grief? How long would it last, and how real was this commitment to change?

Immediately, Peter felt guilty. How deep was his own grief at losing Lucy? How much was he mourning her loss? He pulled on his boots. Deep. Real. He'd give Walter the courtesy of believing he had loved "Mrs. Smith" as much as he loved Lucy.

⚜

Peter wandered through the Institute and Museum of the History of Science. Why hadn't he come before? He could spend the entire day here. Galileo's own instruments! Scientific devices from the Renaissance! Surely, these must be some of the first thermometers ever made. They even had some of the most recent devices for measuring electromagnetism.

The Institute must keep current on research. Peter tried to find where the labs were. He went back to examine the display about electromagnetism.

Why wasn't anyone else here? In his eagerness to study the museum's holdings, Peter had forgotten his purpose. He glanced around. Only one other man. Thin, well-dressed, a nervous-looking mouse of a man with pince-nez glasses pinched a little too tightly on his nose.

The man caught his eye and approached him. "Ah, are you a fellow traveler?"

"Yes," Peter said.

"On Grand Tour perhaps?"

"Precisely. Do you know any other Englishmen in your *pensione*?" Peter hoped he could find Lady Shelford or Lucy through this man.

"Ah. No. Arrived a few days ago," he said. "Hoping you could introduce me to a few, actually."

The man's voice had an annoyingly nasal quality. Peter could hardly imagine spending hours with him, but the man seemed desperate to make Peter's acquaintance. He must have been traveling alone.

"Let me give you my card," Peter said. "Chelmsford. My brother and I are in Florence for a few weeks. I'll give you the direction to our lodgings. You're welcome to join us for dinner."

"James Oxley. Pleased to make your acquaintance. Fine collection here."

Peter turned back to the display of gadgets. "Yes. It reminds me of the Great Exhibition. Did you visit that?"

"Of course," Oxley said.

"I studied chemistry at Cambridge, so I'm trying to work out the mechanism on this device."

Oxley peered closely at the glass. "You're a scientist?"

"No. I'm going to be a vicar," Peter said. "And you?"

"Lawyer," the man said briefly.

They moved to the next display.

Oxley leaned over a model, then looked up at Peter. "Ah, a vicar, and yet you are a man of science, nonetheless."

Peter pointed at the exhibit. "This is an intriguing concept. Do you see how old it is, and yet the application is still being used?"

Oxley laughed. "You have the mind of a philosopher."

"I shall teach the boys in the village well, then," Peter said. "And content myself with Christmas lectures in London."

The lawyer looked over his shoulder. "Well, pleased to run into a fellow countryman." He tipped his silk topper, which was slightly askew, and left the room.

Something seemed odd about the encounter. Peter followed his instincts and continued into the next room with Oxley, trailing behind him.

The lawyer checked over his shoulder. His eyes widened. He hastened his step and hurried to exit. Peter increased his pace, gaining on Oxley, and followed him out of the building.

Mr. Maldon waited at the bottom of the stairs. Lucy! Was she here, too? Peter searched the busy walkway and street.

The lawyer rushed down the stairs, walking stick in hand, his hat askew, trying to distance himself. The motion drew Peter's attention back to the gravel path, where Mr. Maldon and Oxley rushed to join the crowd.

Peter grinned. Finally, the search was over. He wouldn't let them escape. He took the steps two at a time, all dignity forgotten.

"Mr. Maldon!" He pushed his way into the throngs of tourists. Mr. Maldon had neatly steered his lawyer into an avenue swarming with visitors, businessmen, and residents. Pigeons fluttered and scattered as Peter strode across the street.

He could see the lopsided silk topper still askew on Oxley's head.

Peter lengthened his stride, trying to regain his composure. For a pair of short-legged men, they moved remarkably quickly. Finally, Peter saw them turn into a side avenue. Cornered. He knew this part of Florence. That street led to a tiny plaza with no other way out.

Peter sauntered casually through the alley, crossed the square to meet the men, and pretended to study the church's façade. "Elegant. A church in every piazza in Florence."

Oxley groaned while Mr. Maldon merely chuckled.

"That was no chance encounter, Oxley," Peter said. "Well met." He extended his hand.

The lawyer reluctantly shook it.

"Shall we discuss your real business here in Florence?" Peter asked. "Did you come to ascertain my whereabouts? I'd like to speak with your employer."

Mr. Maldon extended his hand. "Peter, my boy. Well met, indeed." He chuckled again. "Thought I lost you."

"So did Lucy," Peter said, a trace of humor in his voice. "She's hidden herself well, but I'd like to speak with her and apologize. I've done wrong, and I'm sorry. I have a proposal for you, sir, and one for her."

"Walk with me," Mr. Maldon said, pulling at his shirt. "I'm not used to this heat."

Peter enjoyed a dinner of Florentine steak, freshly shelled peas, and pasta with a thick, rich marinara sauce. He was going to miss this

when he returned to England. Walter ate quietly, evidently preoccupied with his own thoughts.

"I've got it," Walter said after dinner. "Forgot to tell you."

"What?"

"The address. Found someone at the Foreign Office. Simply told
him Lord Chelmsford required Lord Shelford's information.
Simple. Why didn't we try it earlier?"

Peter put down his utensils. "You waited until after dinner to
tell me? I assumed you didn't get any information." His brother
had kept this to himself, as if it wouldn't concern Peter? After all
the searching he had done? True, Peter was hiding information as
well, but he had a good reason. Hopefully, he would visit Lucy
tomorrow morning, and then he could tell Walter everything.

Walter signaled to the waiter to pay their bill. "I was hungry."

They began to walk through the cobblestone streets toward their
pensione. Walter stopped at a bronze sculpture of a boar.

"Give me a coin! Please," Walter said. "Smollett wrote about
this. Put a coin in the mouth and let it fall through for good luck,
then rub the snout."

Peter took a few coins from his vest pocket.

Walter rolled a coin through the jaws of the great boar. "Wish
me luck with Lucy tomorrow." He sighed. "This is it. Farewell, Mrs.
Smith."

Did his brother realize they were rivals? Did he know this was a
terrible idea, that Lucy never wanted to see them again, and that both
of them would have to beg for forgiveness? He heard the coin clink
through the grate below. "What if Lucy doesn't accept your apology?"

Walter rubbed the pig's nose vigorously. "I know I treated her
abominably. I don't have a leg to stand on, but we are legally entan-
gled. I hope she'll take me as I am and give me a second chance. All
I can do is beg. I'm not acting like Father if I bring her flowers, am
I? I don't want to be a complete cad, but I want to be respectful."

Walter rolled another coin. It landed perfectly again. "Perhaps
that is why Father wants me to marry her. Mother needs a daugh-

ter, after having raised four sons. It would make Mother so happy, and I am eager to return home now."

Peter decided to roll a coin for luck after all. It hit the boar's tusks and missed the grate, hitting the street below with a dull thud. He didn't rub the snout.

Luck was for Walter. Peter intended to fight for Lucy, but he had to be very careful how he approached this battle. Walter thought he had changed, but he still believed in omens. He was still ignorant of Lucy's wishes and desires.

And Walter was still legally engaged to Lucy.

Peter was risking everything by speaking to Lucy without Walter's permission. He would almost certainly be disowned and lose the living at Chelmsford, if she would even agree to see him.

But he had a plan.

And her father might just be willing to entertain it.

CHAPTER 26

Lucy paced back and forth in the drawing room. She had barely finished breakfast when Papa announced she could expect a visitor in a few hours. He seemed delighted with himself. She went to the window and watched the street. Who could it be? Papa loved surprises. She hated them.

Lucy played a few notes on the piano. Where was Eleanor? She needed someone to help pass the time. Lucy checked the street again.

Walter? She threw back the curtain and collapsed onto a sofa. Not him. Why would Papa want her to speak with him, after everything she'd told him? He could not be insisting that she still marry him. She wouldn't.

It had barely been half an hour since breakfast. He was far too early for Papa's appointment. He was far too early for anything.

"Stout!" She called for Eleanor's butler.

He appeared in the entrance to the drawing room. "Yes, Miss Maldon?"

"Will you please ask my father to join me?"

Lucy tried to collect herself. She couldn't. She continued to pace up and down the room. She wanted something active to do instead of being trapped in this room. She had allowed her father to push her into the engagement, but she would refuse to marry Walter.

How could Papa even consider him?

The doors opened, and she quickly seated herself.

"Lord Chelmsford," Stout said.

"Lucy!" Walter rushed over to her. He covered her hands in his own. "I am so sorry for the terrible things I said. I've treated you abominably these many months." He stared at the floor. "I am so very ashamed. Please forgive me for the hurt I've caused you. How are you?" He searched her face.

"And Mr. Maldon," Stout intoned in his emotionless voice. Papa rushed into the room. He looked perplexed and angry. Perhaps he was as surprised as she was.

Seeing Walter again brought back too much pain. Lucy withdrew her hands. "I don't understand why you're here or how you found us." She felt a pang of panic. Cecelia. Someone needed to warn Cecelia.

"We are engaged," Walter said. "I came to fulfill my obligation to you."

Lucy turned aside. "You came from Mainz? I don't understand."

"Peter learned of your destination."

But Lord Shelford had given instructions for the footmen to tell them about Berlin. Something was wrong. How could he have found her? Only Rachel could have given him their direction, and Rachel had felt as shaken by the Chelmsford brothers' betrayal as she had. "Does Peter know you're here?"

"Peter? Why? No, I left him at home. I could not sleep."

"You and Peter have not discussed this?" Lucy asked.

"Of course we have," Walter said. "He supports me. He knows how important this is to me. I will be the best of husbands. I am a changed man."

"Ah, no. Lord Chelmsford," Papa said, "that may not quite be true."

Which part? Every part of that was wrong, except that Peter supported Walter's decision, because he had never loved her. He helped Walter before, and he was helping him now. Her pain was replaced by anger.

"You made it quite clear that you had no intention of honoring our engagement. Nor do I." Lucy tried to distance herself from Walter.

He moved to face her. "Please, Lucy. I will devote my life to you. I made a terrible mistake. Forgive me."

His voice was sincere. He seemed pained. He looked so much like Peter, with that dimpled chin that barely showed through the thin beard and his endlessly dark eyes. It was too much. He had hurt her too deeply, and his brother had broken her heart.

"You love someone else, Walter. Let us end the engagement," Lucy said.

Mr. Maldon crossed the room to Lucy. "Do you want me to send him away?"

Lucy felt a surge of relief. Papa supported her. He would not force her into this.

"I want you to get Oxley and cancel the marriage contract." Lucy studied Walter. "I know you're sincere. But I could never be happy with you. I cannot trust you to be faithful or truthful."

Walter got down on his knees, as he had in front of Cecelia. "I've seen the pain that dishonorable men cause. The misery they wreak. The lives they destroy. My father was not honest, but I swear that I will be. I will spend my life earning back your trust and proving my loyalty."

Lucy walked away from him. "No, Walter."

He followed her. "Please. I ran away from duty and obligation. I could not shoulder responsibility." Walter straightened. "I apologize. I meant to ask you, please, will you hear me? I will honor my responsibilities and duties now. I will marry you tomorrow. I am ready to be the man I should be, to take up my title, truly, not just in name as I have for almost three years, but in all regards."

Lucy turned around and faced him. "I don't want to be an obligation. I want to be loved. I believe you. I see the change in you. I commend you, but I'm not part of your penitence."

"I will be constant—" Walter began.

Lucy put a hand on his arm. "Walter, you can be faithful and still break my heart. I would know that you loved another."

He was silent.

"I'm breaking our engagement. Perhaps you already have. I don't know, but my father and his lawyer are here. I will ask you to step into another room with them and make whatever legal arrangements are necessary."

Walter swallowed. He looked up to the ceiling, then put his hands behind his back. His dimpled chin trembled.

"You're a good man. We part on good terms. We will remain neighbors and see each other for the next fifty years."

Walter tried to smile.

"So let us shake and be friends." Lucy extended her hand.

Walter pressed her hand to his heart. "I would not have deserved you," he said.

"No." Lucy smiled at him. "Perhaps not."

Papa joined Lucy in the drawing room shortly thereafter. He brought Cecelia with him. "Not to worry. Chelmsford is secreted with Oxley," he said.

Cecelia stared at him.

"Walter is here," Lucy said. "Sit with me, dearest." This would be a shock, and she did not know whether it would be welcome or not.

Papa rubbed his hands. "Oh, this is working out better than I imagined. I've got to send for a few people. I'll be back in a moment." He bustled out of the room.

"Please excuse him," Lucy said. "When he begins to work on contracts with Oxley, he loses track of everything else."

"Why has Walter come?" Cecelia asked. "What does he know?"

"Nothing." Lucy moved to sit next to Cecelia. She plumped a few pillows. "He came to propose. He feels like he has to marry me now that he thinks Mrs. Smith has passed away."

Cecelia nodded slowly.

"I told him 'no' at once. They are signing the legal papers or whatever nonsense is required to end the engagement right now," Lucy said.

Cecelia picked up one of the pillows and held it tightly. "You know, even when I'm not holding Sarah, I still find myself trying to rock her to sleep."

Lucy put an arm around her. "He is changed. Quite sorry. I almost trust him, but I have been so hurt."

Cecelia laid her head on Lucy's shoulder, and Lucy put her arm around her.

"I daresay, if Walter knew you were here, he would fly to your side and beg your forgiveness the way he begged mine." Lucy put a hand on Cecelia's head and stroked her hair. "And I almost think it would be safe to allow it." She knew Walter well enough to recognize the change in him. He had a softness about him that she'd never seen before.

"Men leave when times are difficult," Cecelia whispered. "They abandon us."

Lucy curled her feet beneath her on the couch. "I have the same fear. Rachel and I discussed it at length. Men change their minds so easily. But the Chelmsfords crossed the European continent to find us," Lucy said. "It took weeks of looking in Florence. That speaks of determination. Dare we trust?"

Cecelia's voice grew even quieter. "Sarah cries. She wakes in the night. No man wants to marry and begin with a wife who has already given birth. He may think he does, but he will tire quickly of the demands. I am weary."

Lucy ran her hand over Cecelia's blond hair. "Of course you are. It is hard to imagine any man wanting to step into that situation." She thought of her time with the Chelmsford family before Walter left England. "Walter is the oldest of four brothers. He knows about responsibility and raising children."

Cecelia's voice could barely be heard. "What if he does not love Sarah the way I do?"

They sat together for a moment. She wasn't sure why she was arguing Walter's case for him, after all he'd done to her. She saw two unhappy people and couldn't stand to see them separated, if they truly loved each other. No, she should not interfere, especially when she could not forgive Peter herself.

"It is a lot to ask of anyone." Cecelia raised her head. "I have not come to expect the best from men."

"We have not seen their best, it is true. You and I are blessed with papas who are devoted, even if they are imperfect." Lucy thought of the times she disagreed with Papa. She never doubted his love, even when she objected to his decisions.

"When did you lose your mother?" Cecelia asked.

"Ten years ago," Lucy said. "A sudden illness one winter." She still missed her, and especially at times like this. She wanted a mother to guide her through these painful emotions and difficult choices. "And you?"

"Eight years," Cecelia said. "She had been sick for years. She was Papa's whole world, and now I am."

Lucy felt wistful. "There must be other magnificent men out there. The world must contain more than two good men. Eleanor thinks her husband is wonderful. Three men."

Cecelia laughed. "These men must grow into their nobility a little at a time. Lord Shelford would never do for me, and my mama used to tell me such stories about Papa when they were first married. He was not always like he is now."

It was as if something obvious had never occurred to Lucy. "Of course. Eleanor said she loved Lord Shelford not because he was perfect, but because he forgave her as often as she forgave him."

"There must be a lot to forgive." Cecelia looked at Lucy. "Is it possible to heal after this kind of betrayal? Can we believe them?"

"Walter would fall at your feet and worship you the rest of your days," Lucy said. "I know it. His mother is the best woman on earth. All of the Chelmsford brothers adore her and treat her well."

Walter seemed sincere. He did not know Cecelia lived, so he had pursued Lucy to Florence. Peter, on the other hand, knew his brother wanted to marry her and supported his decision. Her hurt felt too deep to ever heal.

Papa carefully cracked the door open and slipped inside the room. "Well. That's set."

"Papa?" Lucy asked. "Will you sit with us a moment?"

"Of course." He settled himself across from the two women. "What can I do?"

"Do you trust the change in Walter? Do men alter in time for the better? Could Cecelia rely on Walter, or would it be heartache in the end?" Lucy rushed through the thoughts in her mind.

Cecelia sat up and watched Lucy's father carefully. "Were you always a paragon as you are now?" She smiled. "I should ask my papa, as well. I know what my mother would have said."

Lucy's father laughed. "No, I was foolish and imprudent. Your mama had a lot to forgive many times. She never thought me a paragon." He sobered. "I was unreasonable and hasty to rush you into a marriage contract with Chelmsford. I'm still a careless fool, sweets. Any man will be a bit stupid at times. We all are. You live with us, and you know our faults."

"Thank you, Papa," Lucy said.

Cecelia turned to study her. "If I were able to forgive Walter, would you forgive Peter?"

Lucy leaned back on the sofa. "That's different. He never loved me."

"Ah," Papa said. "Yes. Our visitor will have a bit more to bargain with than he expected. That's good, that's good."

"I thought Walter was the expected visitor," Lucy said. "Who's coming?"

"Eh? No." Papa grinned. "Peter. He's in for a treat."

Lucy stood. How did her hair look? She smoothed the front of her dress. What had she worn today? Oh, dear. She should change. She didn't want him to see her in this dress. "What did you do, Papa? I don't like the look in your eyes."

"I wonder whether he did love you, Lucy," Cecelia said softly. "And whether you still love him."

"Sit down, sweets," Papa said. "I gave him our direction and invited him over." He chuckled. "I've arranged a little interview for him."

Lucy began to pace around the room. She pulled the curtain open to check for Peter. Not yet. When would he arrive? "Why? When did you see him? Why is he here?"

Never mind. Peter had sent Walter to marry her. She would refuse to speak with him. Lucy forced herself to sit down. She gripped her hands in her lap and held her head up high. "I have nothing to say to him."

"Ah, but you do, dear heart. He's given me a business proposal. You and I need to talk."

CHAPTER 27

Peter crumpled the note and tossed it into the fireplace. Walter left without him? Without leaving the address?

Since when did Walter wake up before noon?

He entered the *pensione's* grand dining room. He had time for a simple breakfast. He wanted to have enough strength to carry out his plan.

Because it would take a lot of energy to strangle his brother.

Peter dressed quickly and went downstairs to the dining room. How soon could he get to Lucy's apartments? How would he explain his previous appointment to Walter when he arrived? Did Walter already know?

Things were too complicated for seven-thirty a.m.

Peter had risen earlier than usual to ensure he arrived at Lucy's home well before his brother woke. Walter had already left for the walk across town. It would take at least half an hour to get there. Walter had called on Lucy at eight o'clock in the morning? Eight-thirty? How long would it take to walk there?

Well, the Shelfords and their household were all early risers. Lucy was probably awake and dressed, unlike many other women of their acquaintance.

At least Walter had the decency to leave a note explaining his absence. It had burned beautifully, like his relationship with his brother. Gone up in flames.

He felt so angry he could hardly eat. He tore the roll a little harder than necessary and buttered it with a vengeance.

Why hadn't he told Walter in Mainz? A month ago? This was his own fault.

He had told him, but his brother didn't believe him.

But Lucy promised she would never marry Walter.

He felt a brief flame of hope. Lucy would turn him down.

She'd be a fool to refuse Walter, if she did. It would be social ruin for her. Walter was wealthy, titled, and penitent. He'd probably treat her well and be faithful. He'd make a good husband now.

Peter chewed violently. Why had he waited so long to say anything?

Because Walter always slept in.

He thought he'd wake up first, go and visit Lucy, and then come back and tell Walter what he'd done. Last night, lying in bed, he'd worked it all out.

Walter could react any way he wanted, once Peter had secured Lucy's forgiveness and affection—employment with her father.

Turns out, Walter had imagined the same early morning-visit-Lucy-alone scenario, but he'd beaten Peter to it.

And Walter was with Lucy right now. What if she agreed? Had she merely been saying that she didn't want to marry Walter, in order to cover the pain caused by his rejection?

Lucy had accused Peter of trying to distract her from Walter. What if she had only turned to Peter as a replacement? Was he a substitute until Walter became available?

He finished his meager breakfast as quickly as possible and went back to his chambers to contemplate his attire. Two minutes. He would give himself that much time. He carefully brushed his hair and polished his dusty boots. Where was Kempton when he actually needed him to pay off his bet?

He checked each button in the small mirror, each piece of clothing.

He needed to look perfect to impress Mr. Maldon, and he was finally going to see Lucy again. He could use every ounce of confidence that a well-pressed suit could give him.

Peter felt like a disaster yesterday, running after him, completely wild, not at all a gentleman. His only thought—Lucy; his only emotion—desperation. Today was supposed to be different. Instead, here he was again, rushing after his brother, already behind again.

But what if she'd already agreed to marry Walter?

Peter couldn't walk fast enough to follow the directions to Lucy's apartments. His walking stick hit the cobblestone sidewalk, echoing in the morning air. If Walter were there, too, he would find out soon enough what she had decided. He wanted to run but decided against it.

Mr. Maldon had given him a specific time to arrive, after all. He checked the pocket watch from his father. Early. He slowed down. Better to arrive looking unruffled.

How would Mr. Maldon react to his proposal? Peter tugged at his collar. One chance. That was all he had. No time for hesitation. False confidence. How many times had he presented his findings to fellow classmates during a seminar at Cambridge? He knew how to tamp down nervousness and project a calm exterior.

Half an hour more. Peter fiddled with the chain on his pocket watch. That was a bad sign, if he were watching for omens as Walter did. If Lucy had turned him away, his brother would have returned an hour ago or sooner.

Peter examined the building as he waited. Tuscan stone. Four stories tall. Wrought iron balconies and wide-open windows. He found a bench across the street and watched cats running between the terracotta planters.

Peter's stomach began to churn. He should have eaten more for breakfast than half a roll. Who else was inside that building? Large crowds made him even more nervous. He examined the metal grates and balconies. It would be time to pull in the flower boxes soon, even in Italy. Nearly October.

He checked his watch again. Finally, it was time. He crossed the street and knocked. One minute early. Just in case Mr. Maldon valued punctuality.

The footman led him into the dining room. Odd. Not the drawing room.

Mr. Maldon greeted him and shook his hand. "Come in, Peter. You don't mind, do you? I think of your brother as Chelmsford. Too confusing to have two of you in the room."

Peter stared. Walter sat across the dining table, along with Shelford, a man he didn't know, Oxley, and Lucy. *Why was his brother here?* This could make things uncomfortable.

Mr. Maldon joined them and indicated Peter should sit on the opposite side of the table.

Lucy looked more beautiful than ever. Her hair was swept up, revealing that tantalizing neck. Sapphire drops dangled below her ears. Her cheeks were pink and her lips—it took all his self-control to pull his eyes away from her.

And that dress. White muslin with small blue flowers. She had kept the fabric, after all, and had a dress made. It fit every curve perfectly.

Mr. Maldon cleared his throat, and Peter realized he was staring. Peter pulled out a hard, wooden chair.

Six people on one side of the table, and he sat alone on the other. Why were they all there? Had Lucy agreed to marry Walter or not?

"Peter, welcome. This is Mr. Robert Browning, the poet. You've met my lawyer, Oxley. You know Lord Shelford, your brother, my daughter." Mr. Maldon pointed to each. "I asked them to join me today to continue our conversation, as you requested yesterday."

He didn't want to embarrass himself in front of so many people. The celebrated poet? One of the most eloquent men in Britain? He had not requested an Inquisition.

Mr. Maldon leaned across the table. "I've already spoken with your brother, who has cancelled his marriage contract with Lucy.

Chelmsford, what are your plans concerning Peter's future employment?"

Peter blew out a breath. He relaxed his white-knuckle grip on the chair. It was done. After all these months, the engagement was ended. She had refused Walter. Now to convince her to accept him.

Peter heard an odd tapping sound, like a boot striking stone. Heads turned toward him. He stilled his leg, and the sound stopped immediately.

Walter looked confused. "He's going to take orders when we return."

"I see. Is he under any obligation to do so?" Mr. Maldon peered down the table. His usual, jolly face changed entirely. It was serious and businesslike.

"I suppose not. I've always expected it. I've got three brothers to support, and the current vicar will be happy enough to retire," Walter said.

Mr. Maldon regarded Walter. "In how many years, precisely?"

He paused. "He's been hinting around about leaving, but I suppose he could remain a few more years, if I asked him."

Mr. Maldon turned his attention to Peter. "I understand you prefer science."

"Yes, sir," he said. It wasn't brilliant, but it hadn't embarrassed him.

"And my daughter."

Peter blinked. Walter was staring at him. Peter tried to catch Lucy's eye. She was avoiding his gaze and staring straight ahead. He had never wanted to have this conversation with Walter. He had delayed again and again. Now, he had to tell Walter in front of Lucy and her father and Shelford. And a man who wrote love poetry. And a lawyer.

He squirmed in his chair. "Yes, above any other woman."

"Under normal circumstances, I might expect to hire a man with experience at your age and pay him fair wages. But you don't belong to the middle class." Mr. Maldon considered Peter. "And yet you have the mind of an engineer."

He seemed to await an answer. "Yes, sir." He was going to have to say more this time. "I studied chemistry at Cambridge."

"And will you be content to toil away, day after day? Is that really the life you find satisfying? I have Shelford and Mr. Browning here to advise you on the social ramifications of leaving the upper class and lowering yourself to accept paid work."

"Yes, Mr. Maldon." Peter turned toward Walter. When he'd first made the proposal on the crowded sidewalk yesterday, he never imagined this conversation would also take place so publicly. "I don't imagine lowering myself in any way by accepting paid work, nor do I imagine leaving the upper class simply by joining your company as a safety advisor, should you accept my proposal."

"Shelford will advise you on the more conservative elements, perhaps," Mr. Browning said. "I will, of course, always be an example of the more radical course of action. Follow your heart, lad."

"Most members of the gentry would view your actions as a step down. You may lose connections and respect from certain members of the aristocracy," Shelford said.

"What work are we discussing? Joining Mr. Maldon's company?" Walter asked. "And what did you mean about Peter preferring Lucy? You're serious?"

"Yes. Let's start there," Mr. Maldon said. "I expect any employee to speak frankly. Peter, are you able to express yourself in clear terms to your brother?"

This was it. His one chance. He had rehearsed his haphazard scheme over and over on his walk. Now, to address the proposal to Walter instead.

"Sir, thank you for this opportunity. I appreciate your consideration. I am seeking employment as an engineer in Mr. Maldon's company, Walter, because I fell in love with Lucy in Mainz."

Silence. He forged ahead. No one had stopped him, and that was all he could ask. Walter hadn't disowned him yet.

"You may have noticed she was upset with me when she found us at—."

"Cecelia," Lucy said. "Her name is Cecelia Duxford."

"Miss Duxford's home," Peter said.

Walter stared at him. "No. I was more focused on Miss Duxford's reaction, honestly."

"I had proposed earlier that day, and Lucy had accepted. I was trying to tell you that, when she arrived at Miss Duxford's home. I intended to ask you to break your engagement with her, but then she discovered I had not been completely honest. I apologize to you for that, Lucy, and Mr. Maldon, and Walter."

Silence. Walter looked at him, confused. "You asked Lucy to marry you while I was engaged to her?"

"At the same time you sought Miss Duxford's hand," Peter said. He knew he should own his actions, but he couldn't help feeling a little defensive. "Yes. And I kissed her. More than once." He may as well get it all out there.

Shelford barked a loud laugh.

"Bravo," Mr. Browning said. "I'd hire him."

"I am here to regain her trust, apologize to her, and seek employment from her father." Peter let out a deep breath. He risked a glance at Lucy. She gazed stonily ahead.

Mr. Maldon seemed neither surprised nor upset by Peter's admission. Lucy must have already told him.

Mr. Maldon cleared his throat. "Yes, he offered his services as a safety engineer for my mining firm," Mr. Maldon said, considering him. "You assume the position is available and unfilled? That I have no other technical advisors working to prevent accidents and deaths in my mines?"

"No, sir," Peter said. "I would argue that I am better qualified than they are."

Mr. Maldon chuckled, then assumed a serious demeanor once again. "What pay rate are you expecting?"

Peter regarded Mr. Maldon. How much could he ask for? If Walter disowned him, he would have to make his own way in the world. He scrambled to remember lectures he had attended on coal dust and their contribution to explosions in recent mining disasters to try to impress Mr. Maldon.

He couldn't ask for too much, but he had to act more confident than he felt. He could tell that Mr. Maldon respected impertinence and brash conversation. *Be bold*, he told himself. *For Lucy.*

"I need high enough wages to support a family, sir," Peter said.

Mr. Maldon smiled. He did seem to love a challenge. "And what are your qualifications?"

"I have recently graduated from Cambridge with a degree in chemistry."

"And no practical experience. Most of my men have worked in the mine since they were nine," Mr. Maldon said.

Peter folded his arms. This wasn't about mining. It was about Lucy. "But they haven't analyzed the safety and explosion reports. I have attended chemistry lectures in London every Christmas for years, in addition to my regular course of research, and I under-stand the complex factors involved in mining disasters."

Mr. Maldon leaned forward. "In theory. Not in practice."

Just then, the door opened. "Miss Maldon. Your friend has sent a note that she would like to speak with Lord Chelmsford after all."

All eyes turned toward Lucy. She drew a deep breath. "I do apologize. Peter, if we may interrupt your job interview for one moment."

He nodded. Lucy had looked at him for the first time. He smiled at her. She frowned and folded her arms.

"Walter, before I proceed, do you give your consent to allow your brother to work for my father's firm, should the firm decide to hire such a clearly untrustworthy and unqualified applicant?" Lucy's tone was icy.

He shrugged. "If Peter wants to work for you, I have two other brothers who can become vicars. You were serious, Peter? All those times you talked to me about Lucy? If I'd known, I never would have pursued her for myself."

"I offered to marry her when we were all in Mainz," Peter said. "In front of you."

"You meant it?" Walter asked. "I didn't realize."

"Walter." Lucy's tone was firm. "When Colonel Loughton told you that Mrs. Smith was no more, that she was gone forever, that she had died…" Lucy paused. "Well, he meant that Cecelia would not use that false name anymore. That is all."

Walter gaped at Lucy. He pushed his chair back from the table and ran from the room.

Lucy had lied to him, too, causing his brother unnecessary pain and deep sorrow. Peter couldn't fault her or be sorry. It had worked a change in Walter. Perhaps she would understand or forgive him more easily, if she understood the urge to protect someone she loved. Peter felt an inkling of hope.

"You can resume, Papa, if you wish to. I maintain that he clearly lacks experience and expertise," Lucy said.

Mr. Maldon steepled his hands. "You made your opinions clear earlier. So, what position do you expect to start at, boy?"

Peter thought quickly. It was a lot to take in. Mrs. Smith was alive. Her name was Cecelia Duxford. She wanted to see Walter. *Lucy lied!*

Lucy also did not want to speak to him or meet his eyes. This was his only chance to persuade her.

But she made a dress from the fabric they selected together, and she was wearing it today.

"As I said, sir, I am hoping to marry."

Lucy huffed.

He kept his focus on Mr. Maldon. "I want to support a wife and family."

"Most of my men marry at twenty-eight or thirty. Maybe twenty-six if they're lucky. But you're getting a late start in mining. How old are you?" Mr. Maldon studied him.

"Twenty-two. Nearly Twenty-three."

Mr. Maldon turned to Shelford. "How old are you?"

"Twenty-four."

"And how old were you when you married, Mr. Browning?"

"Thirty-four."

"Oxley?"

"Twenty-eight."

Mr. Maldon fixed Peter with a stare. "No past experience. Asking for a pay raise before you're even hired. Let me ask you this. I have to worry about people stealing secrets in my industry." Mr. Maldon leaned forward. "Can anyone here testify in favor of your character? Can anyone vouch for your integrity?"

Peter remained silent. They all knew the answer.

"By your own admission, you have lied to my daughter. And what kind of commitment can you give? How many years before you leave and take my secrets to a competitor? Or will you tire of working and return to the easy life of the aristocracy? I mean no offense, Shelford. You and Chelmsford put in hard work, managing your estates, but many others simply live on the earnings of others."

"None taken," Shelford said. "You'd work hard as a vicar, too, Peter."

"Psh," Mr. Browning said. "The boy needs a challenge."

"I will work as many years as it takes to rise to the level needed, Mr. Maldon," Peter said. He really hoped it wouldn't be long. Mr. Maldon was testing him, and Peter would not back down.

"Leaving the aristocracy? Entering the working class?" Mr. Maldon asked.

Another test.

"I maintain that many younger sons work and do not leave the upper class. Society respects their need for financial stability. I feel perfectly confident in my course of action," Peter said. "I am proud to associate with your business endeavors. You are a land owner and fully belong to the gentry yourself, though a business owner, and many accept you in social circles. Lord Shelford's presence here, as well as Mr. Browning's, attest to this fact."

"You understand how your mother and brothers may feel about this? Your uncles and other relatives?" Shelford asked. "Have you seen the way Lucy is treated in town? Can you accept that same treatment?"

"Yes," Peter said. He tried to catch Lucy's eye. He'd do anything to be with her. "Although I do not believe she will continue to be treated that way when we marry. I will not stand for it. I will confront any shop owner and withhold our business and cut any acquaintance who slights my wife. We can shop in London."

Lucy huffed again. "If," she said loudly. "If we marry. Not when."

At least she considered the possibility. That was progress. She no longer dismissed him outright.

"Then I'll leave the decision with the new managing partner in my firm. Lucy?" Mr. Maldon turned to her. "Dear heart?"

She shook her head. "Papa, you cannot call me 'dear heart' during business meetings. Or 'sweets.'"

Mr. Maldon's face returned to businesslike. "What do you think of this candidate?"

"I'm not convinced," Lucy said. She finally looked at Peter. "Why would you work for my father's firm?"

Peter sat across from four men and Lucy. This wasn't the place to declare his love, although he had tried. That wouldn't work with her. He had to convince her to trust him again in a way that she would understand.

"Is there some kind of conditional hire in your industry?" he asked. "I know you doubt my sincerity. Will you allow me a trial period?"

"Capital idea!" Mr. Maldon said. "You could use an underman-ager to oversee safety."

"Three days," Lucy said.

They all turned toward her.

"Perhaps six months," Oxley said. "Standard clause."

"Three days," Lucy repeated. "I'll give him that much." She stood and pushed back her chair. "Are we finished here?" She took a deep breath.

She was getting away.

"Am I hired? Peter asked.

Shelford rose. He nodded to Mr. Browning. They left the dining room.

Oxley followed them. He paused at the doorway. "Shall I draw up a contract, Mr. Maldon? What level of wages did we decide?"

"I'll be with you shortly, Oxley," Mr. Maldon said. "Lucy? Can you give him a little longer? Six months would be standard. Perhaps three months?"

Lucy folded her arms, her posture stiff, and repeated herself. "Three days."

Mr. Maldon nodded his head toward Lucy and winked at Peter.

Very well. If her father was encouraging him, he'd try.

Peter considered Lucy. Her blue eyes sparkled with antagonism, but he could see the vulnerability. "It's past mid-day. I've already lost so much time." He wanted to pull her into a hug, but he knew she was barely able to stay in the same room with him. "Four days?"

Mr. Maldon stood next to her, watching Peter closely. He widened his eyes, as if to urge Peter on. How well did Mr. Maldon know his daughter? Was this a terrible idea?

Peter started walking around the table to speak with her. She remained where she was. That was encouraging. She didn't run away. Perhaps her father knew his daughter after all.

Peter extended his hand. "Shall we shake on it?"

Lucy ignored him. Perhaps not.

Mr. Maldon reached across her to shake Peter's hand. "Good luck, son. Lucy will explain your job duties. I'll let the two of you work them out." He left the room, leaving the door ajar.

"When do I begin?" Peter asked. "The mines are in which counties? How many do you own? Can you tell me about their safety protocols?"

Lucy began to edge her way out of the room. "Your three days start now. You have two and a half left."

Peter followed her, drinking in the familiar smell of her rose perfume. "In that case, put me to work."

CHAPTER 28

Lucy wrapped a light shawl around herself. Papa had suggested Peter take her to explore Florence while they "discussed his job responsibilities." She had agreed, cautiously. It would be a relief to escape the scrutiny of so many people in the crowded apartments and simply walk for a while.

Papa would not force her to do anything against her wishes again. He had promised her that. He had been devastated when he learned her true feelings and all the heartache that ensued from the betrothal to Walter Chelmsford. They had a quick talk after Walter arrived early this morning, while Oxley disposed of the marriage contract.

She explained her true desire to be involved in his business ventures, not to embroider cushions, and he reluctantly agreed to let her have a small say in his dealings.

Lucy hesitated at the entrance of their apartments. Peter hovered behind her, so close she could almost feel him. It made her nervous to spend time with him. Eleanor and Lord Shelford would accompany as chaperones, which would help alleviate any awkwardness.

She still wasn't sure whether she believed him. She glanced

aside at the drawing room door, which was partially ajar. "Would you like to meet Cecelia?"

Lucy nodded to the footman, who opened the door wider. "May I interrupt you?"

Cecelia turned. Walter sat beside her, smiling down at the baby in her arms.

"Please, come in," she said in her gentle voice. "Peter." She held out a hand. "You may call me Cecelia. Cecelia Duxford."

Peter leaned over to catch a glimpse of the child.

Cecelia brushed aside the blanket covering the infant's face. "Her name is Sarah."

Peter offered Sarah his finger. Instinctively, she wrapped her tiny hand around it. "She's precious." He smiled at the baby.

"I'm sorry," Cecelia said, "that we did not start our acquaintance on honest terms."

"You make an impressive medium." Peter laughed. "Walter stole the slates from your home."

She turned around. "You did?"

"I have them at the *pensione*," he said. "They were my only memento of you."

"Oh, Walter." Cecelia laughed. "You know it was all an act?"

Walter looked sheepishly at her. "I do now."

"I have been pressed into labor," Peter said. "We must leave you now. Farewell, Miss Duxford. Walter, a word before I go?"

Walter startled. His gaze was fixed on Cecelia holding the tiny child in her arms. "Now? Can we not talk here?" He turned toward Peter and gave an almost apologetic look. "A moment. Of course." He stood, turning back as though to drink in the sight of Cecelia.

"I'll be here when you return." Cecelia laughed.

Walter grinned and stepped outside the drawing room to join Peter.

Lucy sat near Cecelia. "How do you feel?" she asked. "I've never seen Walter so natural and unassuming."

Cecelia shook her head. "He is afraid I shall vanish again.

Walter is truly a different man, as you said, and yet the things I loved have not changed. Are we being deceived?"

"I cannot tell," Lucy said. "He does not seem to mind that you deceived him."

Cecelia smiled and laid a hand on Lucy's arm. "What reason would they have to hide the truth? I bring nothing but scandal and complication into a man's life. I have a child. Why would Walter seek me out?" She looked at Lucy. "Why would Peter risk his place in society and seek employment with your father, unless he cared? If I, who has so much more reason to distrust men, can hope and give Walter a chance, then surely you can give Peter an opportunity to prove himself."

Lucy swallowed. "It is difficult."

Sarah made fussing noises. Cecelia rocked her and held her close. "But he pursued your carriage, learned your address, and then he followed you to Florence. He even fought with your father, I hear." Cecelia began to rock the baby. "Your papa did not make it easy for him, I suspect."

Lucy smiled. "He interrogated him, and I made it harder still."

"Yet he did not leave. He has no reason to lie to you now. Walter said Peter refused the living at Chelmsford. What nobleman would give up his easy life and secure position in the aristocracy unless he truly loved you?" Cecelia's voice was soothing.

Eleanor said Peter loved her. Cecelia was telling her the same thing. It was easier to trust her friends than her own heart. Her fears echoed loudly. What if he changed his mind? What if he had another reason for acting this way? How could she be certain of his sincerity?

"He's waiting," Cecelia whispered.

Lucy looked at the door. Peter watched her, as if uncertain of what to do. Walter stood beside him.

"May I?" Peter held out his elbow.

Lucy hesitated. She feared she wouldn't think straight if she were too near him.

She crossed the room and lightly rested her hand on Peter's

outstretched arm. She waited for Peter to pull her toward him and prepared to resist, but he didn't.

She almost felt disappointed, then angry with herself. He was appropriately distant, just as she wished him to be. That was safest. She could think rationally this way.

"I'm sorry," Walter said as she passed him. "I apologize for my behavior. It was inexcusable. I didn't know." He inclined his head toward Peter. "Well, I suppose he told me, and I didn't listen." He shook his head.

"Thank you," Lucy said, and they left to descend the steps to the hired carriage in the street below. What had Walter not known or not heard? That Peter was lying? Or that Peter loved her? Why was it easier to trust Walter, who had treated her ill, than it was to believe Peter?

They settled onto separate seats. Lucy ran her hand across the plush velvet lining as she waited for their chaperones. The vehicle swayed and began the journey across town toward the Palazzo Pitti and the Boboli Gardens.

Peter cleared his throat. "Lord and Lady Shelford took another carriage. They're meeting us there."

"But—" Lucy stopped herself. She required a chaperone. She didn't want to be alone with Peter.

"Lady Shelford insisted," Peter said.

She nodded. Eleanor was trying to give them time alone. It was completely improper, and entirely like Eleanor, now that she was married.

Peter studied his hands. "Walter is grateful to you."

"Cecelia makes her own choices," Lucy said.

He looked at the ceiling of the carriage. "Walter has always had a void inside himself that he tried to fill with the wrong things. Ever since he thought Miss Duxford died, he has viewed the world differently." Peter blew out a breath and leaned back into the carriage seat. "He is running toward responsibility eagerly now, instead of running from it. I believe he's found a permanent way to fill his emptiness."

"By caring for someone else," she said softly.

"He has an entire family to cherish now." Peter played with the ring on his finger, twisting it. "You broke your engagement." He glanced over at her. "Formally. It is legal now. Binding. Or rather, unbound."

Lucy nodded. She felt wary. This conversation could get into dangerous territory quickly.

But Peter let the subject drop.

She had plenty of time to search her feelings as the carriage drew closer to their destination. Peter had argued passionately and persuasively this morning. Everyone else believed him.

If she believed him—*if*—then there was still the risk that he could hurt her again. He might seem sincere now, but he had lied before. How could she trust him again?

It was well past mid-day by the time they reached the gardens. Perfect weather greeted them—sunny with a slight breeze, an ideal Italian autumn afternoon.

Peter reached in his pocket to pay the driver.

"Papa already paid," Lucy said.

He frowned. "I would like to take care of you."

"Employees do not pay for the carriage." She moved toward the entrance of the Pitti Palace, where Eleanor and Lord Shelford waited.

Peter remained where he was. "What *do* you need, Lucy? You have everything."

She stopped. "I often wonder what it's like for Queen Victoria. Married, but ruler of the nation. Prince Albert dotes on her."

Peter advanced until he stood at her side. "So, my job is to dote on you?"

Lucy wasn't sure she was ready for that. "That's not what I said."

"Is it what you want?" He offered his hand. When she tentatively accepted it, he rested it lightly atop his arm.

Peter glanced sideways. "I never got a firm job description from your father."

They walked to the entrance of the palace, the gravel crunchily underfoot as Lucy tried to phrase a response. "Duties to be determined," she said at last.

"Hello, darling," Eleanor called. "Lovely place. Quite romantic."

Lucy wondered whether it was a good idea to come with the Shelfords.

"What shall we see first?" Peter asked. "The grottos? The lemon house? The garden of Ganymede?"

"Lead the way," Lord Shelford said. "We may get lost. Terrible sense of direction." He held a map and guidebook.

"Meet you back here in two hours." Eleanor winked at her.

The Shelfords moved into the garden without looking back. Lucy's cheeks burned. Terrible idea to come with them.

An awkward silence descended. Eleanor had left her alone, unchaperoned, on purpose, with Peter. Part of her wanted to return home immediately and stop this charade.

But she'd promised to give him three days.

"You are my hired guide," Lucy finally said. "I require your expertise."

Peter grinned and affected a formal air. "Indeed. Then we shall begin at the obelisk."

They wandered through the palace and began to stroll through the gardens. Lush greenery surrounded them everywhere. Oak trees grew in the distance. An amphitheater was dug into the hillside. A semi-circle of polished granite benches surrounded a grassy basin. In the center of the grass, an Egyptian obelisk reached to the heavens.

"Ramesses II," Peter said. "The obelisk came from Heliopolis. It took four months to move it from Rome to Florence. The granite basin accompanied it."

Lucy studied the ancient relics. "You don't have a map or guidebook," she said.

"I've been here several times, trying to find you," Peter said. "I've memorized the map."

He spoke in a matter-of-fact voice, looking straight ahead.

Perhaps he could sense how wary she felt. She felt a little of the hurt melt away, ever so slightly. He'd beaten paths all over Florence for weeks, looking for her.

"Looking for yourself or for Walter?" Lucy couldn't help asking. "He said you approved of his efforts to marry me." That still stung.

Peter guided her up a set of stone steps. Immaculately trimmed hedges and towering chestnut trees lined the path. "May I explain?"

They reached the top of the stairs and turned to look back over the view.

Lucy wanted to hear. She was ready to listen, even if she was still angry. She nodded.

Peter guided her through an archway made of branches to a bench in the shade. He turned toward her, his brown eyes somber and sorrowful. "Walter left to see you this morning while I was still asleep. As you are aware, he arrived very early. Unfashionably early."

Lucy smiled. She'd barely finished her breakfast.

"He usually sleeps until nine or ten at least, and I thought to arrive at my appointed time with your father before he would awaken. I underestimated the strength of his sorrow and repentance, but I have made other, equally grave mistakes. Let me count the ways."

Lucy caught her breath. She had memorized Sonnet Forty-Three by Mrs. Browning. Everyone had. Peter was apologizing in the language of a love poem.

"First of all, I was wrong to withhold Walter's address when we first met in Mainz. Second, I was also wrong to agree to Walter's requests. Third, I should have told him the truth more forcefully long ago. Fourth, I am entirely to blame for the hurt caused. And lastly, I am not sorry."

Lucy sat back in shock.

"I regret the pain and distress caused by my actions and apologize, but I cannot regret the time I spent with you. I came to know your fine qualities and to love you. I could not have done that any other way."

Lucy had not expected any of this. His frankness. His apology. His non-apology.

Peter continued to gaze into her eyes. "Walter thought Father would send him a message if he attended a séance. He is afraid of his burdens. He inherited many things, including sure evidence of our father's inconstancy. He wanted to run away from marriage, so he would not also be unfaithful to you."

Lucy's shock deepened. "But he was."

"And he hated himself for it. These past weeks have been torture for us both," Peter said. "Knowing that our father dallied, and seeing ourselves in the same light, has been the worst revelation to us."

"Shall we continue walking?" Lucy said. She thought better when she could move. She could see that Peter was telling the truth. It would take a little time to sink in, though.

They proceeded through the branch archway to a path lined by cypress trees on either side.

"I'm not used to talking," Peter said. "I much prefer listening to you. Will you tell me how you feel? Anger, indignation, anything. I want to restore our bond and make amends."

They approached an island basin. Water encircled an ornate fountain with Neptune in its center.

It felt so good to walk with Peter. He smelled like soap and shaving cream. His beard was carefully trimmed, barely visible, just like she liked it. Not one of those thick, wild sets of whiskers that so many men preferred. His suit fit him perfectly. The Italian air gave a slight wave to his thick, dark hair.

"I find that I have little to say, for once." Lucy tried to smile. Peter returned a weak attempt. They passed some Roman statues along the way to an ornate coffeehouse. "I have missed you. I have raged at you in my mind and wanted to tell you a thousand things. Right now I am afraid of you," Lucy said.

Peter stopped on the gravel path. "Why?"

She pulled her shawl around herself. "Because believing you means you could hurt me again." She still felt wounded, but she saw his remorse.

They continued walking again, passing the coffeehouse and following the pathway toward a set of statues.

Peter's voice was serious. "I don't know what Walter said to you, Lucy, and I don't want to sound like my brother, but we've had an awful month. We've both done some thinking and neither of us liked what we saw. I swear to you that I was sincere in my affections and intentions in Mainz, as I am now."

And she believed him with her heart, too, not just her head.

"I changed my mind," Lucy said. "I'm glad we hired you for this temporary period."

They wandered down a sloping lawn, past a figure of a boy with an eagle. Neither seemed inclined to talk. Both were lost in their thoughts. Lucy warred with herself. She felt hope, excitement.

Peter loved her. She loved him. She might be willing to give him that second chance. It felt so much better than her anguish and worry. She could ask for nothing more from him. He'd apologized and asked to remedy his wrongs.

She could meet him partway. She had withheld the truth about Cecelia from them. She could try Eleanor's answer—forgiveness.

It was just three days, and a large portion of humility.

"And what will my wages be?" Peter glanced aside at her, interrupting her thoughts. "I don't believe we discussed a final salary." He seemed nervous.

Lucy felt nervous, too, but she couldn't truly give him a trial period unless she let go of her fear. She wanted this to work.

"Name your starting price," she said. "And we'll negotiate."

Peter considered her for a moment. "Medieval wages."

Her heart skipped a beat.

"You never claimed the prizes you won in Mainz," Lucy said. "At least one of them."

"I'm ready to claim them now." Peter patted his vest pocket. He pulled out her handkerchief, just enough to show her it was there, and tucked it away again.

Lucy's heart began to beat faster. He'd kept it, all this time. Would a man who was play-acting do that?

He led her toward a grotto. They passed through stones that formed a column-like frame and entered the dark, secluded cave. Marble lined the cavity. False rocks and stalactites hung from the ceiling and crevices. Colorful mosaics covered the floor. Carved animals capered and played along the walls.

Peter slowed and came to a stop. Lucy craned her neck up to inspect the ceiling.

"Lucy," Peter said in a thick voice.

She turned her head toward him.

Peter watched her intently. He looked at her neck and up to her lips. "How can I earn that pay?"

She let out a breath. She had chosen to believe him instead of her worries, and she would forgive instead of fear.

"Have you heard of back wages?" Lucy asked. She moved in front of Peter and slid her arms around his waist. "My father sometimes owes his men for work they've already done."

Peter put his arms around her. "I like that."

Lucy gazed up at him. She had to crane her neck again. "You won two contests in Mainz and only collected one kiss."

Peter pulled her closer. "My mistake. Cheek kisses are half-wages. I'm owed one and a half kisses. Which rounds up to two."

Peter bent down and covered her lips with his own. Lucy responded hesitantly. He drew her to him, kissing her tenderly. He brushed her hair with his hand and held her close.

It ended almost before it began. Lucy checked her emotions. She felt safe. No regrets about her decision to let go of the past.

"That's one," he said. Peter searched her face, as if waiting for her. She put a hand on his cheek. If she were going to move forward, there was no reason to wait.

Immediately, he leaned down. Lucy allowed herself to fall into the kiss, resting on Peter's chest. She had to stand on her tiptoes.

He wrapped her shawl tightly around her and pulled her into his arms. She pressed her lips more fervently against his, feeling a longing grow. It was overwhelming.

They broke apart and Peter put his forehead against hers. He gazed into her eyes. "I like employment," he said. "Put me back to work." He pressed a quick kiss to her lips and glanced around. "I'm eager to dote on you."

Peter guided her to a set of stairs that led down into the grotto. He picked her up and Lucy's eyes grew wide with surprise. He placed her one step above him.

Now she was the perfect height. They stood nearly eye to eye.

"I owe you some overtime. Is that what they call it? I'll stay late." Peter pulled her handkerchief out of his vest pocket.

Lucy put her hand on his chest. Every time she thought of him carrying it over his heart, she felt adored. It was surprisingly sentimental of him.

"You've paid me for the tournament." Peter tucked the square of cloth into her reticule, rearranged her shawl around her shoulders, and then encircled her waist with his arms.

Lucy wavered. "I suppose your guide services have amassed some earnings."

"How many?" Peter smiled roguishly. "One for the obelisk, the amphitheater, the coffeehouse, and the grotto? Perhaps the fountain or cypress lane?"

They were an inch apart. She closed her eyes. "Yes."

Peter hugged her to him. This time, she didn't have to stand on her tiptoes. She tilted her head and lost herself in the feel of his lips. There was a sense of relief and homecoming.

When they broke apart, Lucy threaded her arm through his. They climbed the steps together and left the cave. She allowed herself to walk close to him this time. It was so easy to be with Peter.

He blinked at the sun as they left the cave. "There are other grottos in the gardens," he said. "Would you like to explore them? We still have an hour." He raised his eyebrows at her.

"I don't know," Lucy said. "I honestly don't." She laughed. "Make your case."

They followed the path and climbed down another set of marble steps.

"It's possible that you miscalculated my wages," Peter said. "It might have been one kiss for each location, not one kiss for all of them."

Lucy allowed herself to enjoy the euphoria of falling back in love with Peter. The beauty of the gardens, the brilliance of the sun, the gentle breeze, and the brilliant blue sky combined to give her a sense of peace.

They rounded a geometric hedge. The gardeners must have worked tirelessly to trim the tall bushes into unusual shapes.

Peter stopped in front of two enormous marble pillars that marked the entrance to another grotto. He reached up and brushed a lock of hair from Lucy's face.

"That will do for today," Lucy said. She could feel his sincerity. She still needed time to trust her own emotions, but it was getting easier. "Your trial period has begun well so far, even if you are a complete novice." She smiled at him. It felt good to joke and tease. She could feel her anger ebbing away and joy replacing it.

"Excellent," Peter said. "Have I earned a bonus yet? Or did you indeed miscalculate my wages?"

"You are relentless. You're going to make a shrewd business-man," Lucy said. She took him by the hand and led him into the next cave. "Maybe just one more."

CHAPTER 29

Peter straightened his bow tie in the bedchamber's small mirror. Back to work. He grinned.

Lucy loved him. He knew it, even though she had never accepted his apology. She had been uncharacteristically quiet in the gardens, but beneath her hurt and anger, he could sense the longing that mirrored his own hopes.

And the second half of their walk went better than the first.

He really needed to know if her father's mining firm would hire him. It wouldn't all be garden walks. He'd have to spend hours at a desk and really learn about the concepts he had toyed with in school.

The thought was invigorating. He'd much rather spend his time doing that than teaching Latin to schoolboys.

Peter and Walter had talked late into the night. Peter explained what happened in Mainz. Walter, ecstatic, newly reunited with a doting Cecelia, found it hilarious.

"So my former fiancée will be my sister-in-law?" Walter slapped his knee and roared.

"Only if I can convince Lucy to be my fiancée," Peter said.

"I don't know if I can convince Cecelia to marry me," Walter said. "You and I both have work to do. She has told me about her past, and I want to hunt down the coward who forced himself on her."

"Would you really consider marriage?" Peter asked. "I know you are enamored, and I know we will have more time to court them here, but is Cecelia prepared for the rigors of running an estate?"

Walter put his arm around Peter's shoulders. "I have thought deeply. She was raised as a gentleman's daughter and has performed in the courts of Europe. I fear I am the one who will need to learn etiquette from her. I have no doubt she can command the attention of any audience."

"And the scandal?" Peter asked.

"It will pass," Walter said. "We will weather it. By the time we return from our wedding trip in six months, hardly anyone will raise an eyebrow. I will not countenance slander."

Peter understood. He felt fiercely defensive of Lucy, and this time, he'd be on Walter's side, protecting Cecelia, too.

Walter seemed certain that Cecelia returned his regard, at least. Nothing could upset him or dissuade him. Of course he and his brother could overcome anything.

Peter had felt less certain yesterday. Today he was hopeful. They'd visited three grottos in the Boboli gardens. That amounted to six or eight kisses. Perhaps he'd get to the point where he no longer had to count because they were so plentiful.

He'd been afraid in the Shelfords' dining room, when he admitted openly to Lucy's father and Shelford that he'd kissed Lucy and proposed to her without asking her father's permission. He assumed Mr. Maldon would roar with rage and throw him out. He imagined Shelford and Mr. Browning escorting him out, the way the colonel and Shelford had done in Mainz.

Instead, Mr. Maldon fought a grin, Shelford laughed, and Mr. Browning whole-heartedly approved. It was Lucy's opinion that mattered, however.

The brothers walked together to the Shelfords' apartments.

Peter noticed several carriages lined up in the street as they drew near.

Cecelia waved him over. She waited outside a carriage. "It's the first time I've left the house," she said. "Eleanor decided it's time I see the city like the rest of you. Walter, would you care to ride with us?"

Mr. Duxford sat inside with baby Sarah.

"Sir?" Walter asked. "May I join you?"

"Sure, sure," Mr. Duxford said. "How else will we get to know each other?"

Peter could sense Walter's relief. Mr. Duxford had granted Walter permission to court his daughter, but Peter knew that Walter still worried about correcting the bad impression he'd created.

He could understand. Mr. Maldon stood outside a carriage with Lucy and Oxley. Peter had no idea what Lucy's father truly thought of him. He'd tried to create a good image of himself yesterday, but he had a lot to overcome.

The Brownings and Shelfords climbed into the third carriage. Peter walked over to Lucy.

"Join us, my boy. Eleanor's got another scheme today," Mr. Maldon said. "Expeditions all over the countryside with the Shelfords. Never a moment's peace."

Peter could tell Mr. Maldon approved of Eleanor, even if he seemed to complain about the chaos she caused in his life. He respected her. He hoped Lucy's father would come to feel the same way toward him—glad that he turned their lives upside down with his pursuit of Lucy.

Because his own life was in shambles. He meant to incorporate himself into their lives relentlessly until Lucy realized she needed him as much as he needed her.

Mr. Maldon moved over to sit beside his lawyer. Peter climbed the steps into the carriage and settled next to Lucy. Time to act confident again, even though he was desperately unsure, and entirely hopeful.

"Am I earning back wages?" Peter whispered in Lucy's ear. "No pay today." He looked meaningfully at Lucy's father and Oxley sitting across from them.

Lucy fought a grin. She gave the tiniest of nods.

His confidence grew. Exchanging secret glances was an excellent step toward falling in love.

"Sir, since we have this opportunity to talk," Peter said, "may I ask you about your current ventures?" He felt excited about the prospect of working. He loved an intellectual challenge.

Mr. Maldon smiled broadly. "You have no idea what you're getting into, son. Settle back."

Lucy leaned forward. "This is so much better than embroidery, Papa. Truly. Have you been able to acquire the flooded mines? Will you be able to drain them?"

Mr. Maldon glanced at Oxley. "What have I done? Letting her into the business?"

"I'd rather go to Exchange Alley than Almack's, if you'll let me. I mean it, Papa. It's invigorating."

Mr. Maldon chuckled. "You know what you're signing up for, Peter?"

He watched the passing countryside through the carriage window. "Absolutely not. Tell me more."

Mr. Maldon talked non-stop until they reached the outskirts high above Florence. Lady Shelford had decided to have a picnic luncheon in Fiesole, overlooking the city.

Peter settled himself on a bench near Lucy, after making sure she had a full plate of grapes, cheese, bread, and ham. He would always make sure she had the best seat, with the best view, but especially today. His actions needed to show that her desires mattered to him.

They sat in a green field surrounded by Roman ruins. Rows of stone benches had been laid into the hill. Stairs led up to more ruins. Arches stood by themselves without any structure to support. Foundations and parts of pillars dotted the grassy slope and field. Sculpted hedges and tall pines lined the walkways. Florence lay in the valley below.

"It reminds me of the harvest festival in Mainz," Lucy said. "Except there are olive trees instead of vineyards here."

He had hurt her feelings that night. Was she remembering the end of the evening or the beginning? He had to restore her trust in him, but he couldn't think how. He could only think of the most obvious thing to say.

"There are vineyards on the slope across the way here, too. Can you see?" Peter leaned across Lucy and pointed to the nearest hill.

She swayed into him, then pulled back. She must still be unsure. He had to try harder. The old, passive Peter was gone. He tried to think of something.

Peter studied her. The gentle breeze playing with her careful chignon. Her light blue eyes shining in the sunlight. He could hardly resist her. The pull he felt toward her was as much emotional and intellectual as it was physical. When she began to argue with her father about his business, he felt her charm increase tenfold.

A woman who could outwit him as well as bewitch him.

Peter spied a row of hedges. Tall hedges. Ideal for collecting wages or redeeming himself. "Would you care to take a stroll?"

"I'm enjoying the view," Lucy said.

"So am I," Peter said and winked at Lucy. He'd never winked at a woman in his life before.

She put down her plate. "I cannot resist your dimpled chin." She looked around and lowered her voice. "Or cheek."

"I think you've resisted them before," Peter said. He offered her his hand.

"My mistake." Lucy took his hand. "Where are we walking?"

Peter pointed toward the hedgerow. "I enjoy talking with your father."

"You ask intelligent questions," Lucy said, "for someone so unqualified."

Peter nudged her. "Am I unlikely to be hired?"

"Depends on which position you apply for," Lucy said.

They crossed the field and moved toward the secluded path.

Peter felt his confidence increasing. She was teasing him, which was always a good sign.

"What are my options?" Peter said.

Lucy drew closer to Peter. "I require a lifetime commitment."

"More than three days." Peter led them around the hedges. "Agreed." She was encouraging him. This was a different Lucy than the day before. More confident.

"A non-competition clause. Papa insists on those in his industry," Lucy said.

Peter stopped and checked. Yes. The intertwined shrubs grew tall, thick enough for concealment. "There's no one like you."

"But there is the matter of your qualifications." Lucy smiled at him.

"I haven't told you about the lectures I attend at Christmastime." Peter decided it was time to act.

Lucy stared at him. "Are they relevant?"

"Very." He put an arm around Lucy's waist. "The Laws of Attraction." He put his other arm around her back and drew her in. "Principles of Magnetism."

She looked up at him. "You might be qualified after all."

Peter searched for one of the scattered stones that dotted the landscape. He lifted Lucy off her feet, drew her to his chest and placed her at eye level. "There are demonstrations at all the lectures," he said. "Practical applications. Allow me?"

Lucy grinned.

Peter leaned in and embraced her. He touched her lips gently with his own, then felt Lucy respond. He deepened the kiss, letting her response guide him. She pressed her fingers into his back, bringing herself closer to him. He held her tightly, scarcely allowing himself to breathe.

She opened her eyes. "You're hired."

"I love you," Peter said. "I want to marry you, whenever you will allow me. Whenever your father will. I will wait as long as you require to trust me. Years. Whatever it takes."

"I don't want to wait years," Lucy said. "I love you, and I believe you."

Peter crushed her to him. "Can you really trust me again?" He hugged her against his chest, then rested his head on hers. She'd given him this second chance, and he'd tried his hardest to convince her. After so much misery and uncertainty, it felt unreal.

Lucy gazed up at him. "Only a man in love would listen to Papa speak about drills and coal dust for nearly an hour." She ran her hand along his cheek. "If you didn't truly love me, why would you still be here?"

Peter laughed. "That's it? After everything, that's all it takes for you to fall back in love with me? Drill bits?"

Lucy traced the dimple on his jawline with her finger. She kissed his cheek tenderly and moved to kiss him on the mouth. "That's your pay for the carriage ride."

Peter brushed her face with the back of his hand. "I enjoy working for you."

"You mentioned that before," Lucy said.

He gazed into her eyes. She needed to know how deeply he loved her. "I'll tell you every day for the rest of your life."

Lucy considered him. "Does this mean I'll have a mother?" Her lip trembled.

Peter resisted the urge to kiss it. "If I'm not mistaken, she'll be gaining two daughters."

"When I left you and Walter behind, it meant losing your mother as well," Lucy said. "I had none of my own, again, though I had grown to love her."

Peter moved his hands up her back and drew her into a hug. "Lucy."

She rested in his arms, then tilted her head up. "Do you know why I trust you? Really?" She searched his face.

He regarded her skeptically. "It wasn't the drill bits?"

Lucy peered up at him with wonder in her eyes. "Because you listen. You see me. Even when I wouldn't meet your eyes, I saw the way you looked at me. I can see your whole soul. I know you're steady and sincere."

Peter felt the same amazement, that a woman like her could love a man like him. He kissed her again. "Will you employ me? Put me to good use?"

"I would marry you, even if you wanted to be a vicar. You don't have to give up your life among the aristocracy. I will not require you to report to me as my undermanager," Lucy said.

Peter drew her close. "I like getting paid. I will be happier going to Exchange Alley with you than Almack's, too. As long as there are dark corners somewhere in the alley."

"Then you're hired," Lucy said, "for life."

EPILOGUE

Late October 1856

Rachel basked in the warmth of the Italian sun as she waited outside the stone church in Florence. Cypress trees lined one side, hiding a brilliant red building. On the other side, a wrought-iron fence surrounded a churchyard. The walls were an apricot-pink, the color of an early morning sunrise.

She'd attended Eleanor's wedding just three months ago. Lucy had made detailed plans for her own wedding while engaged to Lord Chelmsford. She had bored Rachel with fashion plates and all manner of minutiae. Now, Lucy was marrying in Italy in a simple ceremony without even ordering a special gown.

Lucy.

Who loved to buy dresses with lace and rows of tassels. All the latest fashions.

She wore a simple cotton muslin gown, white with blue flowers on it. No decoration. Just a tasteful, ordinary day dress. Lucy told Rachel she preferred this dress above any other in the world, because Peter had given it to her.

Cecelia's dress was a confection, something Eleanor had ordered for her in Florence. A green floral design repeated along the sleeves and hem. A scarf wrapped around the waist and tied in a simple knot. Pink, purple, and peach flowers danced up the front, the colors fading to a gentle grey as they crossed the shoulder. A simple lace collar folded over the front, which buttoned up the front. The skirt was full, but not overly so. No ruffles.

It was as though a Romantic artist had overlaid a watercolor from a canvas onto a simple white dress. It was elegant and stunning. It fit Cecelia, and the occasion, perfectly, just as Lucy's dress seemed right for her.

The brides marched up the aisle past Gothic arched pillars. Sunlight streamed through the stained-glass windows. There were no decorations: a few simple flower arrangements and the brilliant fuchsia bushes outside.

Peter and Walter waited at the far end of the church. Rachel had said her farewell to Peter two months ago and made her peace. She felt truly happy for Lucy, even if she didn't understand. Lucy and Cecelia had left Mainz heartbroken, and now they were at the altar. How did one recover from such pain?

After Peter and Lucy left, Rachel had thrown herself into studies, working hard to understand both German and nursing. She had received an urgent dispatch from the telegraph office. Lucy was engaged to Peter. He'd found her.

Rachel wondered if she'd done right or wrong by giving Peter the hint. Lord Shelford wanted to protect Lucy and Cecelia, so Rachel should not have told Peter where Lucy went. She hadn't given him her exact address, and it had taken him weeks to find her. If he was willing to try that hard, perhaps her breach of conduct was excusable. She could not, after all, be angry with Peter for lying, and then withhold the truth from him herself.

In order to enable Rachel to attend the wedding, Colonel Loughton had insisted on accompanying her. Alice and Mrs. Glenn came as well, since he couldn't travel alone with her.

The colonel had made special arrangements with the Institute to hold her place in the nursing school while she was away for three weeks to travel to Italy and back.

Mr. Kempton would attend classes, take notes, and tutor them when they returned.

The simple ceremony ended quickly. The dowager Lady Chelmsford, recently arrived from Essex, held baby Sarah. Rachel was amazed at how much the infant had grown since she had last seen her.

Rachel stood with Alice and the colonel, waiting to congratulate the couples. She looked around at the sculpted bushes and fountain with its statue. It was so green and lush here in Florence. In Mainz, the leaves had changed color and were beginning to fall from the trees.

The dowager Lady Chelmsford approached the group, holding baby Sarah. Eleanor brought over a handsome stranger. "May I introduce the Duke of Woodford?"

He took Rachel's hand. "Miss Wickford, a pleasure. Miss Loughton, always good to see you."

Lord Shelford clapped him on the back. "Set things to right. Glad you're on the Continent."

The duke shot him a repressive glance.

"What do you mean?" Rachel asked.

Lord Shelford leaned in and spoke in an uncharacteristically quiet tone. "Shall we say that Cecelia will not be troubled by her past? Chelmsford would not rest until I acted. Woodford's sent out a telegram to every Foreign Office. The sun never sets on the British empire. Felsted will have a hard time of it now."

Eleanor rapped him on the arm. "Don't say that man's name."

"Right." Lord Shelford straightened. "How's the embassy in Paris?"

The duke was nearly as tall as Colonel Loughton. "Mother's settling in. Daresay she'll invite your mother any day," he said. "She's already talking about it."

The dowager Lady Chelmsford held out her hand. "And I must thank her for the telegram and travel arrangements, Your Grace. I wouldn't have missed this ceremony for anything. A double wedding."

"Of course." The duke bowed over her hand. "If you wish to stay with us in Paris, anytime, she'd be delighted to have company."

The doting grandmother smiled as she snuggled baby Sarah to her chest. "Thank you. I'll be traveling with Lord and Lady Chelmsford to care for my granddaughter. If Paris is on the way, I'd be delighted to meet your mother in person. Please send my thanks to her."

"Miss Wickford, Miss Loughton, I hope you'll visit us on your way home from Germany." The duke's smile was breathtaking. His eyes were deep and drew Rachel in.

Colonel Loughton cleared his throat. "Thank you, Woodford. Not sure of our plans yet."

The couples emerged from the church. They must have finished signing the register or completing whatever paperwork was necessary.

Rachel hugged Lucy and Cecelia. "Let me see your hands," Rachel said.

Lucy held out Peter's keepsake ring on her middle finger. Cecelia had a thin gold band with a blue stone.

"Oh, congratulations," Rachel said. "Where do you go from here?"

"Eleanor's arranged a luncheon of pasta at a Tuscan villa some-where," Lucy said, "instead of a proper English wedding breakfast."

Rachel laughed. "Of course she has." Lucy and Rachel loved Eleanor, even though she was so different from them. Neither of them truly understood her, but they adored her.

"And where will you honeymoon?" Alice asked. "You're already in Italy."

"We'll go to Rome first, then up to Vienna in the spring," Peter said. "Walter and Cecelia made separate arrangements."

"And Papa is trying to buy every painting he can without bank rupting himself, but he'll return shortly as well." Lucy smiled. "He wants us to live with him at first. I suspect he's buying the portraits so he'll still have someone to talk to when we leave."

"Will you ask him to send my love to my mother? I'm glad she is well without me," Rachel said.

Lucy reached out. "I'm sure she misses you. I will miss you."

Rachel steadied herself, pushed down the emotion. "And I will miss you. I'm famished," Rachel said. "Lead the way to the carriages."

Rachel watched Eleanor and her husband chatting. Lucy and Peter strolling arm in arm. Cecelia and Walter, already a small family. She would be the last one to go into dinner at every party now. What a strange feeling, having all of one's friends married.

At least she had Alice. Colonel Loughton and the duke walked a distance behind them.

"Promise me you won't marry soon," Rachel said to Alice. "You and I are the only ones left."

"Oh, I intend to never marry," Alice replied. "Miss Nightingale is my example. She's turned down more than one suitor. Some have tried for years."

"Really?" Rachel didn't know about this.

"Yes. Nine years, I believe, one man courted her. She insists that God called her to nursing, and she will never marry."

Rachel pondered the thought. Could that be her destiny? It had been such a relief to think about medical lectures instead of Peter when he first appeared in Mainz. Keeping busy meant she had no time for uncomfortable emotions.

"Perhaps I shall do the same," Rachel said.

From the corner of her eye, she saw Colonel Loughton speed up. He grew level with her and cleared his throat. Rachel turned toward him. He would try to convince her not to make this pledge. He was one of the reasons she should.

"You wish for Alice and me to help establish the new training hospital with Miss Nightingale?" Rachel asked.

"Yes," he said. "But you can assist in many ways."

"Once a woman marries, she has her own family and children. Social obligations. Confinement. Child rearing. The more I regard the matter, the more I believe Alice is right. Consider Lucy. She's left the school because of Peter."

It was best if she warned the colonel now that he should not develop any feelings for her. She did not wish to presume that his attentions showed a deep regard, but Alice thought he had a preference for her.

"You needn't leave the school if you married," Colonel Loughton said.

"But I cannot very well spend my days training other nurses and assisting you the way Miss Nightingale will require, if I were married. Yes, Alice," Rachel threaded her arm through hers. "I shall join you in your pledge."

Colonel Loughton tried to walk beside Rachel, but the narrow pathway only allowed room for two people. He fell behind again and rejoined the duke.

"Consider, Miss Wickford. There are alternatives," he called from behind her. "No need to make any hasty decisions."

"Too late, General, my mind is made up. Consider how well I shall be able to support your work." Rachel felt relief. Men were disappointment, confusion, and heartache. She'd seen the crushing weight of grief that both Lucy and Cecelia experienced in Germany. Had they truly healed? She would avoid that pain entirely. "I'm never going to marry."

ALSO BY LISA H. CATMULL

An Inconvenient Grand Tour, Book 1 of the Victorian Grand Tour Series

She needs to hide. He's tired of being overlooked. It's going to be a long two years.

Eleanor Barrington has one rule: don't draw attention to yourself. She has one goal: marry a Peer to protect her family. When her father decides on a last-minute Grand Tour, Eleanor spends a dangerous amount of time with a man who cannot help with either goal: her brother's best friend.

As the younger son of an earl, Percy Hauxton has to fight for everything. A Grand Tour is the perfect opportunity to pursue his ambition to work for the Foreign Office, but traveling with Eleanor isn't part of the plan.

When circumstances draw them apart and a secret from the past threatens to unravel everything, Eleanor has to decide one thing. Can she marry for love, or does she need a marriage of convenience?

A Disorderly Grand Tour, Book 3 of the Victorian Grand Tour Series

She's sworn she'll never marry him. He's sworn to change her mind.

Rachel Wickford has vowed to devote her life to nursing, like her heroine, Florence Nightingale. She'd rather avoid the heartache of love, but it's hard to evade the man who's already head over heels for her.

Colonel Curtis Loughton needs experienced nurses to help Miss Nightingale's new school, but he needs a wife even more. He's willing to wage war to win over his true love, but he's never encountered opposition like this before. It will take all his ingenuity and grit to prove his devotion.

In a battle of wits, with underhanded insubordination on one side and a determined campaign on the other, can anyone claim victory, or will their hearts be the casualties?

An Attempted Engagement, Book 4 of the Victorian Grand Tour Series

Only one thing stands between Alice Loughton and the man of her dreams: her brother.

Frederick Kempton calls her his "little mouse." She's been shy and quiet ever since he met her at age three. But when timid Alice Loughton decides it's time to marry, there's only one man for her. The one man who doesn't frighten her. The only man she can talk to without wanting to run and hide. Her brother's hired secretary and closest friend.

But her brother knows Frederick Kempton too well, and he's not about to give his consent for a courtship, not when plenty of other men are pursuing Alice, too. And so obedient Alice, who has never broken a rule in her life, is forced to take drastic measures.

And she's dragged Freddie along with her. Can he walk the fine line between loyalty to his oldest friend and a chance to woo the woman he's secretly loved?

A swoony story of hidden messages, love letters, and stolen kisses

ABOUT THE AUTHOR

Lisa went with her family on BYU Study Abroad to Vienna when she was twelve years old. The college students voted her "Most Likely To Return Without Her Parents," and she did.

As an undergraduate at Dartmouth, she lived in Mainz, Germany, for three months, then lived in England during part of her senior year of college.

She's lived in seven states, four countries, and moved almost forty times. Lisa enjoys traveling, but her favorite journeys are in books.

She taught English and History for seven years before quitting to pursue screenwriting. None of her screenplays hit the theaters, but she met her future husband the day she moved to Los Angeles.

After leaving L.A., she decided to write books instead of movies. Lisa lives in Utah with her husband and two rambunctious children.

HISTORICAL NOTE

Hi there. You know I'm a liar. I mean, I made this whole book up. Here's a partial list of the fibs told to make the story flow.

I've taken liberties with the layout of the Boboli gardens. If you examine a map, you'll see the path that Lucy takes is complete rubbish. The fountain of Neptune is in a completely different location than where I placed it to make the story work. You'd have to zigzag all day to walk the way she does.

I was more circumspect with the geography around Mainz. The locations, descriptions, and travel time are based both on my experience living there and on online research.

The deaconess institute on which the story's nursing school is modeled was actually in Kaiserwerth, Germany. I moved it to Mainz because I knew the area better.

Séances and table-tipping were a thing back then. Not a lie. Magic tricks and stage magicians became popular in the Victorian Era. Charles Dickens belonged to the Ghost Club, which was actually founded in 1862. Later, Sir Arthur Conan Doyle joined. Thomas Edison sought to record spirits' voices, driving his research. Harry Houdini sought to discredit mediums as frauds.

Fountain pens? True story. True timeline. Not faked at all, just the idea that Lucy's dad bought shares in the company.

Let's talk about pregnancy. I didn't lie about anything. I'm just not sure that the words I used are the same words they would have used. I did some research and found a few phrases, but let's be honest. None of the characters actually speak the way people spoke in 1856. I hope the book is both approachable and authentic at the same time.

The University of Mainz, established well before this time, only taught theology in 1856. It is named after Johannes Gutenberg. He's the city's most famous citizen, and he invented the printing press.

Many telegraph lines were established before 1856, but I'm not sure which lines connected to each other. The Electric Telegraph Company formed in 1846 in Britain and was nationalized in 1870 by the General Post Office. Our characters would have been able to send and receive telegraphs when in England. I don't know exactly where or when the telegraph lines connected to and from various points in Europe. We're going to pretend like they all did by 1856.

Werner von Siemens and Georg Johann Halske laid down lines all over Germany beginning in 1847. By 1850, a telegraph could go from Salzburg, Austria, all the way up to Cuxhaven, Germany, on the North Sea coast. The Submarine Telegraph Company successfully laid a line between Dover, England, and Calais, France, that began working in October 1851. One of the largest investors in the company was Thomas Russell Crampton, who made the locomotives our characters ride.

Lastly, let's address those beards. Victorian men loved beards. I don't know about the women. One theory is that medieval knights had beards, and that drove the popularity of whiskers. Chivalry and medieval honor were considered the standard of behavior for men in the Victorian era, so it's a thing in this book. Check out the poetry of the time.

That's all for now! I hope you enjoyed the ride.

SOCIAL CUSTOMS IN THE
VICTORIAN ERA 1837—1901

There's so much to try to wrap my head around when I'm doing research. I'll give you a few insights that relate to this book. There might be spoilers. FYI.

Settlements. Lucy's father spent months negotiating a marriage settlement with Walter Chelmsford. Marriage contracts or settlements protected women. They delineated where the dowry went, how much pin money she would have, and anything else the father saw fit to specify. Otherwise, the woman was powerless.

Men owned women and their property the moment the marriage occurred, unless a loving and shrewd father had arranged otherwise.

There are historical examples and exceptions. They are important to note, because Lucy aspires to be more like them. Lady Jersey retained full control and ran a bank. She remained in the top echelon of society and was one of the few exclusive women who granted vouchers to Almack's.

Marriages occurred three ways: by having banns read for three weeks in the parish where each resided, by license, or by special license. Our Happily Ever After wedding would have occurred by license in Europe. Marriages legally obtained in foreign countries were recognized in Britain.

There were laws about remarriage. If a woman was widowed, she could not marry any of the male relatives of her deceased husband. If her husband died, she was considered the sister of her brother-in-law, and she could never marry him in England. Some couples left the country to marry and live on the Continent.

Parents. Let's talk about the mamas and the papas. Why does Lucy call her father that name? If you read Queen Victoria's diaries, you'll see that she does, too. It's what women did. They used the name "Mama" or "Papa," or else spoke of "my mother" and "my father." Men called them "Mother" and "Father." Some Latin speaking families would use "Mater" or "Pater."

Precedence. Servants, such as grooms, had a social pecking order, too. George, the stable hand who broke Lucy's heart before this book began, was lower in precedence. He was not the head groom. He would have been called by his last name, "Forde," if he had been the head groom.

Butlers had a higher social status than footmen. The house-keeper ruled over the other female servants. There were levels within levels of precedence, even for them.

So, why does Rachel worry that she'll be the last one to walk in to dinner? Married women walk in before the single women. Rachel's papa was a gentleman, but he had no title. Rachel is the lowest ranking lady anywhere she goes. She's single with barely enough income to maintain her lifestyle.

Lucy used to be ranked lower than her, because her papa was new money. He worked in business and owned an estate, so he barely qualified for the gentry. After Lucy marries, she'll be ranked above Rachel.

Chaperones. Women required chaperones until they were engaged, then they could walk with their fiancé alone. I fudged a little in this book. I let her walk alone with Peter while she was engaged to Walter. Probably wouldn't have happened, but I took a little license there.

Pregnancy. They had all sorts of different ideas. The only pain killer available was a few drops of chloroform on a handkerchief. Queen Victoria herself used this method. Women wore special corsets, but still wore them for the first two trimesters at least. There were debates about cleanliness, the heat of the room, whether men or women were better at delivering babies, and other topics. 1856 was a year when things were changing rapidly in a lot of areas of Victorian life. We'll get more into pregnancy and delivery in Book Three. Stay tuned.

For more historical information, join my newsletter or follow me on social media. Links are on my website, www.lisacatmull.com.

SOCIAL HIERARCHY IN THE VICTORIAN ERA 1837—1901

Titles can be confusing because there are three ways to address people: (1) the way one addressed an envelope to them and the way someone announces their name formally, (2) the way one addressed a letter to them, and (3) the way one speaks to them. The graphics on the following pages illustrate the way one would address someone in speech.

I used examples to demonstrate. Victoria and Albert London are the hypothetical people. The title name are also London for our purposes, although the family name and title would not usually be the same.

Notes on the children of the aristocracy

Daughters of a duke, marquess, or earl are called Lady and their first name (Lady Victoria)

Daughters of a viscount or baron are called Miss, but not called Lady (Miss Victoria)

Younger sons of a duke or a marquess are called Lord and their FirstName, but they don't hold a title (Lord Albert)

Younger sons of an earl, viscount, or baron without titles are called Mr. (Mr. London)

254   SOCIAL HIERARCHY IN THE VICTORIAN ERA 1837—1901

Peerage and Titles Explained

Peers are the dukes, marquesses, earls, viscounts, and barons. They are the nobility and the title holders. They sit in the House of Lords.

A duke is called the Duke of a Place, like the Duke of London. Marquesses, earls, viscounts, and barons are always called Lord LastName, like Lord London. They are never called Baron Title or Baron LastName. It is the House of Lords, not the House of Marquesses, Earls, Viscounts, and Barons.

A baronet or knight is called Sir FirstName, like Sir Albert. His wife is called Lady LastName, like Lady London. The female equivalent of a knight is called a dame, and her husband is called Mr. LastName, like Mr. London.

Peers sat in the House of Lords and often attended Parliament. It often began January thirty-first and ended August twelfth, although it ended on July 29, 1856, the year this story takes place. Eleanor and Percy got married on August 1, 1856, after the Season ended for that year.

Although some families were in town in February, most Peers brought their families back after Easter. Parties, balls, excursions, and art exhibits were in full swing during May, June, and July.

Baronets and knights are not Peers and do not sit in the House of Lords.

Men often referred to other men by their title or last name only, like London, instead of Lord London or Albert.

Men and women did not usually call each other by their first name or given name. It was a sign of increasing intimacy or appropriate for childhood friends who had grown up together, like Lucy, Rachel, Eleanor, Walter, and Peter. Women might call each other by their first names once they became friends, like Alice, Rachel, and Lucy.

The oldest daughter was Miss LastName, like Miss London. Her younger sisters were Miss FirstName LastName, like Miss Victoria London and Miss Elizabeth London.

A nobleman often held more than one title. A duke might also be a marquess and an earl. An earl might also be a viscount. The oldest son or heir would be allowed to use the lesser title.

The *ton* was the Upper Crust that socialized in London. It was comprised of royalty, aristocracy, and members of the gentry. Some wealthy business owners or bankers were included as well.

Servants had a hierarchy of precedence, too. In the lower classes, some servants were called by their last names and others were called by their first names. The housekeeper and cook were called "Mrs." whether or not they were married.

And then there were the clergy. Oh, this is as complicated as everything else! It needs another page to explain…Here are some highlights. There are three forms of address for clergy as well.

For example, clergymen were never called "reverend" as their form of address, just as a title. The Reverend Albert London or the Reverend Deacon Albert London would be the formal address on an envelope, but in conversation or to his face he would be simply be called Deacon London or Mr. London, never Reverend London.

The archbishops and bishops sat in the House of Lords.

An archbishop was called "Your Grace" or "Archbishop."

Bishops, diocesan bishops, or suffragan bishops were called "My Lord" or "Bishop."

A Canon, Prebendar, or Archdeacon was called only by their title.

Other clergy in the Church of England were called "Mr." or by their position: vicar, rector, curate, chaplain, or dean. Someone might say, "Come on in, Vicar. It's good to see you, Mr. London," and be talking to the same person. He was the vicar, but he was also Mr. London. He was not Vicar London.

The illustrations on the following pages have the titles on the top and the names by which they were addressed on the bottom or to the side. Remember, this is the way one would talk to them in speech, not the way one would address an envelope. You would not use a formal title like "Earl" in conversation, like "Good day, Earl London," but would instead say, "Good day, Lord London."

Social Hierarchy in the Victorian Era
1837-1901

Presented in descending order of precedence (rank)

Royalty

Aristocracy

Duke	Duchess
His Grace	Her Grace

Marquess/Marquis	Marchioness
Lord London	Lady London

Earl	Countess
Lord London	Lady London

Viscount	Viscountess
Lord London	Lady London

Baron	Baroness
Lord London	Lady London

- The Duke and Duchess are never called Lord and Lady.
- For Lords and Ladies: the last name is taken from their title, not their family name.

Gentry

Baronet **Sir Albert**	Dame **Lady London**

Knight **Sir Albert**	*His wife* **Lady London**

Her husband **Mr. London**	Dame **Dame London**

Untitled land owners

Military officers

Vicars, curates, and church officials

Solicitors

Land stewards and personal secretaries

Governesses, tutors, and companions

Physicians, sometimes called Dr., like Dr. London

- Members of the gentry are called Mr. or Mrs./Miss unless specified otherwise
- Some men held more than one title. A man with a military rank might also be a knight or a baronet.

Middle/Merchant Class

> Doctors, surgeons

> Wealthy business owners, bankers

- The Upper Class usually called them by their last name only

---

Lower Class/Working Class

> Housekeeper - Mrs. London

> Cook - Mrs. London or Cook

> Valet, butler - London

> Lady's maid/abigail - Miss London or London

> Coachman - Albert Coachman

> Farm workers, tenants - London

- The housekeeper and butler were equals. The valet and lady's maid were equals.

> Servants - Victoria or Albert

> The poor - Victoria or Albert

> Factory and shop workers - Victoria or Albert